SHATTERING THE TRIANGLE

SHATTERING THE TRIANGLE

— A NOVEL —

DICK REYNOLDS

For Mandi,
Wishing you
all the best
in life!
Dick R.

Valentine Press
Vp

A subsidiary of Skyline Publications & Water Forest Press
New York - USA

ISBN-13: 978-0615784076

ISBN-10: 0615784070

Book Design by Victoria Valentine
Cover Art © Rechitan Sorin

Valentine Press
PO Box 295, Stormville, NY 12582
valentinepress.com

Printed in the United States of America

ALSO BY DICK REYNOLDS

Averil, My Anchor

Mayhem in Mazatlan

Nightmare in Norway

Filling in the Triangles

TO THE MEMORY OF

RICHARD KEITH REYNOLDS

CHAPTER ONE

I HAD TO GET OUT OF DODGE REAL QUICK

The giant Lufthansa A340 Airbus shuddered, sending a noisy tremor throughout its fuselage. Plates, trays, and utensils clattered in the galleys, banging on metal cabinets and falling to the deck. An infant in the economy section woke up screaming as the captain came on the PA system, unnecessarily announcing the turbulence, and asking everyone to fasten their seat belts.

Leslie Faye Aronson Krag had also been startled awake and looked around the darkened first class section, initially not knowing where she was. A mild panic swept through her body and she had a sobering thought. *Is this how it ends? After all the crap I've been through, getting myself out of Colorado and a certain prison sentence, to fall out of the sky into the Atlantic and never be heard from again?*

She looked out the window into the black night and started to relax when the aircraft resumed its smooth flight. She rang for the flight attendant and asked for some aspirin to relieve a monstrous migraine caused by overindulgence in alcohol before, during, and after her dinner. She gobbled up three aspirin, leaned back, and willed them to bring her relief. Which they did since even inanimate objects dared not defy or disappoint her.

All things considered, Leslie's emotional state was only slightly more positive than negative. They should be landing at Frankfurt in several hours and, after a brief layover, she would travel on to Rome where her good friend, Maria Borelli, would take her to her rented villa at Castellina in Chianti, a small Tuscan village about fifteen kilometers from Siena. Though it was a bitter cold day in early January, Maria would probably have made a cozy fire in the living room's antique stone fireplace to welcome her.

True, she had escaped a rather nasty legal situation. As good as that was, it only pointed to her not winning back Andrew, her estranged husband. Leslie had returned to Denver just over a month ago in a valiant attempt to reconcile with him. But Andrew had relocated to Leadville, Colorado, found a job with a construction company there, begun a romantic relationship with Sarah Dolan, his employer's niece, and subsequently filed for divorce. Leslie's campaign, which included hiring a private detective to spy on Andrew and this woman, failed miserably.

Leslie eventually took matters into her own hands and drove to Leadville, hoping to provoke a successful confrontation. The calamitous result was her arrival at Andrew's cabin and, not liking what she found, set it on fire. She left the scene, driving frantically to Pueblo where she hoped to catch Sarah at home and persuade her, with a fully loaded Glock pistol, to keep her slutty paws off her husband. But she never got there. She wrecked her car and wound up in Pueblo's Parkview Medical Center. When both the

Pueblo police and the Leadville sheriff paid Leslie official bedside visits, she knew she had to leave the country. Thanks to her best friend, Nancy Moore, she escaped and was now just hours away from her Italian home.

Yes, she had won her freedom but had not accomplished her mission. In her view, Andrew had tossed her away like a used condom. She conveniently swept aside the fact that she was the one who suddenly left him last August and moved to Italy, leaving him a big check and a note that said she thought it best they live apart for a while. Her tactic of having a temporary separation—absence makes the heart grow fonder?—was a gigantic blunder. It only brought home the sorry conclusion that he could live very nicely without her and was actually much better off.

Leslie leaned back in her seat, the headache almost completely gone. Somehow, some day, she thought, Andrew would have to pay for the shabby way he treated her and trashed their marriage.

Leslie's plane landed late morning at Frankfurt's International Airport. The skies were overcast and the wind whipped a light rain across the tarmac. She easily made her connection, departed shortly after noon, and landed at Rome's Fiumicino Airport at 2:00 P.M. The weather in Rome was much better than Frankfurt's. Sunny skies and an outside temperature about 55 degrees F perked her up.

Leslie's sprits rose even higher when she spotted Maria in the waiting area for greeters. The two embraced and Maria's affectionate warmth came through several layers of clothes, prompting Leslie to shed a few joyful tears.

"I'm so happy to see you again," said Maria, leaning back slightly to get a better look. "You mentioned an auto accident when you called from Dallas, but you don't look like an injured person. Perhaps it was not serious, no?"

"Oh, it was serious all right. A concussion that knocked me out for a while with some scrapes and bruises. But you look wonderful, Maria."

They moved on to the baggage carousel and made small talk until Leslie's suitcase appeared. Leslie grabbed it and said, "OK, this is it. We can be on our way."

Maria gave her a curious look. "You had many bags when you left."

"True, but I had to get out of Dodge real quick and left a lot of things in Denver."

"Dodge? What is that?"

Leslie laughed. "An American expression out of the old west. Leaving a place to escape danger."

They drove northwest on the S2 highway in Maria's BMW and agreed to have an early dinner at a restaurant near Siena. On the way, with some prodding by her Italian friend, Leslie began telling the long story of her Colorado adventure. She told of her initial conference with her attorney, Paul Harrington, and hiring Clarke Layton, the 'boy detective.' "He was quite the bumbling incompetent, mostly a waste of time and money without accomplishing anything worthwhile."

"Then why did you do it?"

Leslie sighed. "I just wanted to find out what my husband was up to so I could come up with a plan for getting him back. Turned out he was playing around with all kinds of women."

"Not too surprising with you living here in Italy."

Leslie ignored the comment and ranted about Andrew's lack of marital fidelity, glossing over her own dalliances with two local men. "This was supposed to be a temporary separation, some space and breathing room that would let us think long and hard about making our marriage right again. Only for him it was an opportunity to screw every female who came down the pike."

They were silent for a while until Maria asked, "What was the danger you had to escape? Was it related to your car crash?"

"If I tell you, you must promise *never* to tell another living soul. OK?"

"Of course, on my sainted mother's grave."

Leslie took a deep breath. "I borrowed Layton's pistol and drove to Leadville, intending to have a talk with Andrew, but he wasn't home when I got there."

"You took a gun? What were you thinking? Suppose he had been home and you had an argument. You might have killed him. What would that have solved?"

"Not a very smart move, but I wanted to have a *persuader* with me. Something handy for self defense, just in case I needed it."

Maria shook her head and gripped the steering wheel harder.

"So once inside his cabin, I saw all sorts of ugly things, glaring evidence of what he'd been doing with one of these women. He needed to be taught a lesson so I set the place on fire, sending that horrible love nest of his up in smoke. Ha! I heard later that the place burned to the ground."

"That was a terrible thing to do. Now I understand why you had to leave."

"Yeah, I left Leadville in a big hurry, heading south to Pueblo where my husband's girlfriend lives. I planned to surprise her, maybe wave that pistol in her face and convince her that screwing him was not a good thing for her health. But I never got there. I wrecked my car, they took me to the hospital, and eventually the police came knocking on my door. The jig was up and I knew it, that's why I had to get the hell out of Dodge."

Maria was silent for a brief period. "Suppose, after all you did, your husband agreed to come back to you. What kind of relationship would you expect to have, considering all the things you did to him and his woman friend? How long do you think he would have stayed with you, a clearly demonstrated criminal?"

"I'd make it up to him. He'd see the error of his ways and would be glad to be back with me."

"I think you should see a head doctor, Leslie. You have made a big mess. And I'm only saying this as one good friend to another."

"Yeah, yeah, I hear you. That's what Nancy Moore made me promise."

"So you'll do it? I can recommend some excellent ones."

"I promise to think about it."

"No promises, just do it."

"All right already, I'll do it."

"You are also a woman without a country but you still have a home in the United States. What will you do about that?"

"Well, the house is still up for sale. And they won't go to the trouble of trying to extradite me, that's the good news. As for the rest of my life, I'll start thinking about that tomorrow."

A gray-haired hostess in a plain black dress showed Leslie and Maria to a table next to tall slender windows that gave them a view of fading sunlight on a wintry Tuscan countryside. Their waiter, his black vest about two sizes too small, brought them a bottle of an excellent local Chianti.

After he took their order, Maria offered a toast. "Welcome

home, my friend." They touched glasses and took modest sips. "I will pray for you, maybe a novena, that you have better days."

"Hope you're right about that," said Leslie.

"Why not? You are a free woman."

"Not just yet, Maria. The divorce gears are grinding away and it should be final in a couple of months. But enough about me. Tell me about your Christmas. I hope it was a happy one."

Maria brightened, anxious to talk about herself. "My children were with me for the holidays but it wasn't always a pleasant time. I wanted to take advantage of their visit to introduce them to the man I've been seeing."

"You have a new man in your life? That's wonderful. This is the first time you've mentioned him. Tell me more."

"I only met him several months ago and it has all happened so fast. His name is Marcello and he lives in Firenzi. He manages one of the big tourist hotels. Lucia likes him and they get along very well together, probably because he also has a daughter about the same age."

"That's a good sign but I'm getting a message here, that your son is not exactly thrilled about this. Am I close?"

"Sadly, yes. Pietro is so immature, I think his problem is that he can't visualize his mother sleeping with a man who is not his father."

"But you've been a widow for years and still young enough to have a loving relationship. He should not be interfering with that. I'll bet he has plenty of girlfriends at the university."

"Dozens, I'm sure." She giggled. "Some day we must take a drive to Pisa and visit his campus, perhaps in disguise, to get a better view of his social life."

"Better yet, I'll have a dinner party. You and Marcello shall be my honored guests. And I shall not mind if you and he sleep over at my villa."

Maria laughed and raised her glass. "To a romantic dinner date with interesting and mature adults."

"Speaking of my villa, I trust it hasn't crumbled to the ground."

"Everything is just as you left it. I have taken good care of all your plants and opened up the rooms before I came to the airport. The fresh air will take out all the musty odors."

"Thanks, but I probably wouldn't notice any of that. I'm just going to crawl right into my bed after you take me home."

"Oh," Maria said. "I almost forgot. There was a telephone call this morning. A man asking for Faye Aronson."

"A man? Did he give his name?"

"Holiday or Halliday. I'm not sure, it was a bad connection."

Leslie was stunned. "This is so bizarre. I just met this man yesterday on my flight from Colorado Springs to Dallas. His name is Roger Halliday."

"What kind of man is he?"

"Quite handsome, about my age. Said he's in the import/export business and comes to Italy often on business. Did he leave a message, a phone number?"

"No, only that he would call again later."

Leslie pondered this for a moment. "He must want something."

"Or someone," said Maria.

CHAPTER TWO

DINNER AT FOUR, HANGING AT SIX,
AND NEWS AT ELEVEN

On the second Saturday of January, Andrew Krag left Roscoe
Bartlett's Leadville home heading for Pueblo and Sarah Dolan,
the love of his life. He had just finished a late breakfast with Roscoe
and his wife, Tanice.

Roscoe had hosted a poker game the night before that lasted
until just after midnight. Andrew accepted his boss's invitation to
stay over and bunk in their guest bedroom. Sam Dolan, Sarah's
dad, also played in the game. Just as Sarah had warned, Sam was
an excellent poker player and won a large share of the pots.
Andrew's consolation, besides having a beer-and-cigar-fueled
hootenanny of a time, was not losing a lot of money.

Another plus for last night's festivities, at least in Andrew's
mind, was Sam's not pressing for details about current living

arrangements with his daughter. Andrew assumed that Roscoe had given Sam the pertinent facts and didn't want to cause Andrew any discomfort at the poker table with three strangers present. Besides, he knew that the whole business of Andrew and Sarah's relationship would be broached and fully dissected on Sunday when the Bartletts, Sam and Emmaline Dolan, and the young lovers would be seated around the Bartletts' dinner table.

As Andrew drove his SUV out of the Bartletts' driveway, he decided to make a detour and swing by his cabin site. He received a pleasant surprise when he arrived; Chris and Alex had finished the cleanup and removed all the debris from the fire that had destroyed the cabin. Several inches of new snow covered all the ashes, mud, and other evidence of Leslie's arson, and gave his spirits a boost. *This place will look even better after I build the new cabin.*

He got out of his SUV and walked around the lot, wistfully recalling the cabin's layout and the good times when Sarah had slept over for two nights of the New Year's holiday. A vehicle coming up the driveway interrupted his erotic reverie.

Andrew recognized the Lake County Sheriff when he got out. Eliot Waters wore western boots, a dirty tan duster, a white cowboy hat, and sported a white handlebar mustache. "Morning, Andy," he called out.

"Hello, sheriff. What brings you out here?" They shook hands.

"Oh, just checking up on your place. Wanted to make sure there was no looting or trespassing going on."

Andrew laughed. "Nothing's left that's worth anything. My buddies have cleared the site pretty well and we're ready for the next step."

"You planning to rebuild?"

"That's right. The insurance has me covered well enough. Roscoe and I have been working on plans and filing some permits. Pretty soon you'll see a sign near the road announcing the construction of another quality RBC home."

"Not to change the subject," said Waters, "but I have news about your wife."

"She's been arrested, I hope."

"Afraid not. Detective Hardcastle and I—she's with Pueblo PD—tracked Mrs. Krag from The Springs to Dallas. Then we learned she caught a flight to Frankfurt and on to Rome. She's got some kind of house in Italy I hear."

"Yeah, a villa near Siena."

"I don't see her coming back to Colorado any time soon. Do you?"

"Nope. Our divorce will happen without her presence but she still has a house in Denver. It's been on the market for months, but no takers so far. She'll probably lower the asking price now just to get rid of it."

Waters took several paces away and turned around. "Damn it, Andy, I hate to see someone get away with stuff like that. Hardcastle and I dropped the ball and she should be in jail right now."

Andrew patted him on the back. "Don't beat yourself up on this, sheriff. You did all you could but she knew she'd get nailed and had to escape. I'm not going to dwell on it. Life's too short and I've got a great life ahead. One that I plan to live the fullest way I know how."

Waters shook Andrew's hand and turned to leave. "I like your style, Andy."

Andrew reached Sarah's house around two o'clock and found her in the kitchen, pouring over papers scattered across the breakfast table. She got up and welcomed him with a strong hug and a long kiss. "About time you got here, stranger."

"Hey, I practically flew down I-25. Miss me?"

"Heck no, did you miss me?"

"Heck no." He kissed her back with a persistent tongue while squeezing her buttocks with both hands.

"You are so full of it, Krag. Come sit and talk to me."

He pulled up a chair and sat down. "What's with all the papers?"

"Oh, getting a little jump on taxes. Taking a look-see at my fiscal shape."

He grinned. "If it's anywhere as near as sexy as your bod you'll surely get a AAA rating."

She began collecting papers and neatly stacked them in three separate piles. "How'd you make out in the poker game? Are you wealthy enough to afford me?"

"Sorry, I ended up in the debit column. But I can still take you out to dinner as long as you order only an appetizer."

"Lucky for you that we're eating in tonight. My turn to cook."

"Sounds like a plan. By the way, you were right about your dad. He cleaned everybody's clock."

"I told you so. He's been gambling since he was in grade school. Told me once he took change out of his mother's coin purse just to get into a penny ante game."

Andrew went to the refrigerator, opened a can of root beer and returned to his chair. "What did you do last night?"

"Girls' night out. Donna, Brenda and I—they're also nurses at the hospital—went to Sena's Buffalo Bar downtown. Had some drinks, did a little dance, lots of laughs, a bite to eat, and called it a night before I turned into a pumpkin."

"What kind of place is Sena's?"

"Sort of a body exchange, like your Coyote Cantina in Buena Vista."

"Don't like the sound of that."

"It was fun. We got hit on a couple of times. Met a cute guy from the Air Force Academy but he was much too young for me. Told him I was old enough to be his mother but that didn't faze him. Said he was intrigued by mysterious and beautiful older women."

"Good grief."

"He also liked my glasses. Said they made me look super intelligent."

"What a line of B. S."

Sarah cocked her head. "If I'm not mistaken, Mr. Krag, you said the very same things to me not too long ago."

"And look at all the trouble it got me."

"Keep it up and you'll be in the guest room tonight. No trouble at all."

They stared at each other for a long moment until they simultaneously burst out laughing. He got up and said, "Think that's my cue for a shower. And by the way, Tanice reminded me that we're expected for dinner tomorrow afternoon with your dad and the ever curious Emmaline."

"Yeah, yeah. Dinner at four, hanging at six, and news at eleven."

Andrew leaned over and smooched her noisily on the neck. "Buck up, sweetheart. We'll get through this in fine fettle with no visible scars."

Andrew and Sarah got a late start Sunday afternoon. Sarah seemed to take an extraordinary amount of time in the bathroom getting ready. Andrew suspected that the delay was not so much her concern about how she looked but more a case of nerves and dreading the afternoon with her mother.

They talked little on the drive up to Leadville, preferring instead to enjoy soft rock music from a CD. When they pulled into the Bartletts' driveway, Sarah turned to Andrew and grabbed his arm. "Tell me how much you love me," she said.

He leaned over and lightly kissed her lips. "Tons," he said. "Now let's go have a great afternoon."

Tanice welcomed them at the open front door. She wore a long red velvet dress and her lustrous ash blonde hair fell to her shoulders. After she gave Sarah a hug, Andrew presented her with a dozen pastel-colored roses. "How thoughtful, Andrew, they're beautiful. And so are you two, finally here *together.* Come inside and get warmed up. Your folks are in the living room, Sarah."

Andrew hung his and Sarah's down jacket on a wall-mounted coat rack in the foyer and led her into the living room, her hand gripping his. Sam Dolan got up from the couch and gave his daughter a hug and kiss on the cheek. Emmaline remained seated and focused on Andrew who went directly to her, kissed her on the cheek and said, "Happy New Year. Better late than never, I guess." *God that was lame.*

"Same to you, Andy." Emmaline cooly eyed Sarah's tight jeans and turtleneck sweater. "Hello, Miriam," she said. "Happy to see that you could join us." Miriam was actually Sarah's first name, one she intensely disliked.

Sarah kissed her mother. "Wouldn't have missed it for the world."

Roscoe came in from the kitchen, greeted Andrew and Sarah, and announced he was ready to take drink orders. He wore a white shirt, a scarlet vest, and a bolo tie with a gold clasp formed by the Marine Corps' eagle, globe and anchor. Sam asked for his customary Wild Turkey over rocks and Emmaline wanted the same, only with lots of 7-Up and ice. Andrew and Sarah opted for white wine.

A long awkward pause followed as Andrew and Sarah sat across from her parents. Andrew finally broke the ice. "Today reminds me of Thanksgiving, the last time we were all together like this."

"By golly, you're right," said Sam. "A lot sure has happened since then."

Andrew glanced at Sarah. "And meeting your daughter was best of all."

Emmaline leaned forward. "I was very sorry to hear about your cabin, Andy. Now I hate to bring this up, but I understand that it was your wife who actually set the place on fire. True?"

"I'm sure it was her but she got away. Sheriff Waters told me that she's back in Italy now so I don't expect to hear from her again."

"How does this affect your divorce?"

"It doesn't. Which reminds me, I need to have a talk with The Viper—I mean Vince Burke."

Sam chuckled at the reference to Andy's attorney but Emmaline's face remained rigid. She continued, "Now I understand you're going to rebuild the cabin but you'll need a place to live until it's finished. You know I'm active in real estate and I've got several very affordable places lined up for you to look at. Next time you're up this way I'll take you around. They're all available now and any one of them should be very comfortable."

Andrew glanced at Sarah again and read the look on her face; the woman's going for the jugular. We knew this was coming, he thought, so there's no use in dodging the issue.

"I'm pretty comfortable right where I am," said Andrew.

"Yes, down in Pueblo with my daughter," said Emmaline, "but how are you supposed to earn a living if you're 150 miles away from your job? You surely can't stay on Roscoe's payroll like that, wouldn't be fair to him. And need I mention the moral implications of the adulterous situation that you've put Miriam in?"

Sarah and Andrew erupted at the same moment, each attempting to address Emmaline's statements. Andrew touched Sarah's hand. "Let me speak to that," she said.

Roscoe and Tanice came into the room with everyone's drink. Roscoe, who had probably heard the uproar, looked around and said, "Looks like I got back just in time to quell a riot." He passed out the drinks and offered a toast as he and Tanice sat down. "To a loving family and dear friends."

"What you said, Mom, is not quite correct." Sarah continued, "When Andy lost his cabin, he had no place to go. And he sure didn't put me into any kind of *situation* but he did come down right away to protect me from his murderous wife. She was coming straight for my house but she wrecked her car along the way. The police found a loaded pistol in her car, something I'm sure she planned to use on me."

Emmaline sucked in her breath, put a hand up near her mouth and said, "Praise The Lord Jesus you weren't harmed."

"And another thing. It's not adultery because I'm not married."

"But you're living in sin."

"Mom, please. It's the 21st century. I'm in love with Andy and we're planning to have a life together."

Andrew reached over and took Sarah's hand. "She's right, Emmaline. I love Sarah with all my heart and soul and have never loved anyone more." Sarah squeezed his hand.

"Well, you can gloss over it all you like but it's still not right. People will talk."

Sarah started to say something but Andrew took his hand away from Sarah and waved with a dismissive gesture. "Emmaline. I respect you because you're Sarah's mother and Tanice's sister, but my relationship with Sarah is very personal, just between the two of us. I can tell you this: I'll always be faithful to her, will take good care of her, and will never hurt her." He paused when he saw something in Emmaline's eyes. *Is she going to cry?* "Anyway, Roscoe and I have an agreement. I'm on temporary leave without pay, except when I come back to Leadville and work on short term projects. Then I'll get a motel room. And don't worry, I can afford it."

The faint ring of a bell from another room caused Tanice to say, "That's our dinner, folks. Em, will you help me in the kitchen, please? The rest of you can come to the dining room and find your places."

Andrew offered his arm to Sarah, which she took, but she held back to let all the elders leave the room first. "That was pretty eloquent," she said. "Could you possibly imagine the sweet things I'd like to do with you right now?"

"Oh yeah, but hold that thought until we get home tonight."

After everyone sat down, Emmaline said a rambling prayer of thanks with references to the biblical Miriam, her brother Moses, and her legendary well that accompanied the Israelites through the desert. The look on her face suggested that Tanice had spoken to her in the kitchen about her mother-daughter rants.

Tanice served a standing rib roast with potatoes and carrots that pleased everyone so much it halted conversation. Talk resumed when Tanice congratulated Sam on his good fortune in the recent poker game. This segued into Roscoe's boasting of experiences with Lady Luck during his twenty-six years in the Marines. Sam regaled everyone with exciting tales about his earlier life as a working cowboy and ranch owner in southern Colorado near Alamosa and Monte Vista.

At one point when Roscoe and Sam took a break for air, Sarah joined in with a question for Roscoe. "How is your business doing these days?"

Roscoe looked puzzled. "My business? Well, it's OK but it'll pick up in the spring. Why do you ask?"

"Have you ever thought of expanding? Like setting up a branch office down in Pueblo?"

Roscoe smiled. "Oh, now I see where you're headed. Maybe thinking about putting Andy to work right there in your back yard? Well, to answer your question, I have thought about it. But I don't have the spare capital right now and I wouldn't want to take on the risk of a big loan."

Sarah put her hands together in a steeple. "How about taking on a partner, someone with a chunk of money that would buy her a share in your business?"

"*Her?* You talking about yourself?"

"Could be," she said. "Here's another hypothetical. Suppose somebody wanted to buy your business. What would be the price tag?"

By this time, everyone else had placed their utensils on the table and were looking intently at Sarah. Roscoe massaged his chin and pondered her question. "Right now, I'd put a round number on it, say ten million. But a prospective buyer would have his own appraiser take a closer look."

"All right, here's my proposition. I'll give you two million for a twenty percent share. You'll still be the general manager and I'll be a silent partner. Andy sets up an RBC branch in Pueblo, rents an office, hires a secretary and construction workers, leases machinery, markets the company all over town and—"

Everyone wanted to speak, except for Andrew who looked at Sarah with a new appreciation for her suddenly revealed business talents. Roscoe held up his hands in a request for quiet. "Where on earth would you get that kind of money?"

"While you *boys* were playing poker Friday night, I was doing some research. I've got this stock in Digger dot com from the divorce settlement with Tom. Never paid much attention to it, always thought I'd save it for my retirement. Well, it turns out that Digger has done almost as well as Google and Microsoft. And so, Uncle Roscoe, I've got two million to invest in your company and Andy's future with plenty left over for my golden years. What do you say? Do we have a deal?"

Stark silence followed until Tanice laughed and said, "This is the first time I've seen him totally speechless in forty years."

Sam said, "Looks like a pretty good deal to me. Think you better jump on it before she has second thoughts."

Roscoe offered his hand and Sarah took it. "Deal," he said. "I'll talk to my attorney tomorrow and have him draw up the paperwork."

"And I'll call my broker, sell some shares and have him send me a check."

Emmaline shook her head. "Am I understanding that you're not coming back to Leadville, Andy? What about your cabin?"

"Good question. Maybe you could sell it for me. Or you might want to manage it as a rental. Let me think about it." He turned to Sarah. "You are something else, girlfriend, and continue to amaze me. Looks like I'll be working for you *and* Roscoe."

She kissed him. "No, sweetheart, you'll be working for *us.*"

CHAPTER THREE

YOU HAVE DAMN NEAR RUINED MY LIFE

Leslie went straight to bed and slept for twelve hours. She awoke the next morning about eight o'clock and built a fire in the living room fireplace while the coffee pot burbled away. As she sipped her first cup and stared into the flickering flames, she allowed her mind to drift.

She felt secure but lonely in this recently renovated 17th century quarrystone house situated on 300 acres. Numerous pomegranate, olive, and fig trees surrounded the house, but they had been several months without their leaves. Tall cypress lined both sides of a long driveway going out to the road leading to Castellina.

The modern kitchen and living room were equipped with many up-to-date electronic amenities. A private swimming pool located at the back of the house had been drained and covered for the winter. A small chapel with bell tower also graced the property but Leslie had no interest in going inside and communicating with The Divine Presence.

Instead of dwelling on the question that Maria had asked last evening, what she'd do with the rest of her life, Leslie focused instead on this particular day and the necessary things she needed to accomplish.

She unpacked her suitcase and started a small load of laundry. While munching on a toasted muffin, she flipped through the stack of mail that Maria had left. She smiled when she found a formal note on expensive stationery from Dominic, an older man she'd been seeing before returning to Denver. It was an invitation to a concert and dinner in Florence later in January. Leslie made a mental note to call him that evening and accept his invitation. She would also ask Maria to have Marcello book a suite at his hotel for that evening.

She spread the mail on the table, looking for something from Marco, a much younger man whom she'd also been seeing. She sighed, accepting that there was nothing from him. His style was totally different; Marco would just show up on his motorcycle and expect Leslie to drop everything and hop on for an adventure. He treated her like a *Principessa* and she was only too eager, like a starry-eyed teen, to give him everything he asked for. Plus a good deal more.

Leslie opened a Christmas card from Suzanne Auten, owner of the villa. Suzanne lived in Romanshorn, Switzerland, near Zurich, on the shore of the Bodensee, and owned a small book publishing company. In her card, Suzanne commented that the monthly bank transfer of Euros for the rent was working well. She also reminded Leslie that she would have to vacate the villa for all of June when Suzanne returned to Italy for a summer holiday. Leslie mentally put that aside for the moment; who knew what her life would be like then?

After cleaning the kitchen and finishing the laundry, she took a shower and got dressed. Feeling refreshed and ready to tackle her e-mail, she went to one of the smaller bedrooms, which she'd converted into an office, and turned on her computer. She was pleasantly surprised to find only about thirty e-mails, most of which she deleted immediately. The first one she opened came from her best friend.

Dear Les,
Hope you had a safe trip and are now comfortable in your villa. Please let me hear from you soon. I care.
Love, Nance

Leslie sent her a brief reply, friendly and conciliatory, and promised to write more later. The next e-mail was from her ex-private detective and not so friendly.

Bitch.
You have damn near ruined my life but you won't get away with it. The Denver police paid me a visit along with that cowboy sheriff from Leadville. They found MY pistol in your car and traced it back to me. They had the balls to threaten me with accessory to arson and conspiracy to commit murder. Told me all about your little escapade at Andrew's cabin. What the hell were you thinking? No, you weren't thinking at all, that's the obvious answer. So what did all this get you in the end? Not your husband, that's for sure. He's safe with his honey in Pueblo and you are where? Well I don't care where the hell you are. Being your private eye was the biggest mistake I ever made. I'm getting out of Denver and starting over in some place where they've never heard of Leslie Faye Aronson Krag.
Layton

Leslie deleted the e-mail and muttered, "Good riddance, you idiot." She composed an e-mail to her real estate agent and told him that she wanted to lower the asking price on her home to generate a quick sale. She asked him what the current market conditions were like and also to inform her attorney that she was back at her home in Italy.

After shutting down her computer, she walked out to the road and retrieved the day's *International Herald Tribune*. She took it back inside, crawled into bed, and tried to read. But after scanning the front page she gave up and fell asleep.

Andrew and Sarah left the Bartletts' home around seven o'clock and headed south along a dark U. S. 24. Their conversation was minimal until he asked her, "How do you think it went this afternoon? Are you happy?"

"Yes, very happy. Dad was close to tears when we said goodbye but Mom was still on the frosty side."

"We hit her with a lot but I think she'll come around."

"Right, more like later than sooner. The Bartletts have always been on our side and now Roscoe and I are going to be partners. Can you believe it?" Andrew didn't respond. After a lengthy silence, she added, "Hey, are you OK with this?"

"I'm still trying to get my head around it."

"Which means something's bothering you. Talk to me, please."

"Your idea took me by surprise, that's all. It would have been nice to talk it over before you sprang it on the whole family like that."

"Agreed, but it actually just came to me—poof—right there at the table. All that talk about rebuilding your cabin, what you'd be doing with your free time, hanging out with me in Pueblo.

Seemed like the right thing to do."

"You've known about that stock for years."

"True, but I never paid any attention to it or the stock market. It was something I put away for my retirement." They were silent again for a moment. "Don't you think it's a good investment?"

"I have no idea what the construction business is like in Pueblo. One of the first things I need to do is a market analysis. If it looks good, figure out where to locate the office and how to develop an advertising campaign."

"You can do it, honey bun, I have confidence in you."

"I know that. But while we're talking, I have a favor to ask. Don't put my name in your contract or any of the legal documents."

"Why not?" Her question came out somewhere between a wail and a whine.

"I'm not saying that I don't want the job. I really do, but I don't want you or your money at risk."

"You're not making any sense."

"Your investment should be with RBC, Inc. and not dependent on a third party like me. What if something happened? A serious accident where I couldn't work. You remember that backhoe incident last October when Alex was almost killed? Could have been me in that trench, covered up with tons of dirt. Another thing is doing business with relatives. If there's a financial disaster, it leads to finger pointing, arguments, family disruptions, people not talking to each other for years. It's just not a good idea and I'd hate for that to happen with you and your family. And then there's Leslie, always a threat until the divorce is final."

"Now it makes sense. I'll mention it to Roscoe so he can tell his attorney. But you'll be the boss in Pueblo, spending your time in the office and staying safe."

He turned and grinned. "But I'll have to get out and about, check on my crews, and get my hands dirty in that cool Colorado clay."

"Engineers," she muttered.

They reached Sarah's place shortly before ten o'clock and decided to go straight to bed. Sarah's surgical shift at Parkview Medical Center began at 7:00 A.M. and meant an early wake-up for her. Andrew, in a custom established every morning since he'd moved in with her, set his alarm for 5:30. He'd fix her a small breakfast while she showered; he couldn't sleep in while she went off to a full day's work.

Andrew sat up in bed holding a small tablet and pen. Sarah came out of the bathroom wearing a red plaid Mother Hubbard nightgown she'd received as a Christmas present. "What are you doing," she said, standing in the doorway.

"Making a list, checking it twice, gonna find out—"

She laughed. "You're too late, Christmas is gone."

"Maybe I'm early for next Christmas. No, just jotting down stuff to do tomorrow. Places to go, people to see."

Sarah went back into the bathroom, brushed her teeth, and returned to the bedroom. She walked around to Andrew's side of the bed and made a nudging motion. He moved over slightly so she could sit on the mattress edge. She took his tablet and pen, placed them on the bedside table, and said, "I had a thought."

He grinned at her. "You need some aspirin?"

She gave him a playful punch on the shoulder. "I am *not* Leslie."

"Glad to hear *that*."

"Let me say it another way. I am not going to treat you the way she did."

"Double glad, but I think I'm missing something."

"OK, bottom line. Leslie has lots of money and tonight you learned that I've got several million. I think this bothers you down deep. There's some concern that our relationship may wind up the way yours with Leslie did."

"Damn," he said. "Maybe I'm the one who needs the aspirin."

"Am I getting through?"

"Keep talking, you're getting closer."

"Your wife was a dilettante, spending her days at the country club, playing bridge and tennis, gossiping and partying with all her socialite buddies. I have a nursing career and I intend to stick with it."

"I know that and don't want you to quit."

"Couple of more things. If you want to take off on a hike or backpack, I'd like to go with you. And if you see a fourteener that needs climbing, I'll watch through binoculars from base camp and have some food cooking. But if I can't make it, I'll be waiting at home, not running off to Europe and leaving you a big check."

He pulled her closer and kissed her. "Sounds wonderful. But remember that I didn't go chasing after Leslie when she bugged out. If *you* did something like that, which I don't believe you would, I'd come after you."

She kissed him back and continued, "One last thing. You have a profession and a career, too. I want to see you succeed, that's why I'm investing in RBC."

"I think we already covered that but it's still nice to hear you say it."

"Which reminds me, you worked at a Lexus dealer in Denver before we met. How come you weren't doing your engineer thing?"

"That was one of our sore points. Leslie didn't think I looked dignified enough wearing a hard hat and boots. A coat and tie made me look more professional."

"But you were a car salesman."

"Yeah, and not a very good one," he said. "I hated that job."

"And you think that occupation is a higher class than a construction worker?"

"She did, I didn't."

"Oh boy," she said. "No wonder you two didn't make it."

"Come get under the covers," he said.

She slid into bed and he turned out the lamp. They cuddled for a while, enjoying the familiar intimacy of each other's body. "You know," she said, "you don't have to work in geo-tech engineering. I just want you to be happy with whatever you're doing."

"Thanks, sweetheart, but I wouldn't change a thing."

CHAPTER FOUR

YOU ARE CONSIDERED A FUGITIVE FROM JUSTICE

On the second morning of her return to Italy, Leslie found a new source of personal energy. Almost over the effects of jet lag, she went shopping for new clothes among the *haute couture* shops in Siena. On a sudden impulse while passing a beauty salon, she went inside and got a color and cut. Still parted in the middle, her hair was now a soft ash blonde, cut short to the neck with the ends curving inward, shaping her face within an attractive oval. After a full lunch with two generous glasses of the local Chianti, she went home and took a nap.

Leslie had a dream, something that rarely happened, about Roger Halliday. When she awoke suddenly, she thought the telephone was ringing and picked up the handset. She heard only the disappointing dial tone. *Why hasn't he called back?*

Later that afternoon, she reluctantly called the 'head doctor' in Florence and made an appointment for next week. Maria had enthusiastically recommended Dr. Tonino Bertolucci, saying that he was the brother of the famous film director and screenwriter, Bernardo Bertolucci. Maria also said, "He has treated many people in the movie business so he should be well qualified to help you."

Leslie couldn't quite grasp what Maria was driving at, but promised that she would meet with Dr. Bertolucci at least once before committing to a long term treatment plan.

That evening, Leslie composed a long e-mail to Nancy, proudly reporting that she had followed through on her promise and would soon visit a prominent psychiatrist for help. She also reminded Nancy that she had agreed to come to Italy for an all-expenses-paid vacation, with her husband, Joe. She added that any time would be great, except for June when her landlady would need the villa.

Leslie rejoined her bridge club the next afternoon, the group she belonged to before her recent traumatic experience in Colorado. The seven other women included three well-traveled Italian ladies who spoke excellent English. The others were expatriates: three Americans and one Englishwoman.

The ladies welcomed her back with equal measures of jubilation and curiosity. They knew the purpose of her trip to America and wanted to hear all the juicy details. She obliged them but told a rather fanciful and distorted story; Andrew desperately wanted to reconcile with her but she suspected he wasn't sincere. She told them that she'd hired a private detective, found evidence of his blatant infidelity, and emphatically declared that she'd have none of that. She concluded by saying she was the one who filed for divorce and cautioned the others to beware of handsome young men who wanted only sex and money while giving nothing in return. She omitted mention of a burning cabin in Leadville and the loss of her precious BMW red convertible. The only other topic of conversation centered on the scandals surrounding the Italian Prime Minister and his flagrant appointments of nubile young women of dubious qualifications to government posts. Not surprisingly, little bridge was played that afternoon.

That evening, Leslie received several e-mails. The first came from her real estate agent who recommended the asking price on her home be reduced to $895,000. She flinched when she saw the number, noting that it was $34,000 lower than the current price. She'd probably break even if it sold at the new price, but that was still better than making a large monthly mortgage payment on an empty house. She sent a simple reply, "Do it." *When that place is sold, I won't have a home in America. Am I going to wind up a rootless woman, a stranger only sampling the cities of Europe alone?*

The next e-mail was from her attorney.

Dear Leslie,

I have recently learned that you left the Parkview Medical Center of your own accord and fled the country under suspicious circumstances. I presume that you have returned to your home in Italy.

I was extremely disappointed to hear this news. When I talked to you last, I suggested that you retain counsel from the Pueblo area, an attorney experienced in criminal matters. Now, in the eyes of the law, you are considered a fugitive from justice. This is regrettable because I believe the prosecution would have had great difficulty proving your guilt.

You have several thousand dollars left in your account with me. Any future action on your pending divorce should not be a significant expense. I expect it will be granted within several months so a large portion of my retainer will be returned. When that occurs, it will mark the end of our professional relationship. I shall not, in good conscience, be able to represent you any longer.

With best wishes for your future,
Paul Harrington

Leslie sighed. Sorry you feel that way, she thought, but I don't think I'll be needing you again anyway. Probably no great loss.

She was surprised to find the next e-mail, a short one from Julie, her married daughter who lived in New Jersey.

Dear Mom,

I'm probably the last person on earth you want to hear from but I have no choice right now. I called your home but got a message saying the number was disconnected. Where are you? I need to get away from here for a while and I'd like to see you. Maybe we can bury the hatchet and be friends again. Or at least be civil with each other. Please say yes.

Love, Julie

"I'll be damned," said Leslie aloud. "She was right on target with the first dozen words." Leslie recalled the last time she'd seen Julie, at her wedding to Andrew four and one-half years ago. Julie was drinking heavily and dancing with Andrew; it looked like she was trying to hump him, right on the dance floor. The two women got into a heated argument and it turned physical, both winding up in a flower bed with Julie's dress ruined in the process. She vividly remembered her daughter's parting words to Andrew,

"You'll regret the day you married the old bitch."

Leslie wondered if Julie had tried to contact her father, a wealthy Wall Street investment banker. Richard Grantham, thirteen years older, had dumped his first wife to marry Leslie nearly thirty years ago. Leslie and Richard had lived a full and glamourous life in Manhattan, dining in the best restaurants and frequently attending the Metropolitan Opera and philanthropic events. Their life changed dramatically after Julie was born. Leslie wanted to move to Connecticut but Richard didn't want a long commute every day. As the marriage careened downhill, Richard began an affair with a younger woman at his bank and eventually filed for divorce. Leslie, a shrewd observer of Richard's conduct, knew all the signs of infidelity and kept a detailed record that helped her win a huge financial settlement. For many years after, Leslie wondered if she could have avoided the divorce if she'd been more diligent with her birth control methods. She also believed that her terrible relationship with Julie was caused by her own regret over the matter. As for Julie's current relationship with Richard, she surmised it wasn't a good one. His present wife, just a few years older than Julie, probably wouldn't stand for any competition for Richard's attention.

Leslie shut down her computer, went to the kitchen and poured herself the old standby of vodka on the rocks. She'd have to sleep on Julie's request. Maybe she'd answer her e-mail tomorrow. Or the next day. Or never.

The days passed uneventfully as Leslie continued to mull over Julie's request, but she couldn't make a decision. Julie hadn't sent a follow-up e-mail, so Leslie felt little pressure to respond. She figured that her daughter had probably made other arrangements for getting away.

Ten days had passed since her return to Italy. After dinner, she sat in her living room reading the *International Herald Tribune.* When the phone rang, she thought it was Marie, responding to an earlier message.

"Faye?" said the faint male voice.

"What?"

"Is this Faye Aronson?"

Temporarily speechless, Leslie recalled that she sometimes used her middle and maiden names when her security might be at risk. "Yes, who's this?"

"Roger Halliday, we met recently."

"Yes, I remember. Where are you?"

"I'd like to drop by your place tonight. Is the invitation still open?"

"You're in Italy now?"

"I know you live somewhere in Castellina but tell me how to find it."

Leslie was grappling with this sudden call from out of nowhere. "Um . . . well, from the center of town take the road marked SR 429 north about three kilometers. Stone monuments mark the driveway and one has a metal plaque that says Casa Campana. I'll leave the lights on. When can I expect you?"

He hung up.

"Damn him," she said, glancing at the clock. It was 8:30.

She bustled about the house in a mild panic, straightening up the living room, kitchen, and her bedroom. She also changed from pajamas and bathrobe into a beige sweater and dark brown woolen pants, washed her face, and applied some makeup. She returned to the living room and tried to finish reading the newspaper but couldn't concentrate. She decided to have some vodka to relax her nerves.

Thirty minutes later, the phone rang again. Fearing it was Halliday calling to cancel his visit, she rushed to answer it. It was Maria, returning Leslie's earlier call. "You sound upset, Leslie. Am I calling at a bad time?"

"No, no, it's OK. I thought it was someone else."

"Your message said you wanted to talk about something."

"It's about my daughter, a very long story. Let's do it another time."

"But I have plenty of time to listen now."

"I just can't. I'm too tired."

"Then I will say goodnight. Don't forget your appointment tomorrow."

"My appointment?"

"Doctor Bertolucci in Firenzi. You promised."

"I won't forget. Goodnight, Maria."

Leslie took her empty glass to the kitchen and poured another vodka over ice. She curled up on the living room couch and sipped her drink, wondering what would happen next. The time passed slowly and, by eleven o'clock, she'd heard nothing more from Halliday. She dozed and eventually fell into a shallow sleep but was startled awake by repeated doorbell chimes.

She rushed to the front door and called out, "Who is it?"

"Halliday," came the answer.

Leslie opened the door and stared in disbelief at the man standing before her. He wore black trousers and a long, black leather jacket. Even more bizarre was his black mustache, a scruffy black beard, and a full head of black hair.

"You're not Roger Halliday. The man I met had silver hair and a clean face."

"It's me. I just look different."

"It's after two o'clock. Where have you been?"

"Sorry, but I got here as soon as I could."

She continued staring at him, unsure of what to say or do next. He shivered, shifting his balance from one foot to the other and said, "I'm cold. Can we continue this discussion inside?"

She looked closely at his face and convinced herself that he was the same man she met on the flight to Dallas. "Yeah, sure, come into the living room."

He stumbled to the couch and slumped into it. "Got anything to drink?"

"Vodka and Scotch."

"Scotch . . . and some ice if you have it."

She went to the kitchen and made him a large drink. He took a long sip and pronounced it smooth as a baby's ass. She sat in a chair opposite and said, "OK, Mr. Halliday, talk to me. Why all this mystery and don't leave anything out."

He looked around and said, "You have a nice place. Thanks for the invite."

So that's the way it's going to be. "Where were you calling from?"

"It wasn't Italy."

"Then how did you get here?"

"An airplane. Picked up a car in Pisa and here I am."

"Your outfit doesn't seem to fit the export/import business."

"I do other kinds of business. What I'm wearing works well enough."

"We're getting nowhere fast," she said. Halliday laughed but suddenly doubled up in pain. "Are you hurt? What's wrong?"

He drained his glass and struggled to stand. "I'm sorry but I have to get some sleep. If you'll show me to a guest room, I'll be eternally grateful."

Leslie grabbed his arm and felt something wet on her hand. "You're bleeding. Let's go to the bathroom and look at it."

She took off his jacket and tossed it in the bathtub. He sat on the toilet while she cut a long slit up his left sleeve with scissors. When she found a small piece of skin missing near his elbow she said, "What happened here?"

"Just a little nick, nothing to get excited about."

Leslie washed his wound carefully, dabbed polysporin ointment on it, and made a professional looking bandage with sterile cotton pads and gauze wrap. "There. I think you'll survive, Mr. James Bond. Any more nicks that need patching?"

"No, that's the only one."

She helped him stand and led him to one of the guest bedrooms. He fell directly into bed and she removed his black leather boots. "A favor, please," he said. "My bag's in the car. Can you get it? And my cell phone's there somewhere."

Hands on her hips, she said, "Anything else? Like maybe a Big Mac?" He only groaned and she went out the front door, surprised to find a beat-up Fiat sedan about ten years old. *If this is a rental he should get a refund.* She found a black duffel in the back seat and a cell phone on the floor near the brake pedal. She locked the car and took the items back to the guest bedroom.

Halliday was fast asleep. She watched him from the doorway and was overcome with an intense curiosity, wanting to check his cell phone and rummage through the duffel bag. But she had second thoughts. *He surely has his secrets and I've got mine. It would probably be smarter if we let nature take its course and slowly peel back this onion, one secret at a time.*

CHAPTER FIVE

YOU MAKE IT SOUND SO ROMANTIC

Roscoe Bartlett sat at his office desk, thinking about Sarah's financial proposition and all the work it would take to close the deal. He'd have to get his CPA and attorney to work out the details and that would mean traveling often to Denver. With any luck, he'd meet them both on the same day. But first, he would have to find a qualified appraiser, one who could put a realistic and fair price on the business. This was necessary to protect himself as well as Sarah.

Roscoe had a milestone birthday coming later this year; sixty five and he could start collecting Social Security. But he wasn't sure he should take it now or delay it for a year or two and get a higher monthly payment. He didn't need the money. In addition to his Marine Corps retired pay and Tanice's part-time job at a local bank, he drew only a small salary as the head of RBC, Inc. Profits from the business were plowed right back into the company.

Perhaps, just maybe, he should consider retirement. But what would he do with himself? Tanice wouldn't appreciate him hanging around the house all day.

Originally from a small town in Montana, Roscoe enlisted in the Marines when he was nineteen. After boot camp and basic infantry training, he was assigned to an infantry unit at Camp Pendleton, California. A short time later, he was a grunt rifleman in the 4th Marines, fighting in the jungles of Viet Nam west and north of Danang. He won the Bronze Star for taking charge of his squad when their patrol was ambushed by the Viet Cong and, even though wounded by sniper fire, led his troops in the destruction of the enemy's position.

At the end of his Viet Nam duty tour, he accepted an appointment to OCS at Quantico, VA. This unexpected move surprised his family and friends because he had never considered a military career until that time. After officers' Basic School, he wound up in combat engineering, a field that was seriously shorthanded at the time. Technical schooling followed and he was headed again to Viet Nam for a second tour. But just before leaving the states, he met a beautiful Tanice Johnson one night at a Mexican restaurant in San Diego; she was the quintessential blonde and shapely California girl. He conducted a vigorous courtship by mail throughout their one year apart. When his platoon wasn't building airstrips, roads, or bunkers, he was writing to Tanice. Their wedding shortly after his return was sort of an anticlimax.

They agreed to delay having children, feeling it was prudent because of Roscoe's military career. Unfortunately, as time went by, the idea was postponed until it was too late. This was the only regret either one had during their entire forty years together. Now they doted on two dogs, a golden retriever named Midas for

Roscoe, and Fido, a beagle for Tanice whose name she spelled as Phideaux.

Roscoe retired as a Lieutenant Colonel and the Bartletts moved to Leadville, attracted by Rocky Mountain vistas and the many outdoor activities offered by their immediate surroundings. Emmaline, in her role as a friendly real estate agent, found them a beautiful 2.5 acre building site with excellent views of Mt. Elbert, Colorado's highest peak at 14,333 feet. They built their home with Roscoe acting as the general contractor and Tanice as chief designer. This commercial experience went so well that it prompted him to form RBC, Inc., and build another home, this time for a friend. The business grew steadily from that point.

Roscoe was inwardly quite pleased with the way things were working out. He had hired Andrew last August and considered him not only a valued and trusted employee but also his proxy son. Roscoe wanted to keep family and business matters separate during his company's expansion in Pueblo but he'd bend over backwards to make sure that Andrew and Sarah's future, as well as RBC's business, would be a bright success.

Andrew spent every work day that week gathering information. First on his list was the boss man himself; he called Roscoe on Monday morning and spent nearly an hour picking his brain. For example, he wanted to know just how he got started in Leadville and what suggestions he might have for Andrew. Roscoe fell back on his Marine Corps experience for one tidbit: make a recon. Andrew interpreted this wisdom to make a wide-ranging and comprehensive inspection of the terrain in and around Pueblo and the surrounding parts of the county. Not an easy thing to do since the population was well over 100,000. However, he put many miles on his SUV looking at everything of possible interest. By comparison, Leadville and Lake County had 5,000 people at best. Roscoe's admonition was, "Network, network, network."

Andrew got it. He worked on the design of a qualifications brochure that would later be circulated among realtors, city and county public works personnel, and other likely clients. Consulting a web site designer would come later for more company exposure. He asked Darlene in the Leadville office to e-mail him pictures of finished structures that RBC had built, both residential and commercial. He also asked for a condensed record of major projects completed over the last five years, experience that would be highlighted in the brochure along with his own professional qualifications. His brief career as a Lexus salesman would not be included.

Andrew was concerned about business competition in Pueblo and used his computer to search for data on this subject. He was flabbergasted to learn there were over 300 companies, large and small, that were listed as commercial and industrial building contractors. A smaller number of specialist outfits dealt with excavation, restoration, concrete work, and heating and ventilation. He wondered if there was any room in this mix, any market niche for RBC.

He was also sensitive to the local and American economic situation. A planned development north of the city called Pueblo Springs Ranch had been put on hold and kept there for two years running because of the slow economy. This 24,000 acre property, to be developed by a Nevada company, might be a source of business if it ever got off the ground. He also checked the employment want ads in *The Pueblo Chieftain* and found that skilled construction workers were very much in demand, seemingly a paradox if the economy was as bad as the government said it was. *Who was hiring and for what reason?* If there was a labor shortage and he did win a contract for a project or two, he might have to lure Alex, Chris and Chavez down to Pueblo.

But all was not gloomy. During his reconnaissance, he looked at Pueblo West, a community of nearly 17,000 that straddled U. S. 50. Construction was ongoing but most of it involved accessory structures such as sheds, carports, and garages. The bright spot was that less than 60% of the community's available land had been built on. He saw several new homes for sale by different builders with asking prices covering a large range. This area deserved another visit.

Sarah brought home a pizza on Friday after work and found Andrew in her office, deep in concentration. She bent over, draped her arm around his neck and kissed him on the cheek. "That's enough work for today, sweetheart."

He got up and gave her a hug. "Glad you're home. How was your day?"

"Pretty routine. Pizza's in the oven. Want a beer or a glass of wine?"

"Beer is good," he said. "I'll turn on the gas log."

They met again in the living room when Sarah brought their drinks on a tray. She set his can of beer, a frosted mug, and her glass of Merlot on the coffee table between the couch and fireplace. They sat close on the couch and toasted each other. "Here's to a very nice weekend with you," she said.

"I'll drink to that," he added.

"Pizza will be ready soon. Sausage, green peppers, and onions, your fave."

"I had a light lunch today so even road kill on tar paper would taste pretty good right now."

Sarah made an ugly face and said, "Bleeaaah."

Andrew laughed. "Hear anything from Roscoe today?"

"Just a message on my cell. He has meetings in Denver next week. Told me not to go cashing in any stock just yet. But the deal is moving ahead, just taking a little bit longer than I thought."

"We've got plenty of time. Tomorrow I'd like to take a drive out to Pueblo West. I want to show you some things, a couple of lots for sale in a nice area. Might want to build a spec home or two."

"OK, but you're the expert on home building."

"You know more about it than you think. I want you to see some of the homes out there and get your ideas. It's all part of your investment and having a vote on how your money gets spent."

"Gee," she said, "You make it sound so romantic. How can I resist?"

"It'll be a fun day, you'll see."

A timer bell went off in the kitchen. Sarah took the pizza from the oven and returned with half of it, cut into smaller pieces. After each had devoured a piece, Sarah said, "Oh, one interesting thing did happen. I saw that woman detective today, Hardcastle's her name."

"At the hospital?"

"Yes, visiting another police officer who had surgery. She was the one who questioned me when your wife was in recovery and she remembered me."

"I'll bet she remembers Leslie, too."

"Right on that. She's been talking to Sheriff Waters and she's still mad about letting her get away."

"She'll get over it eventually. I already have."

"Oh. Another bit of news, separate subject. I have a shift change next week, three to eleven."

"Really? How's that going to work?"

She smiled. "Hard to tell, never having you around before."

"So you'll be getting home around midnight but you can sleep in the next morning. *We* can sleep in. Together. In your cozy bed. Has a nice ring to it."

She gave him a messy kiss, her lips coated with sausage juice and tomato paste. "I like the way you think, Krag."

Leslie slept poorly even though she had locked her bedroom door. She was certain that Halliday was sleeping soundly but she wasn't about to take any chances with a strange man in the house. A noise woke her once in the middle of the night, a banging on the side of the house near her window. It turned out to be a loose shutter. She was able to stop the noise but she'd have the caretaker fix it later.

She finally got out of bed about eight o'clock and made a large pot of coffee, anticipating that her guest would want some when he woke up. Her own breakfast, in addition to coffee, was a hard roll with butter and orange marmalade. She looked in on him several times, taking pains to be quiet while moving about the house. During one of the several moments when she stood in the guest bedroom's doorway, Halliday, who was sleeping on his stomach, shifted his body sideways, causing a pistol to slide from under his pillow onto the carpeted floor. A solid 'thunk' startled Leslie but Halliday slept on peacefully.

Leslie decided to shower, get dressed, and leave early for her appointment with Dr. Bertolucci. Just before she left, she wrote a note and left it on the counter near the coffee pot.

> *Roger,*
> *I have an appointment in Florence and will be gone for most of the day. Please take all of your things and leave before I get back.*
> *Leslie*

As she drove down the driveway, she wondered if Halliday would honor her request. She felt ambivalent about whether she wanted to see him again and laughed out loud when she remembered seeing his pistol fall to the floor. *I locked my bedroom door but he was ready to defend himself in case I attacked him. Or was he thinking that someone else might come after him? Too bad I don't have Layton's pistol anymore. We could have some target practice and find out who's the better shot.*

CHAPTER SIX

LOOKS LIKE I'M JUST IN TIME FOR COCKTAILS

Leslie hated driving in Florence. The streets were too narrow, the drivers raced around like they were competing in a Grand Prix, and parking spaces were practically nonexistent. Employing a tactic Maria had shown her on an earlier trip, she parked her Mercedes CL 550 next to a train station on the city's outskirts and took a taxi into the city.

She had an hour to kill before her three o'clock appointment so she decided on lunch at a cafe close to Dr. Bertolucci's office. She ordered coffee, a ham and cheese sandwich, and grappa, an unaged brandy as fortification for the coming ordeal. After consuming all three items, she had another grappa and then another. Perhaps now the coming session wouldn't be so unpleasant after all.

She walked swiftly along the cobblestones, raising her collar to ward off a biting wind that had suddenly sprung up. If snow was coming, she wanted to get home immediately after her appointment.

On the second floor of a large office building, a dowdy woman receptionist greeted her and gave her some forms to fill out. "The cost for today is two hundred Euros," she said, "and one fifty for next visits. How will you pay?"

"Cash."

The forms were in English and similar to the countless questionnaires she'd completed in America. Leslie scribbled her answers but completed only the blanks for basic personal information. She handed back the papers and returned to her seat. Ten minutes later, the receptionist ushered Leslie into an inner office and asked her to sit on a couch opposite a large overstuffed chair.

Leslie looked around the room, her nostrils picking up an unpleasant musty odor that reminded her of wet wool. One wall was total bookshelves, floor to ceiling; the wall opposite displayed diplomas, certificates and a large oil painting of Swiss Alps covered with snow. Long heavy tapestries in muted red and green patterns hung on both sides of a single window that looked out on the street below.

The door burst open and in he barged, rubbing his hands together and flashing a wide smile with perfect teeth. A short man with a slight build, he had a pencil thin black mustache and goatee, a large volume of suspiciously black hair, and wore glasses with thick lenses and heavy black frames. "Hello, hello," he said, "Good afternoon, Signora Krag." He came up closer and took her hand. "Tonino Bertolucci, at your service. It is a pleasure to meet you. Are you comfortable?"

Leslie could only grunt, "I guess so."

"Excellent, excellent," he said, taking his chair and moving it closer. "Then let us begin. Tell me why you are here."

"For my appointment?"

"Let me rephrase my question. Why do you wish to speak with me?"

"I made a promise to my friends, Nancy and Maria, that I would talk to a—that I'd get some help."

He made an exaggerated scowl, followed by an odd laugh, making Leslie wonder if he'd gotten too familiar with the more eccentric people of the film industry. "Help for yourself, yes? And not for your friends."

"Yes, for myself."

"Excellent, excellent. I see that you are American but you are living in Italy. Will you be staying a long time?"

"I'm renting a villa in Castellina but I still have a home in the states. Do you know Denver? In Colorado?"

"Oh yes, I'm familiar with it. I have toured your country several times."

Leslie smiled, feeling more at ease. "But I'm selling it. No plans to go back."

"Then you will become a citizen of Italy, yes?"

His question made her focus on the crucial issue of her future, something which she'd avoided thinking about. After a pause, she said, "This is a problem. I'm not sure what I'm going to do or where I should live."

"Let me ask this. Why are you selling your home in Denver? Is there a reason you don't wish to live there again?"

She sighed. "Well . . . yes. I can't go back. They'll arrest me and put me in prison." She reached into her purse, pulled out a tissue and dabbed her tearing eyes. "I'm a fugitive, I burned down my husband's cabin, and I . . ."

After a moment of silence, "Would you like something? A glass of water?"

"A stiff drink would be nice."

Another pause, then he said, "Please tell me how all this came about."

Leslie started with last August when Andrew went on his backpack trip to the Maroon Bells and she left for Paris and then Italy. She told the doctor about her return to Denver, attempting a reconciliation, but Andrew had found another woman; how she had hired a private detective and how she took his pistol and drove south for a confrontation with Andrew and the other woman. "When I got to his cabin and saw what was going on with him and the whore, I lost it. Burned the damned thing down and drove to Pueblo, hoping to find them together and end it once and for all. A stupid move, all things considered. Wrecked my car, wound up in the hospital, and my best friend came down and helped me escape. Had to do that or they'd put me in jail. Never done anything like that before in all my life." After a pause she said, "Shouldn't you be taking notes on all this?"

"Sorry, I should have explained. For our first meeting, I want to listen carefully to everything you say. Immediately after our talk, I will write a report to myself, pose some questions, a few discussion points for our next meeting."

"OK, you're the doctor."

"Excellent, excellent. When you left Colorado last August, what were your intentions, your feelings towards your husband?"

"I thought we needed some time apart, to think about our marriage and why it wasn't working. I also wanted him to miss me, realize what a great wife he had, and beg me to come back."

"But you gave him a large sum of money and made it easy for him to get along without you. Your actions seem inconsistent, signora."

"Dammit, I was trying to save my marriage." Her voice became louder. "He saw some greener grass and dumped me for a younger woman. Just like that first son of a bitch I married. You can't trust these assholes. You lower your guard for a minute and they shit all over you." She sniffled, dabbed her eyes and blew her nose. "It's not fair."

"So the marriage is over, is that true?"

"Yes, he filed for divorce and it should be granted in a month or two."

"Do you now see this as a reality?"

"What are you driving at?"

"I'm asking if you are ready to accept this fact and put it in your past. Begin to focus on your life ahead."

"Yes, but there is still some unfinished business between us."

"What do you mean?"

"I don't want to discuss this anymore."

He scowled again but didn't laugh this time. "You mentioned a previous marriage. Please tell me about that."

Leslie calmed down and described her affair with Richard, who was married when they met, their marriage of twenty years that produced Julie, their only child, and how he had left Leslie for another woman who was thirty years younger than he. She bragged about winning a huge financial settlement when they divorced. "Andrew Krag did the same thing to me," she said, "and I want my pound of flesh."

"And you are hoping to receive *more* money?"

"Hell no," she said. "He doesn't have any."

Dr. Bertolucci started to say something but hesitated for a moment. "Your daughter, do you have a good relationship with her?"

"Not at all. Haven't spoken to her in years. She was always daddy's girl, his little angel. She was angry when Richard and I divorced. All my fault, you see."

"People take sides when a couple divorce. They tend to identify with either the husband or the wife."

"Strangely enough, I got an e-mail from her the other day. She's trying to find me, says she's in some kind of trouble and needs to get away."

"And what have you told her?"

"Nothing yet. Haven't decided whether I want to open myself up to her brutal attacks and emotional meltdowns."

"Shouldn't you at least inquire? Perhaps ask her to explain her situation before you reach any conclusions?"

Leslie pondered. "Yeah, I guess I owe her that much."

"Excellent, excellent," he said. He glanced at his watch. "Our time is up but I believe we have made excellent progress. Next time I would like to hear about the first part of your life; parents, siblings, schools and so forth. Is that agreeable?"

"We'll see."

He stood and opened his office door. "I would like you to consider making a visit to Assisi or La Verna, locations known to our beloved St. Francis. While you are there, contemplate his prayer of serenity. It may help to bring you peace of mind."

"If I have the time." After he left, she stopped at the receptionist's desk and handed over two hundred Euros.

The receptionist asked, "Would you like to make your next appointment?"

"I'll have to call you later."

Leslie's anxiety level rose steadily while driving back to Castellina, wondering what she would find at her villa. She drove slowly up her driveway in the darkness, looking for Halliday's car, but couldn't see it anywhere. She parked in the small garage, went inside and called out, "Hello, anybody here?" No answer.

She made her way to the bedroom where Halliday had slept and peeked inside. The bed had been made and all traces of him were gone. She hung her coat in a hall closet, went straight to the kitchen freezer, and poured herself a large vodka. After a long pull, she sighed and finally relaxed.

Leslie took the drink to her makeshift office, turned on her computer and composed an e-mail.

Dear Julie,

I've been traveling and just got your e-mail. I'm living in Italy now and have put my home in Denver up for sale. That's why you got the disconnect message.

You mentioned something about getting away for a while. What's going on? Are you in trouble? Please tell me more about your situation.

Love, Mother

She hit 'Send' and went back to the kitchen feeling pleased with herself. She had told a small lie about traveling and only revealed the name of the country where she currently lived. *No chance of her showing up on my doorstep that way.*

While pouring herself a second drink, she heard the doorbell ring. Holding the drink in one hand she opened the door with the other. The man standing at her door smiled and said, "Looks like I'm just in time for cocktails."

Temporarily speechless, she stared at Roger Halliday, transformed to look like the man she met almost two weeks ago. He wore a tan overcoat, his hair was the original silver, and his face shaved clean. "*You again,*" she blurted out.

"Yep, it's me."

"What do you want, Halliday?"

"A second chance. Can we try this again?"

Leslie hesitated before opening the door wider. "Oh, all right. Come inside." He draped his coat over a living room chair and sat on the couch. "You like scotch, as I recall."

"Lots, with a little ice."

Leslie went to the kitchen and made him a generous drink. She returned and sat at the far end of the couch, watching him take a first sip and noting his dark suit, white shirt and maroon tie. "You look a lot more civilized now," she said, "like the man I met on the Dallas flight."

"And you are more beautiful than the woman who sat next to me."

Leslie blushed. "Yeah, well . . . I was in pretty bad shape. Just got out of the hospital after wrecking my car."

He reached over and touched his glass against hers. "To healthier times."

After a taste, she said, "Have you seen a doctor about your arm?"

"It's fine. I cleaned it up this morning and put a new bandage on it."

"Tell me how that happened."

He shifted his body and took another drink. "Doing some

business with an uncooperative customer, unexpected complications with his associates who didn't like the terms of the contract."

"Importing or exporting?"

He laughed softly. "Definitely exporting, but they weren't buying."

"I figured you weren't in Italy. How did you get here?"

"A plane dropped me in Pisa, my associates had a car waiting, and here I am."

Leslie had a thought about the pistol she'd seen but let it go. "It seems that every answer you give me generates a half dozen new questions. Why is that?"

"I have a question for *you*. When we met, you said your name was Faye Aronson. But the note you left was signed Leslie. Which is it?"

She smiled. "Good catch, Roger, if that's *your* real name. My full name is Leslie Faye Krag and Aronson is my maiden name. I use different names, depending on the occasion and situation."

"You're married? Where's your husband?"

She smiled even wider this time. "Are you hungry?"

"Very."

"Then drink up, Roger, you're taking me out to dinner." She chugged her drink, found her coat, and handed him her keys. "We'll take my car."

CHAPTER SEVEN

SOMETHING ELSE SOUNDS ABOUT RIGHT

Andrew woke up around seven o'clock on Saturday morning. He started to slide out of bed when Sarah whispered, "Where are you going?"

"To the kitchen and start the coffee. Stay put and I'll bring you some."

She moaned softly and rolled over.

He turned on the coffee machine and picked up *The Chieftain* and *Denver Post* from the front porch. Andrew had started delivery of the Post shortly after he'd moved in. While warming two huge cinnamon buns in the toaster oven, he read the comics and laughed at Dilbert, Non Sequitur, Peanuts, and Doonesbury. When all was ready, he put cups of coffee, glasses of orange juice and the warm buns, along with the two newspapers, on a breakfast tray.

"Well now, what do we have here?" Sarah wondered when he came back.

"Breakfast for milady. Just a spot of nourishment to tide you over."

She sat up and, supported by two pillows against the headboard, Andrew placed the tray across her lap. She tasted the coffee as he slid back into bed. "Wonderful," she cooed. "Can I look forward to this every morning next week?"

"Sure, just fill out a card and hang it on the doorknob."

Sarah alternated between the bun, orange juice and coffee, occasionally glancing at Andrew who was looking at the *Post's* front page. "Anything interesting today?"

"The usual trouble in Afghanistan. There was an assassination attempt on the governor of Kandahar Province. The hit man had a weapon tucked into his boots instead of hiding it in a turban. The governor's right hand man was killed and one of his bodyguards wounded pretty badly. They're blaming the C. I. A. and the Taliban is trying to rally support against the American infidels. The whole thing is pretty confusing right now."

"And the governor didn't get hurt?"

"No, but the assassin escaped and they believe he was wounded."

Sarah put on her glasses. She raised her cup like the Statue of Liberty's torch and he took it, not needing a verbal mandate, and went back to the kitchen for a refill.

When he returned, Sarah had disposed of the breakfast tray and was reading *The Chieftain.* He crawled back under the covers and they read their respective papers, pausing periodically to comment on something or ask a question. Andrew remarked that the weekend weather looked promising but a snow storm was expected on Monday night or early Tuesday morning.

After Sarah finished her paper, she returned her glasses to the

Shattering The Triangle 67
night stand and slid under the covers so far that only her eyes were visible.

Andrew looked over and said, "Uh, oh. Looks like somebody is having a sinking spell."

She rolled toward him, threw an arm across his chest and tickled the inside of his ear with her tongue. "What I would really like right now is for you to make love to me. Do we have time?"

He pulled her closer and was surprised, no delighted, to learn when he caressed her body's smooth curves, she'd removed her nightgown somehow without him noticing. "We always have time for that," he whispered.

Afterwards they slept for an hour, took turns in the bathroom, and were ready to leave just before noon. "Nothing like an early start," she said with a lewd grin.

"Be sure to wear your boots, sweetheart," he said. "The ground we'll be walking will probably have a lot of snow and mud."

They drove west on U. S. 50 and entered the Pueblo West community near the Desert Hawk Golf Course. This was the oldest part of the development and the neighborhoods were mature and well established. "We'll be doing a lot of driving," he said, "just so you can get a feel for the kinds of houses that have been built."

The homes seemed to vary in size, architectural style, and probable cost with no dominant pattern emerging. Small adobe homes sat next to two story mansions that had at least twice the square footage and one or two more garages.

They reached Juniper Road and turned back east, driving along the edge of Lake Pueblo State Park, then heading south until State Highway 96, and west again on that road. When the highway turned into Siloam Road, they continued for a mile and turned right into the southwest part of Pueblo West. They pulled up to an open area and Andrew stopped his SUV. "Here we are," he said.

"OK, and *where* is here?"

"We're looking at the southern edge of the state park," he said, pointing to a line of pine and blue spruce trees about two hundred yards ahead. "Our home buyers will have privacy and nice views."

"Our buyers."

"Sure. Let's take a hike, *partner.*"

They walked to the trees and back along the road that fronted numerous lots for sale. A light dusting of snow covered most of the ground but the ground was firm because of last night's freezing temperatures.

"Not too many houses out here," she said.

"That's the part I like, the forty percent available to build on. An opportunity to establish a neighborhood." They walked some more and he pointed to a sign advertising a lot for sale by Ron Sebastian Realty. "Did you notice something about this guy?" he said.

"Yes, plenty of signs up. Maybe he'd like to unload a couple real quick."

"That's what I'm thinking. I'll bet if we offered him a package deal—say three lots with some attractive cash—he'd probably jump on it."

"All he could say is no, or come up with a counteroffer."

"OK, here's my plan. Let's pick out the best three lots we can find and have our real estate agent talk to him and put together an offer."

"We have an agent?" She frowned. "Oh no, I don't like where

this is going."

He grinned. "Yep, Mrs. Emmaline Dolan. Hey, she knows the business and might do it for less than her usual commission. It's got win-win written all over it."

"OK, wise guy. But you have to deal with her, not me."

"Done. Let's walk around more, pick out some properties and I'll take pictures. Over lunch, you can tell me what kind of houses I should build on them."

"Buona Sera," bellowed the owner of the trattoria, "welcome to Buitonis." He escorted Leslie and Roger to a table with a flourish of hands and more animated greetings. Roger muttered, "He probably thinks we're an old married couple."

At Roger's request, a bottle of the locally produced Chianti soon appeared at their table along with bread and olive oil. They ordered a shared appetizer of deep fried calamari to be followed by fish and pasta dishes.

"What do *you* think we look like?" said Leslie, picking up on Roger's earlier observation.

"Oh, a couple on their first date, eager to learn more about each other. Perhaps lovers on their third or fourth date, anticipating a romantic evening. Or maybe something else, something beyond our wildest imaginations."

She drank some wine and said, "Something else sounds about right."

He laughed and touched his glass to hers. "Here's to something else." He took a sip and said, "Back at your place you told me that you're married."

"I was hoping you'd forget about that." He smiled and shrugged. She was tired of telling people about her marital troubles, first Maria and then Dr. Bertolucci, but she felt that Halliday was entitled to civil dinner conversation. "Yes, he's back in Colorado but he filed for divorce so I should be single again in a month or two."

"So you'd been with him in Colorado before we met?"

"Yes, trying to convince him that we should stay married."

"Was it a long marriage?"

"A little over four years but we lived together for a year before that."

He shook his head. "Hard to believe he'd leave a beautiful woman like you, so vivacious and intelligent."

"Thanks for that," she said, sipping wine to hide her blushing. She knew it was polished B. S. but she still liked hearing it.

"I know there are two sides to every story," he continued, "especially inside a marriage. Nobody outside of it knows what goes on inside. Sometimes not even the couple themselves."

Leslie laughed softly and felt some of her tension fade away. In the ensuing silence, she thought about what she wanted to ask him. There was no point in discussing his appearance in black the night before, his wounded arm or the pistol she'd seen on the bedroom floor. He'd just refuse to talk about it and change the subject. So she'd have to sidestep the sensitive topics for now and focus on the safe ones. For example, who was the Halliday that wore suits and appeared to be a conservative businessman? "Are you married, Roger?"

"No, but I was once, several years ago. We had a good life for a while but we each wanted different things."

She decided they'd have a more pleasant evening if they didn't swap marriage disaster stories so she shifted her approach. "How about your early life? Where did you grow up?"

He brightened. "All over the country, actually. My father was a pilot, career Air Force, so we moved around a lot. Lived in Germany and later Thailand when I was a kid. Have some fond memories of friends I made. When Viet Nam came along, Dad was all gung ho about it, a chance to fight for our country."

"I'll bet he got his wish."

"Not exactly. He was shot down over North Viet Nam and spent a couple of years in the Hanoi Hilton before he died. The bastards never sent his body back, one of the things on my bucket list to resolve."

"I'm sorry. Maybe we should change the subject."

The look in his eyes told her that this was important and he wanted to continue. "When that happened, I decided that I'd finish the job for him. Metaphorically speaking, of course. So I won an appointment to the Air Force Academy and started my career but I never got to fly. Wound up in a special part of the Air Force, a computer geek with an advanced degree earned at government expense, dealing with communication security, interceptions, cryptography, and all kinds of spooky stuff. But after ten years of all that, I figured I may as well leave the military and make a lot more money doing the same thing."

"And did you?"

"Yep, got started with a company out west called Digger dot com and really enjoyed it for a while. Good money but super long hours."

Something about the company's name triggered a visible response in Leslie that caused Roger to pause. Where the hell have I heard that name before? she wondered. "No, go ahead," she said. "What happened then?"

"They found me and my life changed forever. Courted me like

crazy, the damnedest recruiting drive you ever saw."

"They?"

"Members of our wonderful government from an organization that embraces secrecy like a religion and abhors publicity of any kind."

Leslie smiled and felt the flush of a biblical moment. His story and their mutual experiences over the last two days were suddenly in sharper focus. "So you joined up. I'll bet they offered you plenty of opportunities to avenge your father's death and perform all kinds of patriotic missions for the glory of our country."

"You're a very perceptive woman, Leslie."

"So that's what you're doing. Pretending to be a businessman but traipsing all over the world doing their dirty work."

"Not quite. I did for several years but the internal politics were also dirty and they didn't follow through on their promises. So I quit. Sort of."

"Now I'm confused. I thought I had all this figured out."

A waiter brought their calamari and Roger ordered another bottle of wine.

Roger continued, "Just let me say this. I'm doing the same kind of work but now I'm an independent agent. Or consultant, if you prefer that term. I only accept assignments on a contractual basis, ones that I feel are absolutely necessary and morally justified."

"Give me an example."

"This morning I noticed that you get the *International Herald Tribune.* Take a look through the paper, any day of the week, and carefully read the articles about the violence in the Middle East, Iraq, Iran, Afghanistan and Pakistan. Or shift your attention to the countries in Eastern Europe like Bosnia, Serbia and Croatia. Maybe even a couple of African fiefdoms. Government officials in these countries or their loyal opposition send business my way but I can assure you that I turn down more jobs than I take on."

Leslie was faced with an internal conflict, a stark dichotomy of feelings toward this man. The danger presented by his agent-in-black image repelled her but she was strongly attracted to the well dressed gentleman who professed American patriotism and did the dirty work according to his own ethical standards. "I get the picture and don't need any more detail. But I am curious about one thing. Where do you stay when you're not traveling?"

"I have a home, a very nice one in Vienna, Virginia. Close to the Pentagon and not far from Dulles International for the long flights."

"How did you come to be in Colorado Springs?"

"My mother's lived there since I was at the academy. Unfortunately, she's in a nursing home so I try to see her whenever I can."

Their entrees arrived. They ate and drank more wine while the conversation drifted to safer and more general subjects. Over coffee and gelato, Leslie said, "What do you want from me, Roger?"

"Fair question. I'd like to hang out at your place for a couple of days until I'm well enough to travel again."

"That's it?"

"No, I could also enjoy your company and get to know you better."

"Fair answer. But how do I know I can trust you?"

"You don't. But it's not me you should be concerned about."

"Who then?"

"Various people, unhappy customers who might be trying to find me."

"Good grief."

"But why would anyone think to look for me in a hillside villa outside a small Tuscan village? No, I think we're safe."

Leslie shuddered, wondering how the situation became a 'we' problem instead of his alone. "OK, but just for a couple of nights. Then you have to leave."

He took both of her hands in his and gave her his sincerest smile. "Thanks, Leslie. You're one in a million."

She looked away from his dark blue eyes and noticed that most of the other diners had left. "I think they'd like us to finish up."

When they returned to her villa, they hung their coats and stood close to each other in the kitchen. "Can I interest you in a nightcap?" she said.

"Sorry, but I'm exhausted and have to get some sleep." He leaned toward her and kissed her cheek. "Thanks again, I'll see you in the morning."

Leslie could only say, "Yeah, in the morning," as he lumbered down the hall to his bedroom.

She turned out the lights, went to her bedroom, and removed all her clothes. She lay awake for a long time, thinking about her mysterious guest and what she'd learned about him tonight. That is, if he was telling the truth. She didn't lock her bedroom door this time. If he somehow found a new source of energy during the night, she didn't want a closed door to stand in the way of enjoying that 'something else' he mentioned at dinner.

CHAPTER EIGHT

I SHOULD OPEN A WITNESS PROTECTION CENTER

Leslie dragged herself out of bed at seven o'clock and made a large pot of coffee. She moved quietly about the house, not wanting to wake Halliday in case he was still sleeping. Sipping her first cup, she looked out to the rear of the property, her view obscured by rain beating against the window. Gusty winds had knocked over several pieces of patio furniture.

She bundled up in a heavy coat, backed her Mercedes down the driveway to the road, and picked up the newspaper wrapped in a plastic sleeve. On her way back to the garage, she noticed Halliday's wreck of a car parked away from the left corner of the house, tucked under a tall stand of trees and invisible from the road.

Back in the kitchen and drinking more coffee, she scanned several articles in the *International Herald Tribune.* She zeroed in on a follow-up to an earlier report about an attempted assassination in Afghanistan. After reading the article a second time, she trembled. *That would be my guest for the next couple of days.* She mentally constructed the timeline of events from the incident to Roger's arrival; they got him out just in time and my place was his planned hideout all along, thanks to the invitation I gave him on the plane. This irritated her because she didn't like being used this way. If anything, she would be the one who would do the using.

Still dressed in a peach-colored bathrobe and no longer hungry, she went to her office and turned on the computer. She found several new e-mails, the first one from her daughter, Julie.

Dear Mom,

*It's been a real bitch. I've lost my job and nobody's hiring magazine advertising execs right now. On top of that, Harper's been terrible to me, bordering on physical abuse. I will admit that he has good reason to be pissed but that's all I'm going to say. I'll tell you more when I get there. So tell me **where** is located and how to get there. I'll hop a plane and be on your doorstep before you can say Broke in Hoboken.*

Love you,
Julie

Leslie shook her head, wondering what Julie had done to provoke her husband. She and Harper had married almost three years ago and took up residence in a Newark suburb where Harper had grown up. She suspected that Julie brought in most of the couple's income with her position in New York, while Harper's teaching job appeared to provide only minimal support at best.

She composed a short reply, suggesting that Julie fly into Rome or Pisa. She would meet her and bring her to Castellina where she could stay for a reasonable time in one of the guest bedrooms. After sending it, she made a mental note to make sure that Halliday would be gone before Julie's arrival.

Leslie's next e-mail was from her best friend, Nancy Moore.

Dear Les,

I'm so happy to hear that your first session with Dr. Bertolucci went well. He sounds capable and I hope his treatments will be helpful.

Thanks again for your generosity. How about Joe and I coming for two weeks in May or July? Is that too much time? Be honest now. You also said you would make the travel arrangements so we'll just leave that in your hands. Tell us the dates and we'll block them into our calendars—in ink. I'm so excited about this.

xoxo
Nance

How about that? Leslie thought. Casa Campana is turning into a three star hotel. She had promised Nancy an all-expenses-paid vacation in Italy for helping her escape from that Pueblo hospital; it was time to deliver. She opened her desk calendar to May and wrote a note to herself, in pencil, to purchase airline tickets for Nancy and Joe. She sent a reply, suggesting that the second and third weeks in May would be ideal for their visit. Dr. Bertolucci wasn't mentioned; Leslie wasn't sure when she'd see him again and didn't want Nancy reminding her about it.

Leslie turned off the computer and went to the kitchen, stopping when she saw Halliday standing next to a tall window, coffee in hand, while he looked out through the rain. His flannel pajamas, an off-white with long blue bamboo shoots scattered everywhere like lightning bolts, surprised her. "Good morning, Roger."

Without turning he said, "Morning, Leslie. Lovely weather today."

She went to the counter and poured herself more coffee. "Yes, and certainly unlike Afghanistan."

He picked up the newspaper from the breakfast table. "You've read this."

She smiled. "Yes, just like you suggested."

He sat down, scanned the article about the assassination attempt, and folded up the paper. "Interesting," was his only comment.

"And that's all you can say?"

"They got it wrong, as usual. But it really doesn't matter. What matters is that I didn't get the job done."

Leslie didn't want to hear any more about it so she changed the subject. "Some pretty wild PJs you got there, Roger."

"I picked them up on one of my Far East business trips. You likee?"

She frowned. "Sorry, but I don't do *funny* this early in the morning."

"You've been up for a while, I gather."

"Couple of hours, catching up on my e-mails. Which reminds me, my daughter will be coming soon so you'll have to leave before she gets here."

"You have a daughter? You didn't mention her last night."

"Julie's married but she's in some kind of trouble. Wants to hide out here for a couple of weeks. My God, I should open a

Witness Protection Center."

Roger burst out laughing but Leslie only started when his became infectious.

After their laughter died he asked, "When will she come?"

"Don't know yet, probably in a couple of days."

"Just give me the word and I'll leave." He took a sip from his cup and said, "Julie is from an earlier marriage?"

"Correct. Her father's much older, a Wall Street investment banker."

"Do you know if she asked dad for help?"

"She wouldn't. His present wife is just a few years older than Julie and they don't get along at all."

"I see. Well, I suppose it's better that she comes here instead of you going there. But it's a round trip plane ticket, no matter which way you slice it."

"She has to come here, I can't go there."

"Really? Why not?"

She looked away for a moment. "I'd be arrested and thrown in jail."

He poured another cup of coffee. "Tell me more."

"You don't sound very surprised."

"I felt the vibes last night at dinner," he said. "Some unpleasant business with your husband, I guessed, but I didn't want to push it."

She sighed, thinking she should tell him more because she understood what he'd been doing in Afghanistan. "I had a plan, a way to get my husband back. A temporary separation that would drive him crazy living without me. Only when I went back to Denver, he'd already cleared out and moved to Leadville. He got a job with a construction company and took up with his boss's niece. So I hired a private detective and—" Roger shook his head, interrupting her. "Yeah, I know it was a dumb thing to do but I was desperate."

"Sorry," he said. "Go on."

"So I drove to Leadville, hoping to see him and talk things over, get us back together. But when I got to his cabin, he wasn't there and I saw some pretty ugly stuff. That's when I lost it. I set fire to the damned place and headed south to Pueblo where his girlfriend lives. But I had an accident on the way, wrecked my car, and wound up in the hospital. You know how the story goes from there."

"OK, you're an arsonist. And you believe they'd arrest you for that? What proof do they have? Were there any eyewitnesses?"

"No, but I made another mistake that made matters even worse. I *borrowed* my private detective's gun and shot a few bullets into the bedroom wall. The police found them and told me I'd be charged with conspiracy to commit murder. Isn't that enough to get me arrested?"

"Yes, probably so," he said. "And you're also a fugitive from justice. All kinds of alarm bells might go off when they checked your passport at the airport." He drained his cup. "You hungry? How about I fix us breakfast? It's the least I can do in return for your generous hospitality."

"Sure, but you don't know where anything is."

"Not to worry, I'll just dig around the kitchen and put something together."

Something that Halliday had just said—dig around—jolted Leslie's memory. She rushed into her office and looked for reports from her private detective, Clarke Layton. She found them and searched the pages until she found the connection: Sarah Dolan, her husband's lover, had once been married to Tom Rickenbach, the founder and current CEO of Digger.com. "I knew it," she said aloud. "The idiot did something right for a change." She brought the papers up to her breast and embraced them. *I can use this information. Fate has given me another opportunity to achieve the justice that has been denied. But I will be patient this time and make a plan that can't possibly fail.*

Leslie strolled back to the kitchen and found Roger at the stove. "Something smells delicious. What are you making?"

"A frittata with Parma ham. Make yourself comfortable, it'll be ready soon."

She said a silent prayer, thanking Maria for stocking the pantry and refrigerator before returning to Italy. She set the table with plates, napkins and utensils, and took one of the chairs. "Do you cook a lot?"

"When I'm at home. I get my fill of restaurant meals when I'm traveling."

Roger placed the frittatas on their plates along with buttered slices of toasted panini and two small glasses of orange juice which he'd squeezed. "This is wonderful," she said after taking a bite of her frittata.

He smiled and raised his glass. "Glad you like it."

After several more bites she asked, "Anything particular you'd like to do today?"

"A couple of things. I need to buy some clothes, casual things for travel and hanging out here. There wasn't much in that duffel bag I was carrying the other night. And reading material. Is there an English language book store in Siena?"

"A good question. I'm embarrassed to say that I don't have an answer. I'll call my friend Maria, she'll know."

"Don't mention my name."

"I'll tell her it's for me. But do you really want to go out in this weather?"

"It's not that bad. Maybe it'll clear up this afternoon."

They finished eating. Roger began picking up their dishes but she placed her palm on his wrist. "Relax, I'll do that."

"Thanks, Leslie. If you'll excuse me, I'll be in the shower."

She rinsed off the dishes and silverware and tucked them into the dishwasher. She went to the laundry room, picked up two fluffy bath towels, and walked to the bathroom adjoining the guest bedroom where Halliday slept.

Through the open bathroom door she heard water running in the shower. Drawn closer, she stopped and looked through the enclosure's glass walls, catching her breath while taking in Halliday's naked torso from the back. He was well built with wide shoulders, trim buttocks, and powerful calf muscles.

Leslie was so aroused by his appearance that she put the towels on a chair, slipped off her robe and stepped into the shower behind him. He twisted his head around so he could look at her. "Looks like I have company."

"You obviously need someone to scrub your back." She took a bar of soap and lathered up his back, neck, and shoulders. After a few minutes, he turned his entire body around and reached out, trying to draw her close. "Do something with that," she said, pointing to his erection in a laughing tone. "You're stabbing me."

He made the necessary adjustment and brought her closer, lightly kissing her lips while allowing his hands to slide down to her buttocks.

She twined her arms around his neck, pressed her breasts against his hairy chest, and eagerly returned his kiss. "Mmm," she said, "you taste like panini."

He relaxed his hold and began soaping her neck, shoulders, arms, and breasts. "You're even more beautiful than I imagined."

Leslie hummed softly, enjoying his hands caressing her slippery body. She touched his arm near the wound. "Should you be getting it wet?"

"Soap and water is a good antiseptic. Maybe you can help me wrap a bandage on it when we get dried off."

"I'll do that later. First priority is bed. I want you inside me. Now."

They dried each other off with the fluffy bath towels and Leslie dashed through the chilly bedroom into Roger's bed. She yanked the covers up around her into a cocoon, allowing her to inhale his aroma left from a night of deep sleep, making her even more frantic with desire.

He came to bed from the other side, burrowed under the covers while seeking out her smooth silky body and enveloping her with his arms and legs.

Leslie expected their love making to be an athletic rough-and-tumble event but she was pleasantly surprised by his tenderness, patience, and loving concern for her pleasure. He's good, she thought, and knows how to treat a woman properly. No doubt the best lover I've ever had.

Their physical need eventually brought them to a rollicking mutual orgasm. Afterwards, letting their breathing subside, they lay closely wrapped together. "Awesome, Mr. Halliday, this wonderful 'something else' you mentioned last night."

He kissed her. "Very special, Leslie, so nice."

"Good thing you had plenty of sleep last night, getting your strength back for this."

He laughed softly. "Have to keep in shape for the important things."

"Frankly, I was surprised that you didn't come to my bedroom last night."

"I wasn't sure you wanted it and I didn't feel like pressing my luck. Especially after the way I showed up on your doorstep that first night."

"Well now you know." *He could have had me on that plane to Dallas but I would never tell* him *that.*

Leslie had him so entangled with her arms and legs that he found it difficult to slip away for a short trip to the bathroom. When he came back into bed, he said, "Still raining, but not very hard. Maybe it's clearing up."

She rolled over and lay on top of him, her lips close to his while her toes wiggled his feet. "A good reason to stay right here in bed."

"No argument from me."

"We also have to make the most of our time together before I kick you out."

They both laughed as a playful encore of lovemaking began.

CHAPTER NINE

HE KNOWS WE'RE LOVERS

Roscoe Bartlett sat at a long table in his office with piles of financial papers spread out in some kind of orderly chaos. Across the table sat Jane Schneider, a commercial property appraiser who came to Leadville yesterday morning from Denver to put a value on RBC, Inc. She had gamely tromped around the company's snow-covered premises in boots, down jacket and wool ski hat, taking photos of the main building, the maintenance shed, and major equipment items including graders, backhoes, front loaders, and bull dozers. She spent considerable time in the latter building looking over the work bays, itemizing all the maintenance equipment, both metal and electronic.

Over coffee, she told Roscoe, "I think I have all I need for my report. You've been very helpful and I appreciate that."

"My pleasure. When do you think it'll be ready?"

"I'll start on it first thing tomorrow. Should be able to finish it in two days, three max."

"Any idea yet on the bottom line?"

"Nowhere near your ten million. Closer to eight, I'd say."

Bartlett did some mental arithmetic. Two million dollars from Sarah would give her about a twenty-five percent stake in the company. That was enough for him to keep control without her being involved in day-to-day operations. "That'll work," he said. Jane gathered up many papers and began stuffing them into her oversized briefcase. "By the way," he continued, "I need you to send a copy to my attorney." He handed her a 3x5 card with a name, Denver address, and a phone number. "He'll be putting together a partnership agreement and other legal documents."

She flashed a wide grin. "You got it."

Roscoe had enjoyed her company over the past two days. A perky redhead with a sparkling personality, she kept Roscoe and his male employees amused with stories gleaned from her experience as a Las Vegas blackjack dealer plus a few tall tales about working at a Montana dude ranch as an equine instructor. Roscoe's hometown of Choteau, southeast of Glacier National Park, was close enough to her dude ranch to invoke many fond memories by both parties. But when Jane discovered that they both loved the books of Ivan Doig, one of Big Sky Country's finest authors, their friendship was solidly cemented with literary gorilla glue.

She also flirted openly with many workers and seemed to establish a connection with Alex, the resident expert on backhoes. Another long distance courtship in the making, he thought. Just like Andrew and Sarah when they got started.

Jane glanced at her watch. "Better get moving. Don't like mountain driving in the dark or when snow is blowing."

After she left, Roscoe thought he'd call it a day, but delayed his departure to take a phone call. "Hello, boss," Andrew said, "just wanted to tell you about a great opportunity for the south branch of RBC."

"Whatcha got for me?"

"Sarah and I took a ride out to Pueblo West and found some nice home building lots. Three of them are right next to Lake Pueblo State Park, about an acre each. They're owned by the same guy so he might give us a package deal. I'd like to have Emmaline scope this out if it's OK with you."

"Is Sarah all right with you and Emmaline working this?"

"She is, as long as I don't get her involved."

Roscoe laughed. "I understand. And I like it, keeping business inside the family. You think the seller is *motivated?*"

"I do. We can probably get them for a nice price."

"OK, Andy, you can get her turned on, but don't make an offer until we get the cash in hand."

"Right. Any progress on the legal front?"

"Some. The appraiser just finished her visuals today. We should be able to have a meeting with our attorney next week. I'd like you to come up to Denver for it and be a stand-in for Sarah, looking out for her interests."

"Will do, just give me advance warning. I'll probably drive up I-25 and meet you there."

"Sounds like a plan. Give my love to Sarah."

Leslie awoke from a deep sleep with a floating sensation of luxurious comfort, fully relaxed with a wide smile on her face. She sat up and looked around the bedroom, realizing that her newest lover was no longer there. She pulled the covers over her head and shifted her body to the vacant side of the bed, deeply inhaling his scents, trying to capture his essence and allow it to permeate her entire body.

Momentarily lifting her head, she noticed sunlight filtering through the opposite window. She remembered their earlier plan; she and Roger could now go shopping in Siena, assuming that he had not deserted her.

Leslie slid out of bed, put on her robe, and began moving through the villa, peeking into each room. She was relieved to find him in the office, but irritated to see him working with her computer. He was wearing his loud Asiatic pajamas.

Sensing her presence, he turned his head. "Hope you don't mind me using your computer."

She went over behind him and put her arms around his neck. "You could have asked."

"Had to check my e-mail."

"What's so damn important?"

"I'll tell you later. You notice the weather's cleared up? We can go into Siena if you're still up for it."

"Sure."

He logged off, got up, and gave her a perfunctory kiss. "I'll get cleaned."

After he left, Leslie sat down and checked her own e-mail. One from Julie caught her eye.

Mom,

Leaving Newark at 6:50 PM tonight on British Airways 184 with a layover in London. Arriving next day in Rome at 2:05 PM on BA 554. Could only buy a one way ticket. All my credit cards are now totally maxed out. When did flying get

so damned expensive?
See you soon,
xoxoxoxo
Julie

"Damn," muttered Leslie. "I'll have to buy her a ticket home." *Is she really that broke or is she telling me a lie?* She read the e-mail again and did some calculations; she wouldn't have to leave Castellina before sunrise tomorrow morning.

Roger and Leslie got away about four o'clock, driving to Siena in Leslie's car. Their first stop was Fetrinelli's on Via Banca di Sopra, a store that Maria Borelli had said would have a wide variety of English-language books. Fetrinelli's had a small, unassuming entrance but, after going inside, they found the well-stocked section that Maria had promised.

The couple separated, each browsing fiction according to their own interests. Roger became excited when he found a collection of crime novels by Michael Dibdin featuring the exploits of Aurelio Zen, a Rome-based detective. He selected three books and showed them to Leslie who was holding Jackie Collins' latest. "These are a real find," he told her. "Thrillers taking place right here in Italy. This guy Zen is like the American detective Columbo, a bumbling sort of guy who somehow finds a safe path between criminals and corrupt politicians."

"That's wonderful, Roger. Glad you could find something."

He saw her book. "Does that look good to you?"

"Her usual fare, but it has potential. Rich widow swindled by a ruthless younger man, but she gets her revenge. Maybe I can pick up some pointers."

He took it from her and added it to his books. "Let me buy this for you."

Next was a short walk to Cortecci's, a high-fashion clothing store that offered Armani, Gucci, Versace, and Burberry. Roger knew what he wanted and selected three shirts, two pairs of trousers, two belts, a cashmere jacket, socks, and several pairs of underwear. He also purchased a suitcase, remarking to Leslie that he would get rid of the black duffle bag. She wondered about his pistol but thought it prudent not to mention it.

When the salesman tallied up the bill, it was close to 2,000 Euros. Without hesitation, Roger pulled four purple Euro notes from his wallet and handed them over.

The salesman gave Roger his change and wished him a good evening without any unusual comments. This transaction gave Leslie some food for thought. *A man with his own money, which means I won't have to worry about him chasing after mine. Seems to carry lots of cash and I have yet to see him use a credit card. Probably a good thing to do in his line of business.*

Roger put all his new clothes inside the suitcase. "What next?"

"I'm starving," she said. "Do you realize we haven't eaten since breakfast?"

"We've been too busy. Let's stow these in your car and have an early dinner."

Another short walk took them to an intimate restaurant that had just opened for dinner. The proprietor welcomed them with a noisy greeting and seated them at a table next to a front window where passersby could see them dining. When their waiter appeared, Roger ordered an antipasti appetizer and a bottle of Chianti, asking him to serve it quickly because they were hungry. The wine soon appeared, accompanied by bread and olive oil, with apologies that the antipasti would take only a few minutes longer.

After a generous sip of wine Leslie said, "Did you notice how the owner greeted us? Not at all like last night."

"He knows we're lovers, just by looking at you. You're radiant."

"Thanks, but it was probably the scrubbing you gave me in the shower."

He laughed. "I *love* your sense of humor."

She reached over and placed her hand on his. "I want you to know that this time we've had together has been wonderful, sweet, and very special."

"But?"

"Got an e-mail from my daughter. She gets into Rome tomorrow about two o'clock so I'll have to leave in the morning."

"So be it. I'll pack up and slip out the same time as you. And I'll make sure not to leave any souvenirs behind."

"I'm not sure whether I like that or not."

"We still have tonight," he said. "Let's make the most of it."

The waiter brought the antipasti and conversation halted for several minutes while the hungry couple ate and drank.

"Where will you go, Roger?"

"I'll probably drive north and stop in Zurich. Should be able to catch a flight to D. C. easily enough."

Leslie twiddled her glass between her thumb and forefinger. "Didn't you fly into Pisa?"

"Yes, but I can't go back there. Not good for my long term health."

"Another question. I know you have a gun. I saw it fall off your mattress so I'm wondering . . . what will you do with it? You can't take it on the plane."

"I'll leave it with you. You need one, a woman living alone out there in the middle of nowhere. A good replacement for the one you lost in Colorado."

She shook her head. "I am not believing this."

"All right, if you don't want it, I'll ditch it. I can get another one after I get back home. God knows they're easy to come by in D. C."

"What if I want to talk to you? How can I reach you?"

"E-mail is probably best. I'll give you my address before I leave."

"What about your cell phone? I found it in your car the night you got here."

"I'm ditching it. Don't want anybody zeroing in on my location. But I'll get another one and let you know the number when I do."

"Speaking of e-mail," she said, "you promised to tell me about the one you were looking at this morning."

"A client wants a face-to-face when I get back." He sighed. "Probably another piece of *business*."

"Will you ever come back to Castellina again?"

He placed his silverware on the table, took her hands in his and looked straight into her eyes. "I have no idea where the next job will take me, but I'll be back. I promise. I'd like to see your place in the spring. I'll bet it's beautiful then."

Leslie felt tears welling up and pulled her hands away. "Excuse me," she said, getting up and rushing to the ladies room. *Why does this always happen to me? Every time the possibility of a loving relationship happens, the guy leaves me. This one could get killed in his next job and I'd never see him again. Or he might meet another woman in another country, someone just as sappy as me who will welcome him into her bed and make him forget all about me. And why should I even care? I'll have to talk with Dr. Bertolucci about this and see if he has any answers.*

CHAPTER TEN

THIS HAS TROUBLE WRITTEN ALL OVER IT

Leslie sat alone next to a large window at a refueling island cafeteria along the A1 *autostrada.* She drank cappuccino but desperately wanted something stronger to lift her mood. The gray overcast sky mirrored her depression and weighed heavily on her mind. She'd driven for two hours through intermittent light rain and gusty winds since her departure from Castellina earlier this morning.

She recalled dinner last night with Roger Halliday and how they went straight to bed when they returned to her villa. Having him next to her throughout the night gave her great pleasure. But now, in the cold and oppressive gloom of day, she felt an aching emptiness.

They both got up early, took separate showers, and had coffee and rolls before the inevitable departure time came around like the executioner's sword. Leslie succeeded in holding back the tears but her self-discipline eventually proved unnecessary because of Roger's cavalier attitude. His goodbyes were almost trivial with impersonal comments such as, "I've had a wonderful time," "I'll be in touch," and "See you soon." They made her feel dirty, like she'd been just a convenient screw while he recuperated from his misadventures in a remote hideout.

She had stood in her doorway, watching him speed down the driveway in the battered Fiat, and wondered if the wreck would last until Zurich. And if he did get there, what would he do with the car? Who did it belong to? She sipped her cappuccino and wondered if Roger was hurting as badly. Perhaps his faux humor was a crude attempt to disguise his own reluctance to leave her.

Before she left the villa, she had noticed her calendar sitting near the telephone with a single name written in a square at the end of the month. Dominic. Sitting now in this rest stop, she no longer wanted to keep this date because of the days and nights spent with Roger Halliday. Her attitude was not due to any noble motive of faithfulness but a reckoning that it wouldn't be fair to Dominic. She made a mental note to call him and cancel the date. If pressed for a reason, she'd invoke Julie's sudden presence as an excuse, embellished with motherly concern for her troubled daughter.

She glanced at her watch and finished her cappuccino. *Another hour of driving will put me at Fiumicino's multilevel parking structure, well before Julie's arrival.* It would also give her a chance to have a brief lunch and a long drink, the latter as emotional armor for seeing her daughter again after almost five years.

Leslie almost didn't recognize her when she came through the arrival doors. Julie wore black jeans, a long black leather coat, and her dark brown hair fell down to her waist. More arresting were her large silver hoop earrings, dark eye shadow and blackish-red lip gloss. She smiled broadly when she spotted her mother and quickened her pace, almost banging into Leslie's tentative embrace.

"Oh Mom, it's so good to see you again. Thanks for doing this."

"Welcome to Italy." Leslie recoiled a bit, getting whiffs of a strong alcoholic haze. "Have a nice flight? Get any sleep at all?"

"Some, but it got pretty rough close to Rome." Julie backed away slightly and turned her head left and right. "Where's Andy? He didn't come with you?"

Oh shit, she doesn't know. Well of course not because I haven't told her. "We're not together anymore. He's still in Colorado."

"What happened?"

Leslie noticed that she didn't seem too surprised on hearing the news. "Let's collect your luggage and get on the road. I'll tell you about it on the way."

Julie bent over and picked up a black bag that she'd dropped by her feet. "No luggage, Mom. This is it."

"That's all you brought?"

"Yep, all my earthly possessions. We'll have to do some shopping soon."

Leslie sighed. "I'm parked across the street in the garage, not a long hike. Just follow me." Julie's statement about shopping irritated her. *I'll have to ask Maria if there's a Wal-Mart in Siena.*

Julie, engrossed in the passing countryside, said little until they got on the ring road. "Love your car," she said. "Very comfortable and quiet. I'll bet it handles nice."

"It does and it's just the right size for me."

"So what happened with you and Andy? Do you mind talking about it?"

"Nothing very complicated or exciting. For the last year or so, we weren't getting along well. He lost his job and wasn't too interested in finding another one. Then in early August, he went off by himself on a week's backpack into the mountains and that was the last straw. So I came to Italy, sort of a trial separation. After about three months, I decided to go back to Colorado for Christmas. Have a nice holiday together, but he was having none of that."

"Why not? Didn't he want you back?"

"Ha, in your dreams. He moved to Leadville, a one horse town, and found himself a younger woman. Got a job with a construction company. I flew back to Denver, trying for a reconciliation, but it was a huge waste of time. He'd already filed for divorce and didn't give a damn about me anymore."

"That is so sad, Mom. I feel bad for you. After all you did for him."

"Yes, he dumped me like a sack of rotten potatoes. You know, something gets into these idiot husbands, throwing their wives away for younger women. As if they've discovered the fountain of youth." Leslie glanced over and noticed her startled look. "Yes, I'm talking about your father as well. He pulled the same shit, dumping me for his current bimbo. By the way, have you talked to him lately?"

"Yeah, but my credit line with him is maxed out, just like all my plastic. Besides, Michele hates me. She's got him wrapped around her little finger."

"It's not the finger," Leslie said, a smirk on her face.

Julie giggled and shifted her position, stretching her legs and resting her head on the back of her seat. "It's not the company, Mom, but I'm sleepy."

"You go ahead and take a snooze. I'll wake you up when we get near Siena. It'll be time for dinner then."

Back on the A1, Leslie drove at a moderate speed because of a steady rainfall that was verging to sleet. She glanced occasionally at her dozing daughter and felt twinges of maternal devotion. Around half past four, she heard a noise coming from a lower receptacle on her right, sounding like a ruptured duck quacking for medical attention. She reached in, pulled out her cell phone and saw that she'd received some kind of message. Not fully understanding what she should do, she slowed the car, flipped open the phone, and read a text: CLEARING AOSTA, GENEVA NEXT, MISSING YOU TONS. "Yes," she cried out.

"What?"

"Nothing," said Leslie, "go back to sleep."

Leslie wanted to reply but didn't know how. *Julie would surely know, I'll ask her to show me.* Mildly frustrated, but giddy with relief and full of affection for her elusive boarder, she realized that Roger Halliday actually cared about her.

Leslie woke Julie when they reached the same Siena restaurant where she and Maria had dined just days ago. The waiter seated them and said something effusively in Italian before going off to collect their bread and a bottle of Pellegrino water.

"What was that all about?" said Julie.

"He recognized me and said how honored they were to have such beautiful sisters dine in their humble trattoria. What a B. S. artist."

"Now he'll expect a bigger tip."

Leslie asked, "How hungry are you?"

"Very, but I can't decipher anything on the menu."

"That's all right. I'll order for both of us." She selected deep-fried calamari for a shared appetizer, veal piccata with linguini as the main course, and a bottle of Chianti.

After the waiter left, Julie fished around her black leather purse and pulled out a pack of cigarettes.

"You can't smoke in here," said Leslie. "It's against the law. I don't allow it in the house either."

"OK, OK, I'll take it outside while I'm staying with you."

"You should give it up, it's a terrible habit. I watched my Aunt Evelyn suffer with lung cancer and I can tell you it's a horribly painful death."

Julie stuffed the cigarettes back into her purse as their waiter returned with the wine. After he'd poured both glasses, she asked, "Did you fight the divorce at all?"

The sudden change of subject caused Leslie to pause and calculate how much of her marital combat with Andrew should be revealed. As little as necessary was her decision. "As a matter of fact, I did fight it. Hard. But after several conferences with my attorney, I knew it was a lost cause. Colorado is a no fault state so it will just happen, no matter how much I spend in legal fees."

"Is it going to cost you a lot?"

"Not that it's any of your business . . . but no."

"Sorry. Just wondering if you're going to be OK."

"You don't have to worry about that. We had a pre-nup so Andrew doesn't get a nickel. The house in Denver, totally in my name, is on the market. And when it sells, no more ties to Colorado. Fini. End of story."

Julie smiled, raising her glass. "To your new life, wherever it takes you."

They touched glasses. "Thank you," said Leslie. They took sips and she continued, "Now that we've fully dissected my latest failed marriage, let's talk about your situation and why you had to leave home."

"Promise you won't get mad at me?" said a nervous Julie.

"No." Leslie's neutral tone left plenty of wriggle room.

"OK, it goes back to last month. The agency did well last year, considering how terrible the economy is right now. So the big boss decided to throw a fancy Christmas party for the entire staff. Music, food, drink, presents, skits . . . pulling out all the stops for the last working day before Christmas."

"Did your husband come into the city for the party?"

"No, Harper had something going at his school. Anyway, it was a fabulous party and I was having a great time, dancing a lot with this really hot guy, singing and drinking like there was no tomorrow."

"This has trouble written all over it."

"So we're really getting it on, this guy and me, and he tells me he wants to show me something in the big boss's office, a secret that I'm just going to love, and would hate myself in the morning if I passed up this wonderful opportunity."

"A secret something, huh?"

"Yeah, I know, I should have smelled a rat, but I couldn't say no."

Leslie shook her head but kept silent.

"So we get into this plush office with yards of glass, looking out at a New York skyline all twinkling like stars. And before you can say Hey-Bob-a-Ree-Bob, we're tearing off each other's clothes, kissing and grabbing, ripping and fondling each other on this fab couch, humping away like teenagers."

Leslie's throat tightened and she had to drink some water. "Then what."

"We did our thing, got dressed, and said our goodbyes. I managed to get myself home in one piece before I turned into a pumpkin. Before Harper got there, and that was a good thing."

"Is that it?"

"Not quite. Turns out the boss has a video taping system in his office. He's a security nut and has a bit of Tricky Dick in him."

"Oh God, Julie. *Oh no.*"

"*Oh yes.* Then the computer nerd who works the system saw the video tape and shared it with his buddies. I was the agency's slutty hooker and couldn't show my face anywhere in the building. So the boss canned me and the computer nerd but the hot guy got only an ass chewing and a transfer. Talk about a double standard."

Julie paused for a breath and a sip of wine. During the lull, Leslie recalled a similar party almost thirty Christmases ago when she and Julie's father worked together at the same Wall Street brokerage. At least Richard had been classy enough to take her to a nearby hotel.

"Julie," said Leslie. She paused to gather her thoughts. "The tape . . . did you get the video tape from the computer technician?"

"No, I didn't. Turns out it wasn't necessary."

"What do you mean?"

"The asshole transferred it to his computer and posted it on YouTube. Do you know what 'going viral' means? When Harper saw it, he went ballistic and literally threw me out of the house. So that's the story. You know everything now, no more surprises."

Complete silence followed until Julie said, "Mom, say something."

"I'm disappointed in you, Julie. I would have expected more mature behavior. Twenty-six and a married woman, carrying on like a fifteen year old. So juvenile."

"I know, it was terrible and I'm very sorry."

"I'm angry, too. But I'd be a hypocrite if I stayed mad and didn't do anything to help you. God knows I've done a few stupid things in my life, but that's all water under the bridge. First, I'd like to know why you came all the way to Italy. What are you looking for, what do you want?"

"Just to get the hell out of the country, go some place where nobody knows me or what I did. Hide out for a while and try to figure out what to do with my life."

"How do you feel now about your husband? Do you want to go back to him? Do you think your marriage can be saved?"

On the verge of tears, Julie said, "Yes, I still love him and I want to go back. But I don't know if he'll ever forgive me . . . after embarrassing him like that."

"Fine. So we have something to work with. First priority will be getting you some help. Getting Harper on board will take a bit longer."

"What kind of help?"

"Counseling. I happen to know of an excellent doctor in Florence. I'll call and set up some appointments." *Wonder if Dr. Bertolucci will give us a group discount?*

CHAPTER ELEVEN

I HATE IT WHEN A LAWYER READS MY MIND

Andrew awoke at seven o'clock and made his way quietly throughout the house. He had breakfast, gave Sarah a soft kiss without waking her and was on the road by eight o'clock. His drive north on I-25 was uneventful and he arrived at the attorney's office in downtown Denver just before 11:00 A.M.

He took an elevator to the ninth floor of a modern building that seemed to be fully covered by bluish reflective glass panels. He was impressed when he stepped out of the elevator into the lobby of a prestigious law firm. The carpeting and office furniture were a mix of muted maroon and walnut.

Roscoe, who had been sitting next to the firm's gorgeous blonde receptionist, stood and called out, "Over here, Andy."

Andrew went over and shook his hand. "Morning, boss. Your directions were just fine, no trouble at all finding this place."

"Just chatting with Ms. Fabricius here, waiting for you to show."

The blonde gave Andrew a sparkling smile and said, "I'll let Mr. Goodlake know you're here." She made a quick phone call and continued, "If you gentlemen will follow me, I'll take you to the conference room."

After a short walk down a hallway, they entered a room with a large oval table made of cherry wood. Richard Goodlake, Roscoe's attorney, welcomed them and shook their hands. He introduced another man standing next to him as Donald Whisnant, a certified public accountant who had previously worked with both Roscoe and Goodlake.

"Let's gather at this end," said Goodlake, pointing to several stacks of documents neatly positioned at the closer end of the table.

The men took their seats in expensive looking chairs that continued the walnut and maroon decor. Andrew looked to the west and could see the Rockies' front range covered with glittering snow. The sight of the mountains made him want to be out in the wilderness. Good day for a snow climb, he thought.

Goodlake passed copies of a thick document to each of the three men. "This is the appraiser's report," he said. "Lots of information to wade through but the most important thing is the bottom line where Ms. Schneider put a value of $8,120,000 on RBC, Incorporated. How does this sit with you, Roscoe?"

"As expected, Dick. She called yesterday and gave me the highlights. Seems fair to me."

"Fine," said Goodlake. "Based on this number then, and given Ms. Dolan's investment of two million dollars, this would give her a 24.63% share in the venture."

"I hate fractional numbers," said Roscoe. "Why don't we just round it off at twenty-five percent? We can deal with quarters much easier."

Goodlake smiled. "I thought you might want to do something like that so I've taken the liberty of putting that number into the other documents."

Roscoe groused, "God, I hate it when a lawyer reads my mind. Always turns out to cost me a lot of money."

His comment provoked nervous laughter by Goodlake and Whisnant but Andrew just smiled, knowing how his boss liked to get an edge.

Goodlake passed out another document with fewer pages. "This creates a new business structure, a limited partnership with Mr. Bartlett as the general partner, and Miriam as the sole limited partner with a twenty-five percent stake."

"Everyone calls her Sarah," said Andrew. "She doesn't like Miriam."

"I understand," said Goodlake, "but we're constrained to use her full legal name in all the paperwork. We can still refer to her informally as Sarah."

Andrew felt foolish raising this point. He waved his hand in dismissal, a signal to continue with their discussion.

"As a limited partner," Goodlake continued, "she won't participate in the daily operations of the company. However, at Mr. Bartlett's request, she will have to approve any purchases of real property over $100,000 by the general partner."

Andrew smiled and gave Roscoe a knuckle bump. "Thanks, boss."

Goodlake continued, "I have another paper for you, Andrew. Please have *Sarah* sign in each place that I've marked, in the presence of a notary public, and mail them back to me, along with a cashier's check payable to RBC, Incorporated for two million dollars. The date set for creation of the limited partnership will be February 14, a little over two weeks from today. Is that sufficient time for you?"

"By Valentine's Day? Yes, that's plenty of time. Something else for Sarah and I to celebrate."

"Close to her birthday on the eighth," said Roscoe. "You've got a lot of shopping to do, Andy."

"Don't I know it."

"Please take a few moments to review the document," said Goodlake.

Andrew read the several pages and quickly determined that much of it was legal boilerplate. He was gratified to verify that his name was not listed anywhere but was curious about the company's new structure. "I do have a question," he said. "RBC, Incorporated is going to be dissolved and replaced by a new organization called RBC, A Limited Partnership. Why not just create shares in the original corporation and give Sarah a quarter?"

"Good question," said Goodlake. "I'm going to let Don address that one."

"It's for tax purposes," said Whisnant. "A limited partnership is a flow-through instrument with all profits and losses going directly to the individual partners. This avoids double taxation, once to the corporation, and again to the shareholders when they receive dividends or sell shares and realize capital gains."

"So Sarah gets twenty-five percent of all profits that RBC generates?"

"That's correct," said Whisnant, "and it's taxable passive income."

Andrew sighed. "Sounds like her tax returns will be a lot more complicated."

Whisnant slid a booklet across the table to Andrew. "This will explain all the ins and outs of a limited partnership investment. I've also attached my business card to the front page and will be happy to answer any questions she may have."

Andrew gave the booklet a cursory glance and said, "Thanks, I'll let her know." He added it to his growing stack of papers.

"Any other questions?" said Goodlake. After a brief silence he went on, "Then I believe this concludes our business for today. Thank you, gentlemen, for coming all the way to Denver this morning. A pleasure to meet you, Andrew, and please give my congratulations to Ms. Dolan for making an excellent investment. Now if you'll excuse us, Don and I have to take care of some other business."

Everyone stood and shook hands. Goodlake and Whisnant gathered up all their papers and left the room. Roscoe turned and said, "There you go, Andy. Life in the fast lane with legal beagles and bean counters."

"Makes my head swim. Think I'll review this paperwork at home before Sarah comes in from her late shift."

"You have to go back to Pueblo right away?"

"No, I've got time."

"You ever eat Vietnamese food?"

"Never."

"Then lunch is on me. You're in for a real treat."

Andrew reached Sarah's home about five o'clock. His mood was somber, knowing that she wouldn't be home until much later. He didn't know how much longer she'd be working these late hours but hoped it would soon be over.

He wasn't hungry, still feeling stuffed from a tangy lunch washed down with Tsingtao beer. He chuckled, recalling Roscoe's greeting to the proprietor of the Vietnamese restaurant located near Goodlake's office. Roscoe and the shriveled old man had bantered back and forth in a singsong dialogue, presumably Vietnamese, and Andrew had asked what the man had said. Roscoe had explained, "Your mother defecates in a combat boot." Then he added, "Yeah, it loses something in translation."

Andrew roamed about the house, unconsciously looking for some familiar evidence of Sarah's presence, something that would help ease his mild separation anxiety. What he found only puzzled him: their bed wasn't made, dirty breakfast dishes were sitting in the kitchen sink, and the bathroom looked like it hadn't been cleaned up in a month of Sundays. This wasn't like Sarah, he thought. She must have been in a huge hurry to get out of here this morning. Maybe she overslept.

One thing he needed to take care of, indulging his thinly-veiled obsessive-compulsive complex, was updating the kitchen calendar. He wrote 'partnership' in the block for February 14th and circled the one for February 8th. He also wrote the word 'poker' in the square for February 4th, the first Friday of the month. Roscoe had reminded him at lunch of their monthly game, this one to be hosted by Sarah's dad. That should be OK, he thought. Sarah will probably be working and I can stay over at Roscoe's place like I did last time.

Andrew made a small pot of coffee and settled in with the documents he'd brought back from the morning's meeting. He was in the middle of the appraiser's report when the telephone announced a call from Emmaline Dolan.

"Sarah's not here," he said, "she's at the hospital."

"No matter, I'm calling for you," she said. "I've been nosing around, looking into those three lots for sale out in Pueblo West."

"Did you find anything?"

"You might say so. I learned this Sebastian fellow owns a lot more land out there than those three pieces. He's asking $40,000 for each lot but he had them on the market last summer for $45,000 apiece. So you've got to believe that he could come down some more to get them sold. Maybe we should offer $110,000 for all three. Wouldn't you say that was an attractive proposition?"

"Yes, I'd go along with that."

"Then I can start putting an offer together?"

"It's a little too soon for that. I was in Denver this morning with Roscoe at the lawyer's office. February 14th is the magic date when we have our new business established and the money to work with."

"Well, all righty then. I'll just get all my ducks lined up for that date."

"I'll run this by Sarah, too. She needs to be involved."

The line went silent for a moment. "I don't understand," she said. "I thought she was going to be a silent partner."

"Almost. She has to sign off on any purchase over $100,000. It's written into the partnership papers."

"Well . . . I'll be darned," she said.

Andrew had to muffle a giggle. "That's to protect her investment. I wouldn't worry about it, Emmaline. She's one hundred percent behind our idea to build on those lots."

"Then I'm glad you're working this deal with me instead of her. She has a knack for making things more difficult than they need be."

After the call ended, Andrew had a good laugh, thinking about this small degree of control that daughter now had over her mother.

Andrew was laying on the couch, reading a satiric novel about America twenty years in the future, when Sarah came into the house from work. "I'm in the living room," he called out.

"In a minute," she answered.

He got up when she entered the room. "Hi sweetheart. So glad you're home. It's been—" The grim look on her face spoke volumes.

She ran to him, threw her arms around his neck, and began sobbing. "Oh, Andy, hold me tight . . . I'm so scared . . . this can't be happening . . ."

"What are you talking about? What's wrong?"

She cried harder, unable to say anything. He gently guided her over to the couch where they sat close to each other, his left arm around her shoulder while he held her right hand with his. He said nothing, waiting for her crying to subside. Still wearing her down jacket, she rubbed her eyes with a sleeve.

"Can you talk about it?" he said.

"I found a lump this morning while I was taking a shower."

Andrew felt a sickening jolt to his stomach. "Oh shit . . . are you sure?"

"No doubt in my mind. I check every so often and something's there."

"Have you told anyone else?"

"I drove straight to my doctor and she was able to set me up with a mammogram tomorrow morning."

"Then I'll go with you."

She made a funny whimper. "I appreciate that, but it's not necessary."

"I'll go anyway." He excused himself and returned from the bathroom with a handful of tissues.

After dabbing her eyes and blowing her nose, she said, "Have you ever seen a woman after she's had a breast removed?"

"God, no."

"Well I have. I've been there when mastectomies were being performed and with the patients afterwards. I'm afraid, Andy. I just don't know if I can go through something like that."

"I think we're jumping the gun. Let's find out what the mammogram shows, one step at a time. I'll be with you when the doctor gives you the results." She started crying again and he continued, "You're a strong woman, Sarah. Remember being wounded in Iraq? You had surgery for that and survived just fine."

"This is different," she wailed. "What happens when I lose my breast? I won't be a complete woman anymore and you'll never look at me in the same way again. How can you stay in love with me after that? You want to make love to a woman with only one breast?"

Andrew pulled her closer and kissed her temple. He was stalling for time, knowing that he was entering an emotional minefield. Nothing but explosive wrong answers to choose from. Somehow, he had to pick the safe path ahead. "Look, I know this is a terrible thing for you. But it's difficult to look into some crystal ball and see the future. What I will tell you again and again is how much I love you and nothing's going to change that. I will also promise right now to take care of you, no matter what happens. We're going to see this through and do it together."

She gave him a slobbery kiss. "Thanks, honey, you're right. Guess I overreacted."

He hugged her again. "Want something to drink?"

"No, let's just go to bed."

"You go on," he said, "I'll turn out the lights."

Once they were cuddled up in the bedroom's darkness, she said, "I forgot to ask about your meeting today. How did it go?"

"Fine, I brought home a ton of papers for you to look at when you have time. You'll become a limited partner on Valentine's Day."

"That's a switch. Normally a big day for bed partners."

Andrew gave her a quick kiss, amused by her comment and a good feeling that her sense of humor was returning. "Your mom called this afternoon. She's hot-to-trot on those three lots we looked at in Pueblo West."

"What did you tell her?"

"That we wouldn't have the money until February 14th and—drum roll, please—that you would have to approve it since the price would be over $100,000."

"How did she take that?"

"I think she has a better appreciation of your business smarts."

She kissed him and they were silent for several moments. "Hey Andy," she said, "I've changed my mind. I want you to come with me tomorrow."

CHAPTER TWELVE

MAYBE THEY BURIED SOME SAINTS IN THERE

As Leslie drove from the Siena restaurant, Julie became more alert and visibly nervous about their progress through the dark countryside. They pulled into the villa's driveway, marked by a pair of lighted monuments at the road, and Julie said, "You're so far out in the country."

"It's a big place," said Leslie. "Almost three hundred acres for the entire property. Thank God I don't have to take care of landscaping."

The vehicle's headlights pointed their way up the long driveway. The rain had stopped, but the night was black because of a thick cloud cover. When she finally saw the gray quarrystone structure ahead, Julie exclaimed, "It looks like a fortress, something out of Macbeth or Hamlet."

Leslie laughed. "I've been told that it was built in the 17th century, but it's been renovated since then."

"Please tell me you have electricity."

"I do. Indoor plumbing, satellite TV, plus an internet connection. Not exactly the stone ages."

Julie mumbled aloud, "I can do without the internet for a while."

Once inside the house, Leslie gave her a cursory tour. She pointed out the kitchen's modern appliances, a guest bedroom converted to an office, and the previously unoccupied fourth bedroom with an adjoining bathroom. Leslie had intentionally picked this one for Julie instead of the one that Roger had used. She considered his bedroom a shrine, a holy place consecrated to their lovemaking, and didn't want Julie picking up any 'good vibrations.'

"Everything will look much brighter in the morning," said Leslie. "We can take a little walk around the property, weather permitting. The grounds are still beautiful, in spite of winter weather."

"Thanks, Mom. I'll hit the sack now, if you don't mind."

"Not at all," said Leslie, giving Julie a hug. "Sleep well."

Leslie changed into a pair of light blue silk pajamas and went into her bathroom. She washed her face, brushed her teeth, and combed her hair. When she crawled into bed, she couldn't get comfortable right away, sensing some lumpy fabric under her pillow. She turned the bedside lamp back on and pulled out Roger Halliday's blue bamboo pajamas. She laughed and said aloud, "No souvenirs, huh?"

She gathered them about her head, inhaling his musky scent. *I could put them on and sleep in them. They should be big enough, probably too big, but then I'd have to explain them to Julie in the morning. I'm definitely not ready for that.*

She turned out the lamp and cuddled with the empty pair of pajamas, fantasizing about a naked Roger, somewhere in the house, searching and wanting to do all kinds of wonderful things with her.

Leslie awoke early the next morning with an emotional hangover. She had dreamed about Halliday and that only made her longing more intense. She put on her peach-colored robe and rummaged under the bed covers until she found his pajamas. She thought of slipping them into a plastic bag to preserve his aroma, but decided that would be silly. Instead, she folded them neatly and tucked them into a dresser drawer, under her bras and panties.

After getting a full pot of coffee started, she looked in on Julie. She was sleeping soundly and would probably continue for a while. She sat down with a cup of coffee at the kitchen table, with her calendar, toting up the things she needed to accomplish. Since it was Saturday, she couldn't reach anyone at Dr. Bertolucci's office. She made a note to call on Monday and arrange a session for Julie, more important than her own second meeting with the good doctor. Getting Julie some clothes was an even higher priority. She'd have to call Maria later in the morning and get some ideas about stores where they could shop. And food; she would have to buy groceries and cook meals for two people now.

Leslie took another cup of coffee to her office and turned on the computer. She hoped to see an e-mail from Halliday but there was nothing in her Inbox. She found his e-mail address on the card he'd left and wrote him a message.

Dear Roger,
Very happy to get your text message on my cell phone. I'm going to dig out my instruction book and figure out how to send you one.
Picked up Julie OK and had dinner last night, but not at

*one of **our** restaurants. Wouldn't be the same without you. Have to take her shopping soon because she left home in a big hurry with no clothes. She told me quite a tale about her predicament but I'll save that for later when we're together again. Found that little souvenir you left under my pillow and put it to excellent use. Any more words about that would definitely be an X-rated no-no.*

Please let me hear from you soon,

Leslie

She sent the e-mail, turned off her computer, and returned to the kitchen where she found Julie standing next to a rear window. She wore a ratty green flannel nightgown and had her arms folded around her to keep warm. Gone were the earrings, dark eye shadow, and lipstick. Leslie went up to her and said, "Are you cold, honey? Would you like a robe or something to put on?"

"Sure, Mom, that would be nice."

"Have some coffee while I get you one."

Leslie soon returned with a dark blue robe, similar in style to her own, but made with heavy wool. "This will keep you warm and toasty."

"What's that building out there? It looks like a church."

"It's a chapel. I suppose the people who built this place were very religious."

"Is it pretty inside?"

"Don't know, I've never looked." Leslie paused. "How are you feeling? Did you have a good night's sleep?"

"Kind of woozy, like my body's here, but my brain is over London. Love your coffee, by the way. I should be better after a half gallon or so."

"Are you hungry?"

"A little bit."

"I'll make us frittatas with parma ham. That'll perk you up."

Julie stepped outside with a second cup of coffee while Leslie made breakfast. She glanced out the window occasionally to see her daughter, alternating each hand to her mouth, with either a cup or a cigarette. At one point, Julie disappeared for several minutes, but came back into the kitchen as Leslie was putting their food on the table. "Pretty crisp out there, but warm enough when you stand in the sun."

"See anything interesting?"

"I peeked into the chapel, but it's too dark. Smells kind of musty, too, like maybe they buried some saints in there."

Leslie laughed. "Come sit down, your breakfast is ready."

Julie ate voraciously, but Leslie took only a few bites. *Halliday's definitely a better cook than I am.*

"How long have you lived here?" asked Julie.

"Since last August. I stayed in Paris a short time before moving in."

"I'll bet it's wonderful in the summer, especially by your pool."

"I did get to use it in September, before I went back to Denver."

"Did you buy this place?"

"No, I rent it. The owner lives in Switzerland. She's coming back for a June holiday so I have to camp elsewhere."

As they were finishing their meal, the telephone rang; Maria Borelli was calling. "I was just getting ready to call *you*," said Leslie.

"A happy coincidence," said Maria. "My daughter, Lucia, is visiting from Milan and I would like you to meet her. May we come over about noon?"

"That's amazing. My daughter is here, too. I picked her up at Fiumicino yesterday afternoon."

"Your daughter is there? But I thought . . ."

"What? Is there a problem?"

"Not at all. I was just confused."

Leslie thought about Maria's request. Lucia was probably several years younger than Julie, but meeting an Italian woman close to her own age could be a good experience for her. It might also take some pressure off Leslie's shoulders. "Does Lucia speak English?"

Maria laughed. "Very well, even better than I do."

"Then please come. I'm sure we'll all get along fabulously."

Leslie hung up and said to Julie, "My friend Maria is coming over with her daughter. She's about your age and speaks excellent English."

"Whatever," said Julie, shrugging her shoulders.

Leslie wanted to throttle her, but said, "Take a shower, you'll feel better."

When Maria and Lucia arrived, Leslie invited them into the living room and offered a liquid refreshment, which they both declined. Julie soon made her appearance, introductions were made, and followed by tentative getting-to-know-you talk. Leslie was surprised at the lack of similarity between Maria and Lucia, but even more intrigued by the startling resemblance between Lucia and Julie. They would easily be mistaken for sisters in their tight jeans, black boots, and knitted turtleneck sweaters, albeit Julie's was dark red while Lucia's was white. Lucia's hair was the same color as Julie's, but shorter, and the former wore glasses, while the latter didn't. Still, the familial presence was definitely there.

Leslie spoke to Lucia, "I understand you live in Milan. What do you do?"

"I'm a financial analyst for Bank of America," she answered in English. "My work is about American investments in Italian companies."

"I didn't know—"

"The bank has a long affiliation with Italy. Our founder, Amadeo Giannini, founded the Bank of Italy in San Francisco in 1904. Then in 1928, he merged it with Bank of America Los Angeles. Now we have Bank of Americas all over the world."

"That's very interesting," Leslie replied coolly.

"How about you, Julie? asked Maria. Leslie has mentioned that you live and work in New York."

"Not anymore," said Julie. "I'm kind of between jobs right now. I thought it would be a good time to visit Mom and see something of Italy."

Lucia perked up and said, "I may travel to New York soon on business. You must tell me about it, Julie, all the exciting places to see."

"Sure, I can also clue you in about places to stay away from."

The cross-conversation continued, Leslie talking with Lucia and Maria talking with Julie, until Leslie mentioned the possibility of taking Julie shopping for clothes. At that moment, it seemed that all four women were speaking at once.

When the din subsided, Maria said, "Lucia, why don't you take Julie to the shops that you wanted to see. It will be much more enjoyable for both of you without your mothers watching and giving opinions. Leslie and I will have our own adventure and join you later. Suppose we meet for lunch at Buitonis—say about two o'clock?"

Leslie was delighted with Maria's suggestion and glanced quickly at Julie, only to see panic spreading across her face. *Of course, she has no money.* Leslie stood and said, "Great suggestion, Maria. Excuse me for a moment." She went into her bedroom, dug into her purse, and met a nervous Julie in the hallway. She gave Julie a wad of Euros and a credit card. "Enjoy," she said.

"Thanks, Mom. You're the greatest."

After their daughters had left, Leslie and Maria returned to the living room. "That worked out well," said Leslie. "Was that a spur of the moment thing or were you planning to do it?"

Maria smiled cautiously. "Are you upset with me?"

"Not at all. I think they'll enjoy each other's company. Right now, Julie needs somebody to talk to besides her mother."

"Someone not so critical?"

"You got that right."

"She is a lovely girl," said Maria. "But I have suspicions that she is troubled."

Leslie sighed. "Frankly, she's a mess. She lost her job and is separated from her husband. I'll spare you the gory details but, suffice it to say, she needs a time-out, to think hard about her mistakes and what she's going to do with her life. I'm going to call Dr. Bertolucci's office on Monday and get her an appointment."

"Ah, I understand. I won't press you for more information."

"Speaking of suspicions," said Leslie, "what was that business about being confused when you called this morning?"

Maria twisted her body and momentarily looked away. "I had not expected you to tell me your daughter was here. I thought . . ."

"Something else?"

"I thought your friend was still here, the man you've been seeing."

"What? How do you know about him?"

"You were seen with him, at the book store I told you about, and dining at the trattoria in Castellina. A handsome man with silver hair, I believe."

"I'll be damned. I thought we were so clever."

"This is a very small village, Leslie, and you are a large person. Did I say that correctly? So you are a likely subject of gossip."

"So what?" said Leslie, getting louder. "Why should anyone care?"

"Who is this man, if I may ask?"

"Roger Halliday." Leslie laughed. "You've talked to him, Maria, on the phone that morning when I came back from Colorado. He's the man I told you about, the one I met on the flight to Dallas, and now he's back home in Virginia."

"It seems very mysterious, following you all the way to Castellina."

"No mystery, he was in Foggia doing business. Export-import, dealing in olive oil and other food products. When I met him, I invited him to come for a visit the next time he was in Italy." *Roger would love how I invented that cover story.*

"I would like to meet your friend the next time he comes," said Maria. "Perhaps you could join Marcello and me for dinner one evening."

Leslie slumped. "I'm sorry, Maria, I really am. But the next time he comes—if he comes—we'll get together, the four of us. I promise."

CHAPTER THIRTEEN

THIS IS STARTING TO SOUND LIKE GOODBYE

Andrew and Sarah sat close to each other in the waiting room of Dr. Susan Markoff, Sarah's OB/GYN physician. Sarah had just undergone a mammogram and was awaiting the results. Six other women, mostly middle-aged, were also in the waiting room but Andrew was the only man present. Sarah had been trying to read a three month old *People* magazine but gave up and tossed it onto a table.

Andrew took her hand and said, "How are you doing, sweetheart?"

"I'm sore. You know what they do when you have a mammogram?"

"I've heard it's not pleasant."

"That's the understatement of the year. It's damned painful, clamping down on your boob with a set of metal plates. Like a hamburger patty being squeezed in a waffle iron."

Andrew turned his head, not wanting her to see the start of a giggle. The urge soon passed and he turned back, gripping her hand. "That's the downside of having such a gorgeous figure."

"Wonder if I should just have them both removed? Hack 'em off, just like that, and never have to worry about cancer again."

An older woman with white hair and glasses picked up on her comment and muttered, "Oh for God's sake."

Sarah was about to say something to the woman when Kimberly, a nurse assistant, appeared. "Miss Dolan? Dr. Markoff is ready for you now."

Sarah stood while gripping Andrew's hand. "Let's go see what they found."

Dr. Markoff, a tall brunette in her late thirties, welcomed her. "Sit over here, Sarah, where you can see my computer screen." Sarah introduced Andrew but didn't mention their relationship.

Dr. Markoff sat on Sarah's left and positioned a keyboard on a wooden pull-away pedestal. Andrew sat on Sarah's right. "Here we are," said the doctor. "First, I'm showing pictures of your left breast. Perfectly normal, no unusual objects to be concerned about." She tapped several keys. "Here is your right breast. You can see a small white object in the upper part. I'm surprised you even found it."

"Yeah, but there it is," said Sarah, as Andrew placed his hand on her neck.

Dr. Markoff again tapped her keyboard and a color picture of a tropical beach appeared on the screen. She pushed the keyboard and platform away and said, "Let's talk about the next step."

"Which is?" said Sarah.

"You'll need to have it biopsied. I can't do it but I can

recommend several surgeons who can." She handed Sarah a card. "I'm sure you're familiar with some of these names."

Sarah reluctantly took the card and scanned the list. "I know several from their work at the hospital. Dr. Nadol's the best, but I don't want it done at Parkview."

"I know this is upsetting but we've caught it early. Long term, it's always a good thing because it minimizes the possibility of a later recurrence."

"Upsetting is not the right word," said Sarah.

"I understand, I know just how you feel."

"That's easy for you to say."

Dr. Markoff smiled. "That's right. I've been through it myself."

Sarah stared at Susan Markoff's chest. "But—"

"Reconstructive surgery and no trace of cancer. I'm clean."

Sarah dabbed her eyes with a tissue she pulled from a jacket pocket.

Dr. Markoff wrote on a red and white form and handed it to Sarah. "You'll need to have blood work done before the biopsy. I strongly recommend doing it today so the procedure is not delayed."

Sarah handed the form to Andrew. "OK, I'll go by the lab this afternoon."

"Something else, Sarah." Dr. Markoff pointed to the computer screen. "Isn't that a beautiful scene? I took that picture, two weeks before my own biopsy."

"It's nice, but . . ."

"What I'm suggesting is that you take a vacation, a nice place where you can get all of this out of your mind. They've done some research and found that relieving stress is good for your body in the long term. Besides, it'll take some time before Dr. Nadol can perform the biopsy."

"Just like that?" said Sarah. "Drop everything and rush off to Tahiti?"

"It's something to think about. Meanwhile, I'll send a disc to Dr. Nadol's office with your mammogram results." They stood and the two women shook hands. "Don't worry, Sarah," said the doctor, "you're going to do just fine."

Conversation was minimal after leaving Dr. Markoff's office. Andrew drove to a downtown restaurant for lunch and, after the waitress took their order, he said to Sarah, "What are you thinking, sweetheart?"

"That I should have been born a man."

He smiled. "Would have been my loss for sure." He reached across the table and clasped both her hands. "You've seen cases like this before at the hospital. Be honest now, how do you think your situation compares with the others?"

"That's not a fair question. The cases I've seen are the ones in surgery and they have to be pretty serious to get that far."

"Dr. Markoff seemed to be cautiously optimistic."

"Yeah, but that's her job to be that way."

Andrew took back his hands, thinking that Sarah's outlook on her coming biopsy would remain pessimistic, no matter how he tried to cheer her up. "What do you think about her suggestion . . . taking a brief vacation?"

"Honestly? Probably a waste of money. I'm not like that, Andy. I'd be thinking about it the whole time and it wouldn't be any fun for either of us. I'd rather take a trip when we have some really good news to celebrate. Wouldn't you?"

"You're probably right. We have lots of business things to nail down in the next couple of weeks. I don't think Roscoe would like it if I suddenly left town for a week or ten days. And your parents might have some questions."

"Well there you go, one step at a time. And speaking of business, I believe I have to come up with a large check pretty soon."

"By the fourteenth," he said. "I've got a stack of papers that you should read before then. Couple of them have to be signed and notarized. The CPA guy at the meeting said you'll be getting twenty-five percent of all the profits generated by the new company. That should make your tax situation a bit more complicated."

"Great, just what I needed." She paused and smiled. "Then I'm going to work you real hard, Andrew Krag, to keep our business profitable."

He laughed, sensing that her mood was improving. "Good grief, what have I got myself into?"

"You have no idea, but it's too late to back out. Changing the subject, I saw on the calendar that you have another poker game next Friday."

"I can cancel if it's a problem."

"I'm thinking I might go up with you."

"Really? Aren't you working that night?"

"I can probably get somebody to switch with me."

"That would be nice, but what will you do while I'm playing?"

"Oh, probably hang out with Tanice. Drink some wine, swap girl stories."

"Are you going to tell her about the lump?"

"Maybe."

"Wouldn't you tell your parents first?"

"Not sure. If I told Mom, she'd have a panic attack and be

down to Pueblo in a New York minute, camping out for the duration. Would you want that?"

"Probably not."

"You're the only person I want in that biopsy room. Nobody else."

"I'll be there. But if you told Tanice, that would put her in an awkward position. Especially if Emmaline later finds out what you've done."

"Tanice is cool. She can keep a secret."

Andrew fiddled with his knife and fork. "What about sleeping arrangements?"

"Ah, good question. We should definitely get some sleep."

"Don't be cute, Minnie. You know what I'm talking about." Andrew was using a private nickname, referring to the tattoo of Minnie Mouse on Sarah's upper thigh.

"I'll sleep at my folks' house and you bunk with Roscoe. How about that?"

"Totally hypocritical. We've been sleeping with each other for a month."

"Exactly. That's the way I'll put it to Mom. And Dad will see it my way."

"There are motels in Leadville," he said. "We can make all the noise we want in our own little hideaway."

"After you drinking beer and smoking cigars all evening? I don't think so."

Andrew made a mock face of horror. "Then I'll drink Dr. Pepper and pig out on M&M chocolate peanuts."

The waitress arrived with their food. Sarah picked up a hot French fried potato stick and bit off half. "Don't worry, we'll figure out something."

Andrew took Sarah to a laboratory after lunch where she gave several vials of blood in preparation for the biopsy. When they returned to Sarah's house, she barely had time to get ready for her hospital shift starting at three o'clock.

The next morning, Sarah called Dr. Nadol's office to make an appointment for a consultation. The soonest they could fit her in was on Monday of the following week, the last day of January. She kept that appointment by herself this time; Andrew had been called up to Leadville for a meeting with Roscoe and several others. They were to review a Request for Proposals on a construction contract and devise a strategy for putting their proposal together.

The consultation with Dr. Nadol was quick, professional and very matter-of-fact. He'd already reviewed the results of her mammogram and blood work and gave her an encouraging prognosis. He scheduled the biopsy for February 11th, a Friday, at a small surgical procedure clinic away from Parkview Medical Center. Dr. Nadol gave her a list of things to do before the biopsy, such as fasting that morning and avoiding certain medications for the full week before it.

Sarah left his office with mixed feelings. She had confidence in his medical talents and his fatherly concern for her well being gave her a small degree of comfort. But the delay weighed heavily on her mind. Somehow, she'd have to fill up the days with lots of activity to make them go by as quickly as possible.

Andrew's poker game turned out to be a nonevent. Because two of the regular players were going to be unexpectedly absent, Roscoe made the decision to postpone it to the first Friday in March. Sarah worked her evening shift at the hospital that Friday as planned, telling Andrew that this would make it easier to get a substitute for the day of her biopsy.

On Saturday, they slept late and went to an afternoon movie. On Sunday, they got up early and drove west to the Crestone area. They hiked up the San Isabel Trail on snowshoes and enjoyed a picnic lunch among hundreds of logs covering a large hillside area, avalanche victims that resembled giant toothpicks. The full day of strenuous exercise was a welcome tonic to both. Andrew could see a beautiful glow to Sarah's complexion; her joyful spirits confirmed that she was living in the moment and not dwelling on her medical problem.

On Monday, Sarah went back to working the day shift and they fell back into their regular pattern; Andrew fixing her breakfast while she took a shower.

Tuesday, February 8, was Sarah's forty-second birthday. Andrew made dinner reservations for seven o'clock at *La Renaissance*, the upscale restaurant where they had their first 'official' date just two months before.

The hostess greeted them and hung their coats in a small room near the entrance. Andrew wore a black pin stripe suit and Sarah was in a low cut, black cashmere dress, the one she'd worn New Years Eve at The Brown Palace in Denver. A faux chinchilla shrug draped her shoulders, completing her stunning outfit.

The hostess seated them next to a glass-enclosed fireplace with a flickering gas log that actually produced some heat. After the hostess left, Sarah laughed. "She's the same one we had before. I don't think she recognized us this time."

"You're right. We had on down jackets, ski hats and hiking boots then."

"Our dinner that night is still fuzzy in my mind," she said, "but dessert in your motel room was delicious."

He shifted the leather-bound menu slightly away from his face. "Gets me excited just thinking about it."

They both laughed as their tuxedoed waiter appeared and introduced himself as Max, their culinary caretaker for the evening. "Two glasses of your best champagne," said Andrew. When Max returned with the bubbly, Andrew raised his glass. "Happy Birthday to the most beautiful woman in the world."

She dinged her glass against his. "You are too kind and a little bit biased. There must be other attractions that keep you coming back for more."

"Well now, since you mention it. Aside from the way you've taken care of me when I became homeless, I love your devious brain and goofy sense of humor."

"Hmmm," she said. "Maybe I shouldn't have asked."

"I also love your sense of fashion, always looking glamorous, hair and makeup just so, and clothes that complement your figure. But tonight, I must sadly confess, your wardrobe is lacking something."

"What are you babbling about?"

Andrew reached into his pocket and pulled out a small box covered with gray cloth. He handed it to her and said, "This should make your outfit complete."

She gasped when she looked inside, putting one hand up to her lips. "Oh Andy, it's so beautiful." She deftly removed a ring from the box, a gold band with a large blue sapphire mounted in the middle, surrounded by two smaller diamonds.

"Try it on," he urged.

She slipped it on and flashed it in several directions, catching the table's flickering candlelight in the gems, accentuating their brilliance. "It fits perfectly. How did you know?"

"I borrowed one of your older rings and took it shopping." He was referring to the wedding rings from her first and only marriage, the ones she no longer wore at the hospital to discourage doctors from hitting on her.

She smiled. "Does this signify anything? I mean, like maybe you have a serious personal question you'd like to ask me?"

He grinned. "Can we go steady?"

"You are a piece of work, Krag. But I still love you."

"That's always nice to hear."

Max-the-waiter brought salads, a bottle of Merlot, and later, their entrees of prime rib with baked potatoes. After clearing away dinner dishes, he brought dessert cards and asked if they'd like coffee.

"Two decafs," replied Andrew.

Sarah studied the dessert menu. "These look yummy. Do we have time?"

"Sure, we don't have to rush off to a motel to satisfy your carnal urges."

"Me?" she wailed. "You're the one who couldn't wait. Almost broke my glasses trying to pull my sweater off."

"Then let's have something sinfully decadent right here." Andrew called Max over, pointed to an item on the card, and gave him a wink. He returned with a bowl of vanilla ice cream, a sterling silver gravy boat with hot fudge, and a piece of chocolate cake about three inches square hosting a single lit candle on top. Four waitresses joined Max and serenaded them with a chorus of Happy Birthday, Sarah.

She blew out the candle. "I'm never going to eat all this."

"Too bad we don't have tomorrow off. We could go hiking or skiing and work off all these calories." He put down his spoon, withdrew a heavy cream-colored envelope from his jacket and passed it to her.

"Another surprise?" she said.

"Take a look."

She opened the envelope and took out several sheets of paper. "I'll be damned, it's your divorce decree. When did this happen?"

"Last week, actually, but it came in today's mail."

"Why didn't you tell me before?"

"Because this is your day to celebrate. I didn't want to take away from it."

Sarah balled up her napkin and placed it on the table. "How do you feel about this? Are you upset about having a failed marriage?"

"Are you kidding? Great relief is the biggest emotion I can identify right now. And a sense of freedom, being a single man again."

"This is starting to sound like goodbye."

"No, no, no. I'm not going anywhere. I need you too much to ever think like that. And I want to believe that you need me the same way."

"More than ever, sweetheart."

"All I'm saying is that the divorce is just another milestone in my life, our life now. I always knew it was going to happen, it was just a matter of time." He noted a thoughtful look on Sarah's face. "Were you going to say something?"

"I'm ready to go, whenever you are."

While Andrew dealt with the bill, Sarah felt she was on shaky ground, similar to her experience in San Diego at Christmas during a minor earthquake. His divorce was welcome news but the expensive ring given with such a cavalier comment had shaken her confidence. *If Dr. Nadol gives me bad news on Friday, what will this do to our relationship?*

CHAPTER FOURTEEN

TOO BAD, THEY LOOKED PRETTY HOT

Leslie slept late the next morning. She got dressed, began moving about the house, and learned that Julie was still asleep in bed. She made a pot of coffee and took a cup to her office. Her mood improved several notches when an e-mail from Roger Halliday appeared in her Inbox.

Hello Faye,

I know you don't care for that name but I think it suits you better than Leslie. Such a beautiful name belongs with a beautiful woman like you.

Don't worry about texting me. I'm getting rid of my phone for security reasons and will get another one. Best you contact me by e-mail. Please use this address from now on: daygor@gmail.com

I've taken a new job and it's on the other side of the world.

That's about all I can say. If things work out, I may take the long way home after work . . . if you catch my drift. I'll be checking my e-mail often so feel free to write whenever you wish.

I'm sure you and your daughter have lots of ground to cover. Hope you can help with her 'predicament.' Do you have any idea how long she'll be staying?

Glad you like the souvenir I left behind. Now I wish I'd taken something from you to remind me of the delectable moments we shared. Next time I will.

Take care,
Roger

Leslie turned off her computer and stared out the window. She felt mildly irritated with his plain vanilla response. She wanted more, something tangible, words that spoke not only of his physical affection for her, but personal feelings as well. On top of that, she wouldn't have any idea where he was, what danger he was in, and when she'd see him again. If ever. Not a good basis for a relationship. *Do we have anything now but memories of a brief affair?* She decided not to answer him just then; maybe later today when she felt like it.

Leslie returned to the kitchen and found Julie helping herself to the coffee. "Morning, sleepy head," she said.

Julie yawned with a theatrical groan. "Hey, Mom. You been up long?"

"Not really." Leslie rubbed her hand along the shoulder of Julie's dark blue warmup jacket. "I love this velour fabric and the color suits you well."

"Thanks again, Mom, for bankrolling my new wardrobe. Good

thing I had Lucia with me. That girl knows all the right places and has an incredible sense of fashion. I think we got great value for our money—excuse me, *your* money."

"You and Lucia seem to get along well."

"Yeah, she's a real bud and knows how to handle men."

"How do you know *that?*"

"Couple of guys were giving us the eye at one of the stores. But she said something and they backed off real quick. Too bad, they looked pretty hot."

Leslie gave her a long hard look. "I want you to send your husband an e-mail, telling him you got here safely. You can set up an account on my computer with your own password."

Julie gave her a sneering smile. "If you want. What do we have to eat?"

"There's some cereal in the pantry and milk's in the fridge."

Julie found a box of corn flakes, poured them into a bowl and added some milk. She took a bite and frowned. "Ew, guess we're not in Kansas anymore, Toto."

"They're Italian and need getting used to."

"So, what's the plan for today, Mom?"

"There's a Food Mart open this afternoon but only for several hours since it's Sunday. I want you to go with me and we'll pick out some things you like."

"This could be fun. I'd like to try being creative in your kitchen."

Later, while Julie was taking a shower, Leslie did some reorganizing on her computer, hiding everything related to Roger Halliday that would be hard to find even if her daughter did some snooping. She showed Julie how to use the machine while she cleaned up and, after Julie sent a brief e-mail to Harper, they drove to the

Food Mart on the outskirts of Siena.

Julie walked straight to an outside area near the store's entrance where shopping carts were parked under an open garage. "Mom," she wailed, "I can't get one loose. They're all chained together."

"Welcome again to Italy," said Leslie with a laughing lilt to her voice. "Let me show you how this is done." She extracted a Euro coin from her purse and slipped it inside a metallic device that was fastened to the first cart. When the chain separated, Leslie pulled the cart free. "There you go. When we bring the cart back, I slip the chain back into the coin holder and get my Euro back. Not a bad system."

"I get it," said Julie. "No loose carts rolling around the parking lot."

They moved about the store, examining the items for sale. Julie seemed mesmerized, not only by the food, but also the way it was packaged. She marveled at plastic boxes of milk that needed no refrigeration and coffee packages that felt like bricks. Leslie explained that when the latter was opened and the vacuum seal broken, she would see the familiar dark brown coffee grounds.

They loaded the cart with different kinds of pasta. In the produce section, Leslie pulled two pairs of plastic gloves from a box and handed a set to Julie. "Put these on before you touch anything. They don't want us spreading American germs."

While they were selecting fruits and vegetables, Julie said, "Lucia wants me to come up next weekend. Is that OK?"

"Really? And do what?"

"Oh, hang out. She wants to show me around, meet some friends."

"Milan's not exactly a tourist destination. More like northern

Italy's business capitol. But there is La Scala."

Julie laughed. "I don't think Lucia's the opera type. She did mention Bank of America as a possible opportunity. Something to look into."

Leslie turned to face her, a pear in her right hand that could be thrown if necessary. "Are you thinking of working for a Milanese bank?"

Julie cringed. "Pretty far out, huh?"

"What about your husband? You'd have to get a visa and a work permit. And why would the bank consider hiring an American?"

"Mom, please. It's all iffy, something to think about. Lucia brought the whole thing up so I'll just play along. Probably won't amount to anything."

Leslie tied the top of the plastic bag of pears and placed it gently in the cart. "All right, but I want you to be careful and act like a married woman."

"Thanks, Mom. Lucia said I could take a train on Friday and she'll meet me at the station after work. I can catch another one back to Siena on Sunday and get back that evening. Does that work for you?"

"Sure, I'll take you to the station and pick you up later." They took their fully loaded cart to a checkout lane. "One more wrinkle ahead," said Leslie. "That old lady you see at the cash register will toss some plastic bags at you. Put our groceries in them after she rings them up."

Julie gave her a mischievous grin. "What if I toss them back at her?"

"Then you'll have an intimate meeting with the *Carabinieri.*"

Leslie gave Julie a free rein in the kitchen that evening. She made a Caesar salad with fresh Parmesan cheese sprinkled on top, followed by fettucini with garlic, onion, and bacon bits. Not exactly restaurant quality but, along with a bottle of local Chianti which they finished off, mother and daughter enjoyed a delightful meal.

During dinner, Julie suggested doing some touristy things later in the week. Leslie agreed, subject to the appointments she could get with Dr. Bertolucci. They would plan their excursions around that day in Florence.

Much later that evening, after Julie had gone to bed, Leslie crept into her office and wrote an e-mail to Roger Halliday.

Dear Mystery Man,
Thanks for your e-mail. Guess I can't complain too much if you want to call me Faye. It's my name after all and the one I gave you when we first met.

Julie and I are doing fine. She's already made a friend named Lucia. She's the daughter of my good friend, Maria Borelli. The girls went shopping and Lucia helped Julie buy some nice clothes. Lucia works for Bank of America in Milan and Julie's planning to spend next weekend with her.

What can I say about you—about us—about your damned occupation? About all I can do is hope for your safety. How long do you intend to continue in this insane business?

Please do everything possible to make sure you come back to me in one piece. I don't care if Julie's still here or not. I'll think of something.

Faye, aka, Leslie

After she sent it, she wondered if it was too strong, betraying an excess of dependency on him. She went back to bed and, before falling asleep, decided that her reply was just right. She missed him, she wanted him, and he needed to know that.

Leslie called Dr. Bertolucci's office the next morning and was informed that he was out of the country and would be unavailable for the next two weeks. She made appointments for herself and Julie, on a Wednesday afternoon in the last week of February. This situation gave Leslie the opportunity to plan several tourist trips. She called a friend in her bridge club and canceled her games for the rest of the week.

About noon, Leslie and Julie drove into Siena and took a walking tour of the city's center, treading up and down the cobblestone streets, inspecting churches and shops with a stop for lunch. They joined other tourists in the giant *Piazza del Campo* where the *Palio di Siena*, a traditional medieval horse race, is run in July and August.

Early Tuesday morning, they drove to the coastal resort town of Viareggio and checked into the Astor Hotel on the Esplanade. Leslie assured Julie that they deserved to treat themselves, not only to room service, but be pampered in the spa with massages and facials. That afternoon, they took a taxi to nearby Pisa, and went up into the leaning tower where Leslie had an unexpected attack of vertigo. They took many pictures, several of either Julie or Leslie posed in such a way that the subject appeared to be holding up the tower so it wouldn't fall over.

On Wednesday, they drove to Lucca and spent several hours walking about the old walled city. They found the house and museum ascribed as the birthplace of Giaccomo Puccini, the famous composer of many popular operas. Julie took a picture of Leslie, standing in front of the house with one hand reaching to the knee of Puccini's statue, sitting in a chair with a cigarette in his hand. Leslie urged Julie to see one of his operas at the Metropolitan when she was back in New York.

They returned to Castellina that afternoon. Each woman checked her e-mail account but neither had received anything. This didn't bother Julie so much but it made Leslie irritable. She had plenty to drink that night and went to bed early, pleading exhaustion from all their walking tours.

In spite of that, they were on the road again to Assisi the next day. Leslie parked her car at one end of the city and they took escalators up to the main road which was laid out to follow the long spine of a high ridge from *Porta Nuova* to *St. Francesco*. The sky was a bright blue and empty of clouds, the temperature a mild fifty degrees F. They stopped at the piazza facing St. Claire's church and struck up a conversation with a group of six young priests who had been recently ordained, all taking pictures of one another. Soon, Julie was taking photos of the priests and they reciprocated by taking pictures of mother and daughter surrounded by different priests. Before the men left, the senior one, who also spoke the best English, gave Leslie and Julie his blessing. Leslie protested, saying she wasn't worthy, and adding that it would likely cause a vengeful bolt of lightning to strike them.

The next morning, in preparation for her weekend in Milan with Lucia, Julie did a load of laundry. As Julie was folding her still warm clothes, Leslie came into her bedroom. "Can I help you with any of that?" she asked.

"Thanks, but I think I've got it all together."

Leslie started to turn away. "We need to get rolling soon. I'm not totally sure how to find the terminal and we have to buy your tickets."

"Right," said Julie. "Almost ready." She paused for a few moments and looked up from the items spread out on her bed. "Mom? Where did we go wrong?"

"What?"

"You and me. What happened to *us*? When did our relationship go off the track? And *why*?"

Leslie turned back and folded her arms across her chest. "Well . . . a good question. But I can't point to a date on the calendar and tell you anything specific. One day I do remember is when Andrew and I were married."

Julie laughed nervously. "Yeah, I was a complete shit at your reception. Will you ever forgive me for that?"

"Yes you were, but I forgave you long ago. In the years before that, I was a pretty lousy mother. Divorcing your father, fighting him tooth and nail for money, moving to Colorado, and then starting an affair with Mr. Krag. All contributing factors and my fault as well."

"So we're OK now?"

Leslie walked over with open arms and gave her a hug. "We're great."

Julie returned the hug with even more strength. "This time with you has been wonderful, I want you to know that. And I'm grateful for all that you've done for me, not only since I got here, but for all of my life. I'm going to pay you back for everything, I promise."

Leslie broke free. "We'll see. Now finish your packing."

Julie gathered her new clothes together and began stuffing them into a duffel bag. Leslie went off to her bathroom, tears trickling down her cheeks. After washing her face, she looked in the mirror and thought about the last couple of days of their mother-daughter reunion. She had felt a sense of guilt when Julie arrived and tried to make up for their acrimonious past by being generous with her money. But this morning, she detected a change in their relationship and now had good reason to hope for better times ahead.

Traffic between Castellina and Siena's railway station was heavy, but they arrived a good half hour before Julie's departure time. After Leslie purchased the tickets, they found a wooden bench in the waiting area and sat close to each other.

"OK," Leslie began, "you've got a credit card, some Euros, and you've got my phone number. I want you to buy a cell phone in Milan, one of those throwaway jobbers, and give me a call. If I'm not home, leave a message with your number. I'll call you back as soon as I can."

"Right. What'll you be doing while I'm gone?"

"Taking a break. I've gotten more exercise with you this last week than I've had for a year. I'll give Maria a buzz, see if we can cook up something."

Julie giggled. "You going to miss me?"

Leslie laughed. "Yeah, like a sore tooth."

An excited male voice on a loud speaker rattled off several long Italian sentences causing both women to look at their watches. "That's me," said Julie.

They went outside to the assigned track and found their waiting train. A porter checked Julie's ticket and pointed to a first class compartment ahead. Leslie gave her a hug and said, "Have a good time and give Lucia my best." After another hug, Julie climbed into her compartment and Leslie walked back to her car.

At the villa, Leslie checked her e-mail and found only a few pieces of spam. She heated up a bowl of leftover soup, drank a glass of Chianti, and was about to take a nap when the doorbell rang. Before she opened the front door, she glanced out a window and saw a van with the red and yellow logo of DHL Express.

"Mrs. Leslie Krag?" the driver asked.

"Yes, that's me."

He gave her a form attached to a clipboard and said, "Sign please."

Leslie scribbled her name in the space marked with a large X, the man gave her a large flat envelope, and he left. She returned to the kitchen and opened the envelope with a small knife. A check fell to the floor as she unfolded the papers.

Dear Leslie,

Enclosed is your final decree of divorce from Andrew Krag and a check for $3,250.00, the remaining balance in your account.

This action now completes all of your business with our firm. Please accept my personal best wishes for many years of good health and happiness.

Sincerely yours,

Paul Harrington, Esq.

Leslie picked up the check, put it back into the envelope along with the papers, and poured herself a generous tumbler of vodka. She hoisted the glass in a mock toast, facing what she thought was east, and said aloud, "Enjoy it while you can, Krag. It's not over yet."

CHAPTER FIFTEEN

I'M A NURSE, I KNOW THE DRILL

The alarm made a jarring sound at 6:45. Andrew hit the shutoff button and instinctively rolled over toward Sarah but she wasn't there. He groaned, heaved himself out of the warm bed into a cold bedroom, and slipped on his warmup suit.

As he passed the closed bathroom door, he heard water running inside. *Sarah must be taking a shower.* He continued to the kitchen, poured himself a cup of coffee, and willed himself to have a toasted English muffin with blueberry preserves and a glass of orange juice. He wasn't sure when they'd eat lunch and didn't want an empty stomach when noon rolled around.

When he got back to the bedroom, Sarah was dressed and sitting on the bed, staring into space. He stood in the doorway, content to watch, until she noticed his presence. She looked up and said, "Did you get some breakfast?"

"I did." He glanced at the bedside clock. "We should be leaving soon."

She got up, softly brushed the back of her fingers along his cheek, and went around him through the doorway. "I need some water, then we can go."

Andrew got dressed and they drove to Physician's Plaza, a medical facility about fifteen minutes from Sarah's house. Sarah checked in with a receptionist and was given a black device resembling a hockey puck with the number 13 on top. "Have a seat," said the receptionist. "When the red lights go off, someone will come out and call your number."

"You got one of those things with another number?"

The receptionist gave Sarah an irritated look. After several moments, she slammed a similar device on the counter with the number 42.

Sarah went over to Andrew, took off her jacket and sat down. He reached out and grasped her hand. "How are you doing, sweetheart?"

"How do you think?" she said. She leaned over to him and continued, "Sorry, Andy. I'm here and that's about all I can say."

"It's going to be all right, Sarah."

"What if they cut if off? Are you going to leave me?"

Andrew turned his whole body around to look at her. "I'll say what I've said before. You're jumping the gun. It's only a biopsy to see what's there. But so what? It doesn't matter to me, one way or the other. I know it matters to you, a lot, but I'm not going anywhere. I'm staying with you and we'll see this through *together.*"

Several other patients in the waiting room turned to stare at them but said nothing. Tears came to Sarah's eyes and she squeezed Andy's hand even harder. "You're right, Andy. Forgive me, I just can't stand the waiting . . . not knowing . . . thinking about all the bad things that might happen."

Andrew walked over to a table and brought back a box of tissues. Sarah took a handful and dabbed her eyes, sniffling, and wiping her nose. "You know who the worst patients are? Doctors."

"Not surprising," he said. "Who gets to be second?"

"I'll give you three choices and the first two don't count."

Andrew was about to say *nurses* when Sarah's plastic puck began flashing red lights around its edge. A woman about twenty-five dressed in nurse's garb came out of a door opposite them and called for number forty-two.

"Here we go," said Sarah, rising and heading to the caller. "That's me."

"Ms. Dolan? I'm Cindy. Come inside, room five on your right." Sarah waved to Andrew, indicating that he should follow her. "Is he your husband?"

"No, my dad." Sarah handed her the plastic puck and went around her.

Once all three were in room five, Cindy handed Sarah two folded cotton robes. "Strip down to your panties and put these on. One should open in—"

"I'm a nurse," said Sarah. "I know the drill."

Cindy pulled a green curtain across the front of the room and left. Andrew offered to help Sarah get undressed but sat in a corner when she turned him down.

Sarah sat on the end of the mobile bed, her bare legs extending below the hem of the surgical robes. Andrew came over and massaged her cold feet.

Nurse Cindy and Dr. Nadol soon appeared. "Good morning, Sarah," he said, "all ready for this?"

Sarah grunted something like a *yes* and introduced Andy as

her fiancé. While Cindy checked Sarah's pulse, temperature, and blood pressure, Dr. Nadol went through the standard pre-surgery list of questions.

"No aspirin or ibuprofen for over a week," said Sarah. "I had dinner last night about seven but only water this morning."

Dr. Nadol smiled. "Excellent, Sarah. Now here's what's going to happen. We'll take you into the surgical room but Andrew will have to go back outside. The kind of biopsy I'll be doing is called a needle aspiration. Actually, I'll be using several needles. I'm going to numb your entire breast first so you won't feel anything. But you'll be able to watch the whole procedure while it's happening. I'll remove some cells through each needle, put them on slides, and rush them down to the lab."

"How long? When will you know?"

"Ah. You'll be in the waiting area for three to five hours but Andrew will be able to keep you company."

"Five hours? Damn."

"I know this experience is upsetting," said Dr. Nadol. "Would you like some Valium? You're allowed to have it."

"No, let's just get it done."

"Fine, I'll see you inside."

After Dr. Nadol left, Sarah lay on the bed. Cindy raised the guards on both sides and started an IV in Sarah's arm. "We're taking her now," she told Andrew.

Sarah looked over at him and said, "Come give me a kiss."

Andrew gave her three tender kisses and took Sarah's glasses from the nurse. "See you soon. Be a good girl in there."

Nurse Cindy came into the waiting room and found Andrew reading a magazine. "Ms. Dolan is in room five," she said. "You can go back, *Dad.*"

Andrew smiled, relishing Sarah's earlier remark but not dwelling on Cindy's comment. He went inside and saw Sarah sitting up in bed, still in dressing gowns but without the IV. He kissed her and asked, "How'd it go, sweetheart?"

"As advertised. Now all we have to do is sit and wait."

"Does it hurt much?"

"Not at all. I'm still numb from all the joy juice they shot into me. He said it will start hurting later so he gave me a painkiller."

"That's it?"

A rumbling noise came from the direction of her stomach. "Yep, that's me," she said. "You'd be a real prince if you got me something to eat."

"Really? Anything in particular?"

"A big chocolate milk shake would be absolutely divine."

"I'll see what I can do. Back in a flash."

He drove to Pueblo's center, pulled into a fast food restaurant's take-out line and ordered a giant chocolate milk shake. Sarah's eyes bulged in delighted surprise when she saw the size of the container in Andrew's hand.

As she slurped the cold sweetness, Andrew said, "Take it slow, Honey. You don't want to get a stomach ache."

She took a break, smiled warmly, and took his hand. "Thanks for taking care of me, my one-in-a-million guy."

In between her sips, they talked about every conceivable subject, skating widely around 'the elephant in the room' also known as breast cancer. After finishing the shake with exaggerated bubbling noises, Sarah started to fade. "Would you be upset if I took a little nap? Sure didn't get much sleep last night."

"Not at all. I'll be right here."

Sarah nodded off and began to snore. Andrew went out to his SUV, found a book he'd been trying to get into, and brought it back. He resumed his bedside vigil, alternating his gaze between Sarah and the book. At one point, he went out to the waiting room and helped himself to coffee.

Time passed slowly, no matter how strongly Andrew willed the clock on the wall to speed ahead. Sarah finally awoke just before noon and rubbed her eyes. "Good Lord, how long did I sleep?"

Andrew leaned over and kissed her. "A little over two hours. No news yet."

Sarah was about to speak when Dr. Nadol came in. The look on his face gave Andrew a moment of panic and he grabbed Sarah's left hand. *This can't be good news.*

Dr. Nadol took her other hand. "The news is good, the biopsy was negative."

Sarah covered her face with both hands and wept, her body shaking with convulsions of relief. Andrew gave her a hug and whispered into her ear, "I knew you'd be OK . . . I love you so much." Tears ran down his cheeks and joined with hers. Dr. Nadol smiled and watched them, his arms folded across his chest.

When Sarah and Andrew finally broke apart, Dr. Nadol gave them both wads of tissue. "This is the best part of my job," he said. He paused for several moments so they could recover. "There will be some bruising, Sarah, and possibly a small amount of blood. Don't worry about it but I want you to keep that area clean." He turned to Andrew and added, "Don't want to risk an infection."

"What do I have in there?" said Sarah. "What did the lab find out?"

"A fibrous lump, not malignant. But it's something to keep an eye on. I'll send a report to Dr. Markoff. She'll probably want to talk with you and I want to see you again in six months. So that's it for today, you're free to go."

"Thank you doctor," she said, "thank you so much."

After he left, Sarah got out of bed and started to get dressed. "We don't have anything to do this weekend, do we?"

"Nothing at all," he said. "Monday is Valentine's Day, the same day you become an RBC partner."

"Then let's take a vacation. Now that we know, we can take a real holiday and totally enjoy ourselves. An early Valentine celebration."

"Where can we go? Can't be too far away."

"Let's drive down to Santa Fe. Stay at La Fonda and be real tourists."

"Great idea. Margaritas and dinner at Geronimo's."

Julie had called Leslie on Friday night from Lucia's apartment in Milan. They were about to go out for dinner before trying a dance club. Leslie was happy to hear from her but, like a concerned mother, she reminded Julie that she was still Mrs. Julie Phillips and should buy a disposable cell phone at first opportunity.

Since Julie left, Leslie had caught up on her reading. She got back into *Goddess of Vengeance*, the trashy book which Roger had bought for her in the Siena bookstore. On Sunday, however, she buckled down to the long overdue and tedious task of reviewing her financial situation.

After a modest breakfast of toast and scrambled eggs, she took a cup of coffee to her office and started work. Top priority was the insurance on the BMW she'd totaled in Colorado. Since Paul Harrington had made it clear he could no longer be her attorney, Leslie's last resort was to ask for help from her Denver-based CPA. She sent him an e-mail, asking him to process the claim. She also told him that she was gathering data for her income tax returns. Even though she would probably be an Italian resident for some time, she didn't want to take any chances with the IRS.

Leslie intended next to look at several financial spreadsheets, but something in her e-mail Inbox from Roger Halliday became a higher priority.

Hello Leslie,

There's been a new development here, an obstacle to progress.

I'm thinking of returning to Castellina for a few days until things improve. How is your situation there? Will I be able to see you?

Nothing's definite right now. I'll keep working the problem, but if the 'climate' here doesn't change, I'll hop on a plane.

Kisses, R. H.

The e-mail threw Leslie into a state of nerve-wracking anticipation. *The man is so damned unpredictable. You can't plan on anything with him.* She wanted him to come back, the sooner the better, but Julie would be here. Roger couldn't stay at the villa this time and certainly not share Leslie's bed. Perhaps he could hide at a hotel in Siena or Florence. Leslie thought about it for a while and finally sent Halliday a reply.

Hello Roger,

Sorry to hear about your business problems but the possibility of seeing you again, even on such short notice, could be a silver lining to that dark cloud. As I mentioned in my last e-mail, Julie is in Milan for the weekend and palling around with her new friend, Lucia. The plan is for Julie to be back here late tonight. So if you do return to Castellina, you will have to stay at a hotel. Put on your thinking cap and invent a credible story about the history of our relationship.

Keep me posted. Even by telephone is OK.

Leslie

A half hour later, the telephone interrupted Leslie's concentration. When she answered, the caller said, "Hi, Mom. Did I catch you at a bad time?"

"No . . . sorry, Honey. I was knee-deep in tax papers. How are you?"

"Great. We're getting along famously and Lucia's been introducing me to all her friends, showing me Milan's hot spots. She has a scooter so I rented one and we cruised around the city yesterday. Two wild and crazy chicks on the town."

"Wonderful," said Leslie, in a tone that conveyed it was anything *but* wonderful. "What time is your train getting in to Siena?"

"Um . . . I need to talk with you about that."

"Oh?"

"Lucia has asked me to stay on for a week. She wants to show me around her bank, meet key people, and cultivate important contacts. She thinks there could be a place for me and I should check it out."

"We've been through this before, Julie."

"I know, Mom. I'm an expat and it's hard for Americans to

get a position in this country. But it can be done. I'm not saying I would, but I just want to learn more about the whole operation. Hey, wouldn't it look good on my resume?"

Leslie suddenly realized that Julie's presence in Milan for all of next week gave her that silver lining she'd mentioned in her last e-mail to Halliday. But she couldn't change her mind too rapidly because Julie would be suspicious. "You can't be spending every hour of every day with Lucia. She must have her own things to do."

"True. She's given me some material on Italian banking practices and other commercial activities. I can study them while she's working and, if I get too bored, see a movie or visit a museum."

"I don't know, Julie. That's seems an awful lot to digest."

"No problem, Mom. I can do it. Hey, got an e-mail from Harper."

"He forgave you and wants you back?"

"Not exactly. He was civil and was glad to hear that I'm safe."

"That's something, anyway. Sounds like a good start."

"I'll write him back tonight and be a little more friendly. And a lot more penitent. Tell him how I can be trusted as a mature adult."

"Don't try to bridge that gap in a single day. It'll take time."

"I know. By the way, I'm calling from my new cell phone. Do you have a pencil handy to write down the number?"

"I have caller ID, it's on the screen. How's your money holding out? Can you get by for a whole week on what I gave you?"

"Then you don't mind if I stay?"

"I do, but I guess I have to trust you. I can trust you, can't I?"

"Yes, Mom, you can trust me."

They chatted for several more minutes. Leslie promised to

transfer some money to Julie after she opened an account with Lucia's bank. After the call ended, Leslie wasted no time sending an encouraging e-mail to Roger Halliday.

CHAPTER SIXTEEN

IT'S NOT A SMALL WORLD AFTER ALL

Roger Halliday paced back and forth in the lobby of the Zhonglian International Hotel, one of the better establishments in Dandong, China, a modern city with a population of 2.4 million. He'd finished breakfast about an hour before, followed by a 400 yard walk to a bridge over the Yalu River, the border between China and North Korea. He hiked along the river bank to clear his head, still fuzzy from jet lag caused by a long flight from Washington. An outside temperature of twenty degrees with a biting wind had kept his walk short.

Halliday stopped pacing when he saw a short heavyset man enter the lobby from the street. He wore thick glasses with black frames, held a cigar in one hand, and came toward Roger. "Mr. Halliday?"

"What happened to you? We were supposed to meet last night."

The man removed his hat, revealing a shiny bald head, and motioned to a group of chairs in a far corner. "We shall talk." The man found a large comfortable chair and Roger took one next to him.

"I'm getting the impression there is a problem," said Roger. "Is that true, Mr. Huong?"

Huong took a long drag on his cigar, blew out a cloud of stinky smoke, and tamped long ashes into an ashtray. "The situation has become more complicated. My position within the government and my personal security are in jeopardy. Certain initiatives have not worked to our advantage."

"Like stealing oil from the Norwegians?"

Huong coughed and fumbled with his cigar. "How do you know that?"

"We're not stupid, Huong. Word gets around."

He sighed. "You have just confirmed the wisdom of my plan. Therefore, I must end our negotiations."

"You have nothing for me? No documents or information?"

"It is regrettable, but I had to leave with very little in my possession."

"I could kill you easily, you know. Do your Dear Leader a big favor."

Huong smiled. "And what would be the point? It would only advertise your own failure. It gets nothing in return."

Halliday boiled with anger and frustration. "Dealing with you people is like searching for a pony in a room full of horse shit."

Huong laughed. "You are such an idealist."

"It comes with being an American."

Huong rose and turned to leave. "I will not be returning to my own country. Do not try to contact me again."

Halliday followed Huong to the hotel's front door and watched as he got into a black sedan and sped away. He went to a ground floor room equipped with computers and logged in. He smiled when he read Leslie's recent e-mail, the one telling him that Julie would be in Milan for a week.

He didn't answer her e-mail. Instead, he sent a cryptic message to his contact in Washington, a summary of his meeting with Huong. He ended the report saying that he'd be taking a brief vacation before returning to D.C.

Using the computer, he made a reservation on a China Southern flight to Beijing that would leave Dandong in two hours. He had just enough time to check out of the hotel and grab a taxi to the airport.

Leslie worked for another hour, reviewing her financial papers, before taking a break. She made herself a mimosa and daydreamed about Roger Halliday while she drank it. *How wonderful to have him every night for an entire week. But what will we do when we're not in bed?*

She finished her drink and decided to call Maria Borelli. It was time to discuss a matter which they'd talked about several days ago.

"*Bongiorno,*" said Maria. "I am so pleased that our daughters are enjoying each other's company."

"Me, too. I talked with Julie this morning and she's staying longer in Milan. Lucia's going to introduce her to several people at the bank."

"Do you think she may find a position?"

"Hard to say. If not, it should be a good experience. Learning more about Italy and business in Europe."

"I agree. And how are *you*, Leslie?"

"Better. On Friday afternoon, when I got back from the station, not so good. The DHL guy brought some paper from my Denver attorney. It's official, I'm no longer a married woman."

"You don't sound unhappy. So it was not such bad news after all?"

"I knew the divorce was coming. Just didn't know when."

"As I've said before, you are young, intelligent, and beautiful. Many years to be happy and in love again."

"Perhaps, but I don't intend to marry again. Ever. I've been thinking of what Dr. Bertolucci said about accepting reality. To be honest, I believe that in the past I've defined myself by the men I was married to. No more of that nonsense. From now on, I intend to live life on my own terms."

"Very good, Leslie. You have your self-confidence back."

"I do, but that's not why I called. Do you remember our talk about the man I had been seeing, Roger Halliday? I think he's coming back to Castellina next week. I promised that we'd include you and Marcello in our plans. Maybe the four of us can have dinner one night."

"That would be nice. Do you have a certain evening in mind?"

"Not yet, but I'll call you as soon as I know his schedule. I think it best if we took you to a restaurant in Siena or Florence. That way, I wouldn't have to spend a lot of time in the kitchen slaving over the meal. Is that all right?"

"Certainly. Please call me when you have more news."

"One last thing, Maria. Please don't mention this to Lucia. I want to tell Julie about Roger myself, when the time is right."

"Of course. It will be our secret."

Leslie's telephone rang about four o'clock. "Leslie," said Roger. "So good to hear your voice again."

"Hello there, mystery man. Where are you?"

"Beijing. At the airport."

"My God, is that like . . . China?"

"The one and only. So here's the deal. I'm on Emirates Air leaving at five minutes before midnight."

"What time is it there?" she said.

"About ten, so I've got two hours to kill before takeoff."

"You sound tired, Roger."

"Yes, damn tired. Tired of all this globetrotting with nothing to show for it."

"Guess you didn't solve your business problem."

"Afraid not, but I'll tell you all about it when I see you."

"And when will *that* be?"

"This flight takes me to Dubai but I've got a long layover. I leave there on Emirates 95 and arrive in Rome at 8:05 tomorrow night. Can you meet me?"

"Roger, that's over twenty-four hours from now. Why so long?"

"Contrary to the Disney folks, it's not a small world after all."

"All right, all right, I'll be there. Do you know what tomorrow is?"

"Sure do. Valentine's Day. Think you can handle a little romance?"

She laughed. "I'll get us a reservation at the Airport Hilton. It's a short walk from the terminal through the parking structure."

Halliday chuckled. "Bring my pajamas, will you? The ones with the blue bamboo shoots?"

"No way are you needing pajamas on Valentine's Day, buddy."

Leslie went to her freezer, poured vodka over two ice cubes and took a long pull. *What the hell am I going to do for the next twenty-eight hours?*

She chug-a-lugged her drink and went to the bathroom. She showered and dressed in one of her more fashionable outfits. She drove her Mercedes into Siena where her first stop was Fetrinelli's, the place where she and Roger had shopped for books. She purchased three novels, two by the same author of *Goddess of Vengeance*, and one by Michael Dibdin titled *Blood Rain.* The back cover noted that detective Aurelio Zen has just been given the worst assignment he could imagine, investigating a murder on the island of Sicily. Since she had the time, she'd try it and see if Zen was all that Roger thought he was. The book might even give her more insight into the real character of Roger Halliday.

Leslie took her bag of books to a nearby restaurant, the same one where she and Roger had dined after his purchase of clothes. She was seated at a small table near a window, ordered a vodka martini, and perused the complex menu. When the waiter brought her drink, she asked for more time. But after ten minutes, she decided she wasn't very hungry. She asked the waiter for a bowl of Tuscan wedding soup and a small salad. Plus another martini, of course.

While waiting for her food, she looked around the restaurant. It was early evening and there were only a few patrons. Since it was Sunday, the place would soon be filling up with families.

Leslie was not an introspective person, but tonight, with no dinner partner to share conversation, she began thinking about her situation and events of the last six months. *That bit with Maria about reality was a stretch. Here I am, killing time until I can be with still another man. Do I really need Roger Halliday to make me complete? You are one sorry piece of work, Leslie Faye Aronson. You need to get a life.*

Leslie awoke at noon on Monday, not believing her clock and wondering why she had slept so late. Then she remembered: a restless night of tossing and turning, taking aspirin for a hangover headache, and more sleeping pills than the normal dosage that put her into a deep slumber where time was no longer relevant.

She made a pot of coffee, took a quick shower, and bustled about the house in her bathrobe. After wolfing down a bowl of cold cereal, she gathered clothes and toilet articles and stuffed them into a small suitcase. She stripped her bed and made it again with freshly laundered linen, followed by a light spritzing with an exotic fragrance. Back in the bathroom again, she applied the finishing touches to her face and hair. She rooted around her closet, wondering what to wear for her meeting at the Rome airport. Should it be glamourous and expensive or run-of-the mill casual? She chose tight designer jeans and a rusty orange cashmere sweater *Svelte and sexy tonight. Don't want him to get an inflated ego.*

Around three o'clock, she decided it was time to leave Castellina and drove down the A1 *autostrada* towards Rome. When she checked into the Airport Hilton, she opted for a suite at the top of the building, an appropriate room for a romantic reunion. This would be her Valentine's Day gift to Mr. Halliday.

Once in the suite and facing several hours before Roger's arrival, she relaxed and got back into *Blood Rain,* the one book in the trio that she'd already started. After reading more of it, she understood a lot more about Mr. Halliday. He identified himself with Aurelio Zen, the Italian detective renowned for his integrity and slightly screwy way of successfully solving cases. Zen also enjoyed women and managed to have several affairs though he lived with his mother. Perhaps it's a good thing that Roger's mother lives in Colorado Springs, she thought.

Leslie felt sad when she saw Roger coming into the terminal's waiting area for greeters. His blue suit looked like he'd slept in it and his shirt collar was unbuttoned, his tie loosened and hanging outside of his jacket. The worst was seeing the fatigue etched all over his face.

He perked up when he recognized Leslie and literally stumbled into her arms. "Oh, Roger, thank God you made it." They hugged and kissed, first tentatively and then with familiar affection.

"Had my doubts for a while," he said, "but here I am."

"You must be exhausted." She reached for his single piece of luggage. "Let me help you with that."

"It's got wheels. The hotel's not far?"

"Minutes away, just follow me."

"Hey, you look wonderful, Les. Love those jeans, they fit you well."

Leslie gave her rear end a wiggle and walked ahead.

Once in their suite, Roger hung his overcoat and suit jacket in the closet and collapsed on a small couch. "Are you hungry?" said Leslie. "I can call room service. How about a drink?"

"Nothing, thanks."

"Did you get any sleep on the plane?"

"Not much. It was too crowded, too noisy. All those Arab families with their kids running up and down the aisle. Why are they coming to Rome in February?"

"Not for an audience with the pope, I'm sure." Leslie pulled down the covers and took his hand. "Time for bed, lover."

Roger stripped down to his underwear and crawled into bed. She kissed him and whispered, "I'll be with you in a minute. Don't go away."

She went into the bathroom and came out a few minutes later wearing a sheer black nightgown that reached the top of her knees. She made a theatrical pose in the doorway and called out, "What do you think? You likee?"

Roger's only reaction was soft snoring. Leslie turned out the lights and slipped into bed, cuddling up close and feeling secure in the warmth of his body. She kissed him and whispered, "Happy Valentine's Day, lover."

CHAPTER SEVENTEEN

A PERSONAL MESSAGE FROM THE HOLY MAN

An hour before dawn, Roger awoke and reached out for his bed partner. Leslie, already awake, responded eagerly to his touch and melded her body into his. They made silent love, slowly, and with exquisite patience, each delaying gratification so that a partner's pleasure could be intensified. Only when they were ready, knowing that the mutual summit was about to be achieved, did their final release come.

They lay close together for several minutes, waiting for lungs to refill and heartbeats to resume their normal cadence.

Leslie was first to speak. "That was wonderful, certainly worth waiting for."

Roger kissed her. "It was *glorious*. Sorry I collapsed on you last night. Did I miss anything important?"

"Just my new black nightgown. And undressing me."

"We'll save it for another time."

"Happy Valentine's Day," she said. "Technically, it's already the next day."

"It's still the fourteenth in Colorado."

"Can you stay with me all week? I hope you don't have to go back to China."

"No chance of that. I'm taking a well-earned vacation."

"What happened back there with your *business*? Can you talk about it?"

"This North Korean guy, Huong Pak Chol, was playing both ends against the middle. Working a scheme to siphon oil under the Norwegian tundra and sell it to the Chinese, but the whole thing blew up in his face. Huong was responsible for distribution of drugs and counterfeit bills, raising money for Dear Leader's treasury."

"How in hell did you get mixed up with this guy?"

"They sent me to Dandong to meet him. Pick up some classified documents on their missile development and uranium enrichment. Also talk to him about political asylum in the U. S., but it didn't work out. Guess he'll take his chances in some other country. They say he's got plenty of blood on his hands. A necessary evil for him to get that high in the government."

"I think you'll be safe with me in Castellina."

"But you'll kick me out when your daughter comes back."

"Probably."

"I'd like to meet her," he said.

Leslie stiffened. "She doesn't know about us and I'm not ready to tell her."

"Why not?"

"We've got issues, too many years of conflict. But the big one is her own situation, a problem that she caused. She's married and her husband is back in New Jersey while she's flitting about Tuscany."

"What happened with them?"

"You won't believe this. She went to a Christmas party alone and—"

"She got too chummy with another guy?"

"Sounds like you know about Christmas parties."

"I've been to a few," he said.

"Well, unfortunately, their fooling around was videotaped and later viewed by a cast of thousands, including her husband. So out she went and home to mama."

Roger suppressed a laugh. "OK, I understand."

"You will get to meet my friend, Maria Borelli. We're having dinner one night with her and her friend, Marcello."

"Sounds good. I'll have to put some finishing touches on my cover story."

As they became drowsy, she said, "Get some sleep. We have nowhere to go."

"Right here with you is fine," he said, drifting off with their bodies entwined.

Andrew spent most of Valentine's Day traveling to Denver and back again to Pueblo. The meeting with Roscoe Bartlett, Richard Goodlake, and Donald Whisnant went well. The two million dollar cashier's check was gratefully received, papers were signed and exchanged, and Miriam Sarah Dolan was now a limited partner in the new construction enterprise.

Andrew stopped in Pueblo and picked up a dozen red roses. He arranged them in a vase and placed it in the living room where Sarah would see it when she came home from her hospital shift.

He also made dinner and had it simmering while he worked on his computer. When he heard a squeal of delight coming from the living room, he knew that Sarah had seen the flowers. He went in and joined her.

"What beautiful flowers," she said. "Wonder who they're from?"

He gave her a squeeze and a kiss. "Your not-so-secret admirer. Happy Valentine's Day, sweetheart."

"Thank you, darling, and thanks for the roses."

"Dinner's heating but the corn bread has to be heated. How about a drink?"

"What are you cooking?" she said.

"Good old fashioned Colorado chili, a tasty meal even at 10,000 feet."

"Think I'll have a beer."

Andrew opened two bottles and poured beer into two frosted mugs. He and Sarah sat close on the living room couch, in front of the flickering fireplace, and tapped their mugs together in a toast. "Here's looking at you, boss," he said, "the newest member of RBC management."

She wiped foam from his lips with her fingers. "I'm a partner, *your* partner, and not your boss."

Andrew laughed. "Yeah, but not a silent one. Anyway, the meeting went well. I brought back a bunch of papers for you to look at."

"Ugh."

"No hurry, whenever you get some free time." He took a sip of beer. "How did *your* day go?"

"Pretty good, except for an incident in the OR. Another nurse bumped into me by accident and hit my breast. God, it hurt. Had to pretend it didn't. Another couple of days and it should be OK again."

"Very glad to hear that."

"Yes, me too. Touching will then be allowed."

"I'm not feeling deprived," he said.

"I did have one brief moment of glory. During our lunch break, a bunch of us nurses were talking about Valentine's Day. About what our husbands or boyfriends might be doing for us tonight. When I told them we were having a simple dinner at home, they made some comments, sort of implying that I had a cheap boyfriend. But when I told them about our wonderful weekend in Santa Fe—an early present—they changed their tune real fast."

"Mentioned it to Roscoe this morning and I made some points with him. Treating his niece right is a big deal with him."

"Well there you go," she said.

"I think it might inspire him to do something special for Tanice. Like maybe a trip to Aspen or Vail."

"She'd probably like a week in Cancun or Puerto Vallarta."

"Ha. Wouldn't we all?"

The telephone rang and Sarah reached out for the remote handset. "Hello," she said. After a brief pause, she passed it to Andrew. "For you," she whispered.

"Andrew Krag, speaking."

"Hello, Andy, it's Emmaline calling. I understand Roscoe's new company is now funded with my daughter's contribution."

"That's correct," he said.

"Then I'd like to move ahead and make that offer. The one for those three lots down there in West Pueblo."

"One moment, please. I have to check with the limited partner."

"What?"

"She has to approve all expenditures over $100,000. Remember?"

"Oh for pity's sake. I thought we'd been through all that rigmarole."

Andrew put his hand loosely over the mouthpiece. "Miss Dolan," he said, "do we have your approval to make an offer to Mr. Sebastian on those three lots in Pueblo West that we looked at?"

"How much are we offering?"

"$110,000," he said.

"Approved, but keep me posted on the negotiations."

Andrew removed his hand. "She approved the offer, Emmaline. Let me know how it turns out."

A gruff Emmaline said, "Right," and hung up.

Sarah and Andrew had a good laugh. Sarah gave him a wet, beer-flavored kiss and said, "You now have a brilliant career ahead. Executive secretary, chief cook and bottle washer."

He raised his mug in another toast and said, "To tender touching."

Roger awoke about half past eight o'clock. His first sight was Leslie, sitting on a couch, dressed in a white terry cloth robe and sipping coffee. "He's alive," she called out, coming over to the bed and kissing him. "How about some coffee?"

"You'd be an angel."

She brought him a cup and propped up both sets of bed pillows. "You must be pretty hungry about now."

"Yes, I am. What do you have?"

"I have a strong desire for room service."

He grinned. "And I have a strong desire for you."

Leslie laughed. "Hold that thought for later."

Roger had a second cup of coffee and headed to the bathroom. When he came out, he wore a white robe similar to Leslie's. He dug into his suitcase, found a box wrapped in crimson paper tied neatly with a gold ribbon. "Almost forgot," he said. "Happy Valentine's Day, Leslie."

Leslie ripped open the package and found a jade carving, resting on a rosewood stand that was about six inches long and three inches high. The carving showed a reclining Buddha with a happy look on his face, punctuated with a silly grin. "This is beautiful, Roger. Thank you so much."

"I wasn't sure when I first saw it. Do you like it?"

"I love it. Surely the most unusual gift I've ever received. Is there a story behind the picture on it?"

"Well, the guy promised that it will bring you good luck. Ward off evil spirits and keep the demons away. He also said the Buddha's message is not to be angry or seek revenge. They will only consume you."

She rubbed her fingers across the smooth top of the jade. "How about that? A personal message from the holy man."

A knock on the door signaled arrival of their breakfast. Roger and Leslie took chairs on opposite sides of the table as the waiter unloaded his cart and placed generous portions of food in front of them, including a single red rose for Leslie, compliments of the management.

You know," said Roger, "I've been to Rome several times on business, always in a big hurry, but have never seen anything. How about you?"

"Guilty. Maybe we could visit a few sites before heading back to Castellina."

"What about the Coliseum? Or maybe the Pantheon or Spanish Steps?"

"Any one of those is fine," she said. "Just no churches."

"Spanish Steps then. Isn't the Trevi Fountain close by?"

"Yes, we could walk to it down Via Del Condotti."

"Ah, yes," he said, "the shopping street. Guess I set myself up for that one."

Leslie finished her orange juice and put her folded napkin on the table. "I have a question, Roger. About that company on the west coast you once worked for."

"Digger dot com. What about it?"

"Isn't the big boss a guy named Tom Rickenbacker?"

He laughed. "Rickenbach. Or, as I called him, Old Tom Rickety-back. We used to play racquet ball but he couldn't play golf because of an old back injury."

"Then you must know something about his wife. Or, his ex, I should say."

"Yeah, I remember her. Sarah. A pretty woman, fun to be around."

"Did you know her very well? What kind of person was she? Did she and Tom have a happy marriage?"

"Leslie. Why do you care about them?"

She shifted in her chair. "A coincidence, that's all. My husband is living with this Sarah person in Pueblo right now. The very same woman who took him away from me and ruined our marriage. I'm curious as hell about her."

"That's a *huge* coincidence. But I thought you were over him and what happened back there. Or that's what you told me."

She sighed. "Yeah, I know it's over, but it still pisses me off. Supremely."

Roger reached out to the table's center, and turned the jade carving around to face her. "While I'm in the shower, look at the Buddha and focus on his message."

After he went into the bathroom, Leslie stuck out her tongue and said, "Screw you, Buddha boy."

They arrived at The Spanish Steps about noon, their conversation about Sarah Rickenbach set aside but not quite forgotten. The bright sun and mild temperature made for a pleasant afternoon of walking in Rome. They browsed many shops along the Via Condotti. Leslie bought Roger a wallet at Louis Vuitton, feeling a need to give him something in return for the jade Buddha carving.

They dallied at the Trevi Fountain and tossed coins in the water, each making a silent wish. When pressed, Leslie admitted that she had difficulty wishing for anything specific; she didn't know what she wanted so she settled for an all-inclusive general happiness. Roger hoped for an enjoyable stay with Leslie at her villa.

They drove north in late afternoon and arrived in Siena shortly after seven o'clock. They had a leisurely dinner at a restaurant that neither had been to before and came to Leslie's villa about nine. They agreed to first take care of one item each; Leslie wanted to call Maria and Roger had to check his e-mail. With Leslie's approval, of course. They met up again in Leslie's bed and cuddled close in the darkness.

"Did you reach Maria?" said Roger.

"Yes, we had a nice chat. Everything is going well in Milan with Lucia and my daughter. And our dinner with her and Marcello is set for Friday. We'll pick her up and meet him in Florence. I think she'll probably stay the night with him."

He pulled her closer, pressing his pelvis into hers, and kissed her. "Good, I'll have you all to myself for several days and nights." "Mmmm, I like that. What about your e-mail? Anything interesting?" "They weren't happy about the way things turned out with Huong. But it's not my fault. That's the way it goes sometimes, you can't win them all." "How long do you have?" "He didn't say. Just a snide remark about making my vacation *brief*." She reached down and stroked his firming erection. "Then let's get to the fun part of your vacation. And don't make *this* brief."

Just before dawn, the telephone awoke Leslie from a dream. A panicky woman's voice came from the handset, jarring her nerves and filling her with dread. "Oh Les, it's terrible . . . . I'm so sorry . . . this is awful."

"Nancy, is that you? What's wrong? What happened?"

"Yes, it's me. God, I have no idea of the time. Did I wake you?"

"Don't worry about that, just tell me. Did something happen to Joe?" Leslie paused to let her speak but could hear only crying and sniffling.

"Sorry," said Nancy. "I just came from your house, it's a disaster."

"Something happened to my home?" Leslie was fully awake.

"A fire, lots of smoke, everything up in flames. They tried to put it out but they got there too late." Leslie felt numb, unable to comprehend the situation. "Are you there?" cried Nancy. "Speak to me, Les. Are you all right?"

Roger turned over and said, "Who are you talking to?"

"He burned down my home," she cried. "That no good bastard burned down my home."

CHAPTER EIGHTEEN

LET'S TAKE THIS ONE STEP AT A TIME

"What's wrong, what are you talking about?" Roger was now fully awake.

Leslie turned on her bedside lamp, jumped out of bed and stared down at him. "My house is destroyed and my ex-husband did it, no doubt egged on by that rotten bitch he's sleeping with. I know he set fire to it, probably licking his chops and clapping his hands while the whole damn place went up in smoke."

Roger slipped on his warmup suit. He avoided looking directly at her nakedness, prompting her to turn around. "I'll make a pot of coffee," he said.

"Screw that, I need a drink." She threw on her bathrobe, marched off to the kitchen, and he followed. She poured chilled vodka into a tumbler and took a sip. "Care to join me?"

"I'll pass." He sat at the kitchen table. "Who was it that called?"

Leslie began pacing back and forth, the glass of vodka held

close to her heart. "Nancy, my best friend. She lives a couple of blocks away from me."

"She saw your house on fire?"

"Yeah, but only when the firemen were putting it out. Too late to save anything. Everything gone."

"And you think your ex did it? Why would he do something like that?"

"Revenge," she screamed. "What else? I told you that I set fire to his Leadville cabin. He knows I did it so he's getting even. Eye for an eye, all that crap."

"You don't know that for sure. Do you have any enemies back in Denver? Somebody angry enough to resort to arson?"

She stopped pacing. "Yeah, that stupid detective. Layton was pissed at me for getting him involved. He knew that I stole his Glock, but burning down my house would be a stretch."

"OK, a legitimate element of doubt. It may have been an accident. A lightning strike on part of the house, a faulty electrical connection. You never know."

Leslie resumed pacing. "I don't think so. The house was in excellent condition. My agent hired a home inspection company to check everything out before I put it on the market. No, Andrew Krag did it. No doubt in my mind."

"How about your insurance coverage?" he said.

"Adequate, I think. Oh God, something else I have to deal with."

"One thing to be thankful for. You weren't in the house during the fire."

Leslie poured more vodka into her glass. "You're just too full of cheer so early in the morning."

Roger drummed his fingers on the tabletop. "You'll have to

contact your real estate agent and the insurance company right away."

"Roger," she said. "You once told me that I *might* have trouble getting back into the country. I want you to do something for me."

"Are you actually thinking of going back?"

"You have contacts, right? Find out if I can come through immigration—say, JFK—without my passport being flagged. Can you do that for me?"

"I think so, but what happens when you get to Denver? The police will soon find out, once you start working with your agent or the insurance company."

"Let's take this one step at a time, OK?"

"All right, but before you even hop on a plane, you should talk to Nancy or your agent. Find out what the fire department learned after the fire was put out, what kind of clues they found about how it was started."

"I don't need any of that shit. All I want is to get back there and take charge. Get my life back again and on the right track."

"Good luck on that," he said.

"Damn you, Roger. Don't I mean anything to you? Are you going to help me or am I just some convenient lay between business trips?"

"Haven't heard any complaints from you in bed."

"Answer me."

He grumbled to himself and said, "Yeah, I'll help you, but only up to a point. Nothing illegal, understand?"

She went over, put her arms around his neck. "I understand."

"Get me your passport and I'll send an e-mail to a friend at State. We'll see whether your name is in their data base."

Before returning to bed, Leslie called Nancy and asked for more information about the fire. Nancy had nothing new but promised to call the fire department the next morning. She also agreed to call Leslie's real estate agent and insurance company. While Leslie was on the phone, Roger was sending an e-mail to his State Department contact, asking him to quietly investigate Leslie's legal status.

Sleep for both Roger and Leslie was difficult. Brief periods of slumber were interrupted by segments of tossing and turning. Roger was first to arise about nine, moving silently to the kitchen where he made a pot of coffee. He went out to the road, found the *International Herald Tribune* and read it while having his first cup of coffee.

Leslie joined him an hour later wearing the same bathrobe. She mumbled, "Good morning," and poured some coffee for herself. "Thanks for going out and getting the paper. Any interesting news today?"

"Just the usual unrest in Greece, Egypt, and other parts of the Middle East. All of it pointing to the likelihood of more business coming my way."

"Heard anything from your government guy?"

"Too soon for that. Ten o'clock in the morning here is four A.M. in Washington. And two hours earlier than that in Denver."

"So we wait."

He passed her the newspaper's front section. "Nice weather outside this morning. Good for exploring the countryside."

"Really?"

"Have you ever hiked the grounds of your villa? You told me it has 300 acres. I'll bet there are plenty of beautiful things to see, even at this time of year."

"You want to walk around the villa?"

"Why not? Get a little exercise, clear our heads for making some good decisions and logical plans for our near term future."

She smiled for the first time that morning. "You are certifiably loony. OK, but let's have some breakfast first. Give it a chance to warm up a bit out there."

"Great. I'll whip up some of my legendary frittatas. This afternoon, let's take a drive to the grocery store. Buy food and wine for some delicious meals here at the villa. What do you think, Leslie Faye?"

"Sounds good, as long as you're doing the cooking."

They returned to the villa around five o'clock and carried several bags of food into the kitchen. "Go ahead and check your e-mail," Leslie told him, "and see if your fed guy found anything."

Roger went off and came back ten minutes later. Leslie had opened a bottle of Chianti and poured herself a glass. "How about some wine?"

"All right."

"You don't look happy, Roger. No news, I guess."

"Oh, there's news. You're clean, no problem getting back."

"Then why are you looking so down? That's wonderful news."

"Yeah, and now it means that you're going back to Colorado, the scene of the crime. Putting yourself in jeopardy."

"You obviously don't approve."

"I was hoping for a negative answer."

Leslie poured another glass of wine and handed it to him. "You need to look at this entire situation from another angle," she said. "You've committed a number of crimes yourself—or should I call them business transactions—things that somehow jibe with your ideas about personal integrity and standards of morality. And you even get paid well for it. But now you're with me, helping to get justice for me. The kind that's been denied ever since asshole Krag left me." The thought occurred to her that she could always offer him money, like the folks in D. C. do. But he'd feel insulted and walk out on her.

He took a sip of wine. "That's all well and good, but we don't know what's going to happen yet. And how the hell do I fit in, what's my role in this? We don't even have enough information to come up with a plan."

She moved close to him, put her arm around his neck, and gave him a Chianti-flavored kiss. "Agreed. We've only taken that first step. Let's get a lot more information and see where we go from there."

The 'lot more information' arrived later that night.

Hi Les,

I talked with Captain Dave Stephens this morning, head of the fire station that responded to the fire. He and his people have gone through the wreckage and have come up with a theory on what caused it. His take is that some homeless people got into your house and started a fire in the living room fireplace. Then it got out of control and they probably panicked, which only made matters worse when they tried to put it out with God-knows-what. Stephens is working with the police, trying to locate the people who broke into your house, but he thinks it will be a tough job finding out who they are. Lots of homeless people out there, he says, looking for a warm place to bunk every night. He also wondered how long your house has been vacant, thinking it was a likely target for squatters. I told him that you lived in Italy and the house hasn't been lived in for several months.

I also called your real estate agent and he's on top of things. He's contacted the insurance company and will be meeting with a claims rep soon. He says he'll be e-mailing you with some questions and a progress report.

Wish I could have given you happier news.

Love, Nance

Leslie let loose a stream of profanity that would have made a sailor blush. After she calmed down, she sent Nancy a brief reply.

I think those hose honchos have their collective heads up their backsides. They should be thinking ARSON and tracking down the guilty bastard who did it. Keep me posted.

She deleted Nancy's message, her own reply, and marched off to the kitchen for a calming shot of vodka. She paced the kitchen while sipping her drink, thinking about the contents of Nancy's message. *This is not going the way it should.*

Leslie finished her drink and went to the bathroom, making herself beautiful for her bed partner. She slipped into bed, cuddling up to Roger who had been reading a mystery novel. "Got an e-mail from my friend," she said. "Suspicions confirmed."

"What did she say?"

"She talked with the fire station chief and the police. Definite traces of arson laying about the ruins and wasn't very careful about hiding his tracks. But then he never was the brightest crayon in the box."

"Guess your hunch was on target."

"Ha. It was a no-brainer."

"Then the police should have no trouble building a case against him."

"Well, I wouldn't go putting all my Easter eggs in *that* basket."

"You have some ideas?"

"You bet I do." She took the book away from him and kissed him with lots of teasing tongue. "We can talk about it in the morning."

Nancy had just finished a light lunch and was sitting at her desk, staring at her computer screen. The tone of Leslie's last e-mail made her nervous, as if she was in denial about the possibility of homeless squatters causing the fire. Nancy felt that Leslie was becoming paranoid, thinking that someone wanted to do her harm.

She rooted through her desk drawer, found the business card of Eliot Waters, and dialed his number. "Hello Sheriff," she said, "this is Nancy Moore. You probably don't remember me, but—"

"I remember you very well, Mrs. Moore. The woman who helped Leslie Krag escape from the law. What can I do for you today?"

Nancy almost hung up, suddenly feeling defensive, but she persevered after a pause. "You asked me to call if I heard anything about her."

"I'm listening."

"Well, it's not really about her. It's her home here in Denver. There was a fire and the house had lots of damage. The fire department people believe it was caused by homeless people trying to start a fire in the fireplace but it got out of control."

"I haven't heard," he said, "but I probably wouldn't unless

you called."

"Just thought you'd want to know, sheriff."

"Wonder if Mrs. Krag knows?"

"She does. I called her in Italy when I found out and we've exchanged some e-mails. She's pretty mad about it and isn't buying the story about homeless squatters. She seems to think that it was arson."

"Hmmm." The line went quiet for several seconds. "I can understand why she might think that," he said. "It fits."

"It does?"

"When you look back at what happened to Andrew's cabin, it makes sense."

"Did I do right sheriff?"

"You did, Mrs. Moore, and I genuinely appreciate your call. If you hear anything more, please don't hesitate to contact me again. You have a nice day now."

After hanging up, Sheriff Waters jotted several notes on a tablet. He'd call a police friend in Denver and get points of contact for investigations of the fire. Another call would be to Andrew Krag with a 'heads up.' The last call, and certainly not the least, would be to Detective Sharon Hardcastle in Pueblo. He'd suggest a face-to-face meeting to brief her on this new development. *Don't believe there's a Colorado law that says you can't mix business with a little pleasure.*

CHAPTER NINETEEN

WILL WE EVER HAVE THIS WOMAN OUT OF OUR LIVES?

Leslie awoke at eight o'clock the next morning. She lay in bed for several minutes, recalling the satisfying pleasure of last evening's lovemaking. The sunlight oozing through the windows perked up her spirits even higher.

She quietly slipped out of bed, donned her bathrobe, and padded out to the kitchen. After starting the coffee, she marched out to the road for the newspaper. Though the sun was out, and it was chilly, she didn't care. In her view, the future was again promising. Her life ahead, with Roger's yet-to-be-defined help, would once again be filled with joyous love.

Back in the kitchen, she drank coffee and managed to read the entire *International Herald Tribune* before Roger wandered in. He wore those off-white pajamas covered with blue bamboo shoots. "Morning, Leslie. Been up long?"

"About two hours. Help yourself to some coffee and come sit down."

He gave her a kiss before taking his seat. "Any interesting news this morning?"

"Thankfully, no." Meaning that nothing she read would require him to go running off on some kind of mission.

He stretched both arms and made a pleasing moan. "I feel great."

"Last night's action probably helped."

"Did I hurt you?" he said.

Leslie laughed. "Not at all." She reached out and placed her hand on top of his. "We should deconstruct all those movements sometime, the special sounds and wild words in the heat of passion."

Roger grinned. "Sounds dangerous. Might cause the magic to disappear."

"I've been thinking some more about my house," she said. "I think we should go back to Colorado."

"We?"

"Yes, and stay in Colorado Springs. I'll get us a room at the Broadmoor."

"Hmmm. I've never stayed there. But why The Springs?"

"It's close to Denver and Pueblo, and you'll be able to spend some time with your mom. I can't risk showing my face in either one of those cities."

"What are you hoping to accomplish, Leslie? Or should I say *we*?"

"Get Andrew Krag thrown in jail for torching my house. That's priority one. Maybe take care of Sarah Slut at the same time. And I do need your help, no question about that. Emotional support, coming up with those good ideas, keeping me happy in bed . . . . get the picture?"

"All right, I get it. But how about the situation here?"

"Here?"

"Yes, here. Who's going to look after this place while you're gone? Are you going to leave Julie in Milan or send her back to her husband?"

"I haven't figured that out yet." Leslie got up and began pacing. "She's not ready to go back and Harper's probably not ready for her either. And it's not fair to have Julie bunking with Lucia longer than a week."

"Then bring her back here. She can look after the villa while you're gone. And when you get back, she'll probably be ready to go back to her husband."

"I'm not sure I can trust her."

"How old is Julie?" he said.

"Twenty-six, but—"

"She's old enough. And Maria will help if a problem comes up. You can call her twice a day, or more, to make sure she's staying out of trouble."

"It all sounds so easy when *you* say it."

"OK, then it's settled. When do we leave?"

"I need to be careful about the timing. Maybe you should go ahead of me. I'll break the news to Maria, get Julie to come back here, and set her up with the house and my car. Then I'll join you in Colorado Springs. How does that sound?"

"Complicated. But we can make it work." He got up and poured himself another cup of coffee. "I'll fly to D. C. and spend a couple of days at home, resting up and getting over jet lag. *Again.* You call me when you get to the Broadmoor, then I'll get a flight to The Springs."

"I'll call you before I leave Rome so we can hook up at the Broadmoor."

"Whatever," he mumbled.

Sarah's eyes widened as her jaw dropped. "Are you kidding me?" she almost shouted. She had just come from the hospital and was removing her jacket.

"I'm not," said Andrew, "scout's honor. Sheriff Waters called this afternoon. That guy's a cagey one. Wanted to know where I was the other night before telling me about the fire."

"You can't mean that he actually suspected you of starting it."

"I'm sure he didn't," he said. "He was only being a good lawman, wanting to hear my alibi before saying that a crime had been committed."

"How did Waters find out about the fire?"

"Nancy called him, Leslie's buddy. Leslie seems to think it was arson."

Sarah was silent for a moment. "Ah, yes, and you're the prime suspect. Now that you two are no longer married, you have license to burn her house down, just like she did to your cabin."

Andrew sighed. "She probably believes I did it, or wants to believe it, no matter what kind of evidence turns up to the contrary."

"Is the sheriff going to do anything?"

"He plans his own investigation and will talk to the fire department and Denver police. The whole thing's out of his jurisdiction but he still wants to pursue it. He feels that it's an open matter—Leslie on the loose—that needs some kind of resolution. Meanwhile, he advises caution. Be on guard."

"Will we ever have this woman out of our lives?" said Sarah.

"One of these days, sweetheart. One of these days."

Leslie called Maria after she and Roger finished discussing

their travel plans. "I'm so sorry, but I have to cancel our dinner plans for tomorrow night."

"What is the problem?" said Maria, in a voice that bordered on anger.

"My home in Denver was destroyed by fire. It happened during the middle of the night and the police have solid evidence of arson. So I have to go back."

"Oh Leslie, that is terrible news." She sounded more sympathetic now. "Who would do such a thing?"

"It's rather obvious when you think about it for a moment."

"Not your husband."

"Yes, but he's my ex-husband, still the same worthless piece of trash. Wanting revenge for what I did to him."

"I feel bad for you," said Maria. "When will you leave?"

"Pretty soon. Just have to get a few things organized."

"Shall I look after your home again while you are gone?"

"You are the dearest friend, Maria. But I'm going to have Julie come back from Milan. I know she's enjoying her stay with Lucia but her place is here in Castellina. I'll leave her my car along with some money. She'll be fine."

"Then I shall look after her like my own daughter. Perhaps cook a dinner for her, show her interesting places in Tuscany. Does she see Dr. Bertolucci soon?"

"I hadn't thought about that. Hold on." Leslie checked her calendar. "You're right. Two o'clock next Wednesday. And I need to cancel mine."

"Then I shall take her to Firenzi, introduce her to Marcello, and all of us have dinner together."

"That will be a nice surprise for her," said Leslie.

"What about Mr. Halliday? Is he traveling with you?"

"No, he's going back home. He has urgent business in Washington."

"Your life is so turbulent, Leslie. I do hope it settles down soon. It is not a healthy situation for you."

"That's for damn sure." Leslie paused. "And please don't tell Lucia about this just yet. I'll call Julie tomorrow to break the bad news."

"I understand. Please call me again before you leave."

Sharon Hardcastle, Pueblo Police Department, sat in front of her computer. She was completing a report on her latest investigation when the telephone rang.

"Hello, detective. How are things down in the flatlands?"

She recognized the drawling western voice right away. "Just fine, sheriff. But probably not as exciting as the action up in Leadville."

He chuckled. "Any interesting cases you're working?"

"A financial scam that's approaching epic proportions. Somebody is collecting rent deposits on houses that are already occupied and clearly not for rent."

"That *is* interesting," he said. "Something we don't often see up here."

"What's on your mind, sheriff?"

"Wondering if you're up for a meeting. How about I come down tomorrow evening for dinner?"

"You'd come all the way down to Pueblo for a dinner meeting with me? Is this police business?"

"It is, but I've got a couple of other things to take care of."

"Now I'm intrigued. What kind of police business?"

"Do you recall Mrs. Leslie Krag, our favorite fugitive?"

"Of course. You have something?"

"Her house in Denver was damaged by a fire the other night. Got a call from Mrs. Krag's friend, Nancy Moore, the woman who helped Krag flee the country. You recall us interviewing Mrs. Moore?"

"I remember. What did she tell you?"

"Right now, the fire department thinks it was an accident, some homeless folks trying to get warm. But Mrs. Moore told me that Mrs. Krag wants to believe it was arson. You can probably guess who Mrs. Krag thinks set the fire."

"I also remember her big house, the day we walked around it. That place was vacant, and that was over a month ago. A tempting target for squatters."

"You got it," he said. "An empty mansion that your scammers could work with, trying to rent the place."

"Where are you going with this, sheriff?"

"Knowing Mrs. Krag, and I think I do, it would be just like her to come back here. And if she believes that Andy Krag burned down her house . . ."

"I got it. That woman is just crazy enough to do something like that. This could be another chance to nail her and put her away for a long time."

"I should have some detailed reports from the police and firemen later today. I can bring them down with me tomorrow. That is, if you're available."

"You think Mr. Krag should know about this?"

"I talked with him earlier today."

"Of course you did. Then I'm available. I know a great restaurant. Good food and quiet enough so we can talk."

After the call was over, Sharon smiled and felt unusually giddy.

She hadn't dated for months and was excited that Eliot Waters was coming all the way to Pueblo and take her out for dinner. He could have e-mailed or faxed me that information, she thought. However, being the good detective that she was, she deduced that he wanted to see her as much as she wanted to see him.

Leslie and Roger got up at six o'clock on Friday morning, dressed quickly, and were on the road to Pisa by seven. She parked near the terminal and they walked inside, keeping Roger company as he checked a single piece of luggage for the flight to Paris, the first leg of another long plane trip.

They found a small cafe and ordered two cappuccinos with two Danish pastries. Conversation was minimal while they ate breakfast.

"This really sucks," said Leslie. "I think we should have a long rest period in Colorado before doing any more globetrotting."

"Agreed. We're both going to be so jet-lagged when we get there, it would be crazy to do anything else."

"Where do you go from Paris?" she said.

"Nonstop to Dulles. Should get there about 3:00 P.M."

"Which is . . . what time here?"

"Nine o'clock tonight. I'll call you when I get home." He drained his cup and said, "When do you think you'll fly to Colorado?"

She sighed. "It all depends on Julie. When she comes back from Milan and when I feel I can leave her in charge of my house."

"Don't rush it. I think you'll need to have plenty of confidence in her to handle things. Once you get to The Springs, there isn't much you can do. Except pray."

"Oh, thanks a lot. You're such a great comfort."

He grinned. "Always happy to oblige."

Leslie reached into her purse, pulled out a brown envelope, and dropped in on the table in front of him. "Here's some material I want you to look at. You told me once that you're good with computers. I want you to do some digging and find out everything you can about Andrew Walter Krag and Miriam Sarah Dolan."

He picked it up and made a vertical weighing motion. "Lot of paper here. What's it about?"

"Reports from that private detective I hired. All the necessary info about our enemy, only we need to have it updated."

"What are you thinking, Leslie?"

"I'm thinking our combat will be cerebral instead of physical, with lots of cyber warfare thrown in for good measure. I want you to gather as much intelligence data on these two assholes as possible. Can you do that?"

"I'll do my best. I like your idea, too. Much less dangerous for both of us this way." He glanced at his watch. "Time for me to get moving."

Leslie walked with him to the security station and stayed close for several minutes. Finally, when he got near the detectors, they embraced and kissed one last time. "See you in Colorado," she said.

"Drive safely."

Leslie got back to her villa in early afternoon and found the telephone message light blinking. She played it and heard a brief message from Julie.

Hey Mom, I'm taking the train back to Siena today. Can you pick me up? It gets in at 7:20 tonight. But if you can't make it, I'll take a taxi. Thanks, love you.

Leslie smiled, wondering what had happened to Julie in Milan. *Maybe she and Lucia had a falling out. No matter, at least I won't have to order her to come back here.*

CHAPTER TWENTY

JUST DON'T CALL ME A TAXI

Leslie went back to bed after listening to Julie's message. She needed a nap and wanted to be alert when they met at the train station. They had plenty to talk about.

Two hours later, she awoke and went straight to the bathroom for a quick shower. She dressed, poured two fingers of chilled vodka into a tumbler, and went to her office. She turned on her computer and found two relevant e-mails. The first was from Nancy, brief and to the point.

Dear Les,

I've gone by your home and managed to look things over pretty well, in spite of the yellow police tape plastered all over the place. Now I'm not some kind of fire expert, but your house doesn't look too bad. Lots of ashes over everything but I think they can be removed. Your real estate guy can probably tell you more.

I also talked with Captain Stephens again. He and the police are convinced that it's NOT arson. So I think you should get off that particular hobby horse.

I hope you're not thinking of coming back to Denver because of this. That would be a big mistake and I couldn't be much help to you.

Love, Nance

Leslie was more disappointed than anything and felt betrayed by her best friend's outlook on the situation. She wondered if their relationship had been damaged by her reckless actions in Leadville over a month ago. *Why can't she see things my way? And why would it be a mistake if I came back to Denver?*

The next e-mail was from her real estate agent.

Dear Mrs. Krag,

This is only an initial report, incomplete in several areas, but I did want to give you an assessment of what happened at your house.

First of all, I and the insurance company's claims adjuster believe that your house can be cleaned up and repaired completely. I hesitate to say 'good as new' but it will be in excellent shape for going back on the market. It will take some time to perform all the necessary work but the good news is that you're completely covered by your homeowner's policy.

With your approval, we'll start the cleanup once the police and fire department give us the all clear. I'll work closely with the adjuster to get the repairs done quickly and correctly.

Attached you'll find my detailed report. I went through

each room with a fire department rep and made copious notes.

I'm very sorry this happened. I know it's hard, dealing with a tragedy like this from such a great distance, but I'll do the best I can for you.

Regards, Alan Morris

Leslie began reading the attachment but stopped in disgust after the first page. She sent Morris a brief reply, telling him to proceed and keep her posted. After printing a copy and tucking it away in her file cabinet, she deleted both e-mails. She didn't want Julie reading anything about the fire in case she did some snooping.

Julie stepped from the train, dropped both pieces of luggage, one more than she left with, and gave Leslie a warm hug. "Good to be back home, Mom."

"I see you've been shopping. You look great in those jeans."

"Yep, I gave your credit card a workout. This coat is new, too."

"Are you hungry?" asked Leslie.

"Starving."

"I'm parked outside. We'll talk on the way."

Once on the road, Leslie couldn't contain her curiosity any longer. "Are you and Lucia still friends?"

"Sure, why do you ask?"

"Just wondering. It sounded like she kicked you out."

"She did, but not in a bad way. Lucia has a date tonight, a big one, and she's hoping the guy will stay over for the weekend."

"Ah, that's different. Have you met him?"

"Not yet, but I may some day. He's a banker from Paris, older than her."

"How much older?" said Leslie.

"She never said and I didn't ask." A long silence followed. "Please don't mention it to her mother, OK? She hasn't told her about him yet."

"Right. Guess we have to have our little secrets."

The restaurant was the same one where they had dined on Julie's first night in Italy. They received the same exuberant greetings and were promptly seated at a nice table in a front corner. After placing their orders for wine and food, Leslie turned serious and said, "I have some big news and it's not good. But hear me out before you start jumping all over me."

"I'm all ears."

"My home in Denver was almost destroyed by fire a couple of nights ago. My friend, Nancy Moore, called me in the middle of the night."

Julie placed both hands on Leslie's. "Mom, that's terrible."

"Yeah, and it gets worse. The fire department confirmed it was arson."

"Oh my God, who would do that to your home?"

"I have my suspicions, but that's all I can say." Leslie couldn't mention Andrew's name or the similar destruction of his Leadville cabin. Julie didn't know. Doing so would open up a whole new discussion about Leslie's activities in Colorado before returning to Italy, one that had to remain firmly shut.

Julie pulled back both hands. "How about insurance?"

"That's about the only good news. I'm fully covered but I lost a lot of personal things, keepsakes that can never be replaced."

"What are you going to do?"

"I'm going back. I want to make sure the place gets cleaned up and the damage repaired. But above all, I want to see the guilty bastard put in jail."

Julie frowned and struggled for words. "What about me?"

"We have a couple of options. One, you could go back to Harper. That is, assuming you're both ready for it."

"Give me another one," said Julie.

"You could stay in Castellina while I'm gone and look after the place."

"When will you leave? And how long would you be gone?"

"I'll probably fly out in several days. But first, I want to give you plenty of time to get adjusted. You'll be in charge at the villa and I want you to feel comfortable driving my car. I'll set up a bank account so you won't lack for money. As for how long I'll be gone, it's hard to say. Couple of weeks should do it."

Julie focused on her wine, fingers rotating the glass while she kept silent.

"Well?" said Leslie. "What do you think?"

"I'm not liking it. Getting stuck out in the Tuscan countryside by myself."

"You won't be alone. Maria Borelli will take you to your appointment with Dr. Bertolucci. She and her friend, Marcello, will treat you to dinner that night."

"Big whoop."

"Hey, you'll have a newspaper every day, TV, and connection to the Internet with my computer. You can e-mail your husband as often as you like, tell him how much you love him and miss him."

"What if I need you?" said Julie. "How do I . . ."

"That shouldn't be a problem. I'll call you when I get settled. Not sure where I'll be staying but it will probably be a hotel with e-mail. And you can always call Maria. She's only a few minutes away."

Julie paused for a sip of wine. "This will be a first for me, living alone and responsible for nobody but myself. Guess it could be worse."

Leslie smiled. "You'll do just fine."

On Friday evening, Detective Hardcastle arrived at the Cactus Flower Cantina just before seven o'clock. She craned her neck to look around and spotted Eliot Waters in the dining room. He got up when he saw her coming and offered his right hand. "Hello, detective, thanks for coming."

She took his hand but leaned forward to give him a light kiss on the cheek. "Thank *you,* for coming all this way."

Not prepared for her greeting, he pulled his hand away and complimented her black dress and heels. *Wonder if I could have said anything more juvenile?*

She pulled out a chair and sat down. "Hope you haven't been waiting long."

He sat down. "Just got here myself. Your directions were fine."

A young man placed a bowl of tortilla chips and a cup of salsa on their table. A waitress soon appeared and they ordered house margaritas. When their drinks came, Waters offered a toast to good police work ahead.

"I have a request," she said. "Since we're probably going to be working together again, I think we should use first names. Mine's Sharon."

"I'll drink to that," he said, touching his glass against hers. "Call me Eliot."

"Eliot it is then."

While twisting one end of his mustache he continued, "Actually, you can call me anything you like. Just don't call me a taxi or call me late for dinner."

Sharon erupted in loud laughter and covered her mouth. "Sorry," she said, "but those are awful jokes."

"Yep, I can be a corn ball sometime. But it's nice to hear you laugh."

"On the phone, you mentioned bringing some paperwork. Shall we get our business out of the way?"

He reached down next to his chair and brought up a large brown envelope. "I managed to get copies of the police reports and notes from the fire department investigator. Lots of detail here for you."

She put it aside. "Thanks, Eliot. I'll look it over later."

"I talked with Alan Morris this afternoon. He's Mrs. Krag's real estate guy."

"Probably not a happy camper with her property off the market."

"He's coping well enough. Been in contact with Mrs. Krag, e-mailing back and forth. He sent her a report this morning, listing all the damages, how he's going to act on her behalf to get the place fixed up again. She sent back a brief reply, telling him to go ahead with it."

"Sounds reasonable," she said.

"Except he was expecting a whole bunch of questions. Her reaction didn't ring true, according to him."

"Maybe she has other plans."

"Possibly," said Eliot.

"I had a talk with Sarah Dolan this afternoon over at Parkview Medical. We had some coffee in the cafeteria during her break."

"I can imagine the subject of your conversation."

"I was looking for some woman-to-woman insight on Leslie

Krag. Her emotional persona, what makes her tick."

"And?"

"Sarah thinks there's something wrong with the woman. Well, she didn't put it quite that way, but *not well* is the bottom line. She told me about some things that happened at Parkview, probably in violation of medical ethics, but she didn't seem to care. She also told me a lot that Andrew has told her, mostly about their married life. I agreed with her conclusion; Leslie Krag needs psychiatric help."

"Then she'll be coming back to Denver," he said.

"Back to Colorado, but not Denver or Pueblo. She might be crazy but she's not stupid. I don't see her taking big risks this time."

"How are we going to catch her, Sharon?"

She liked the mellow sound of his voice, the way he said 'we.' "I don't know, Eliot. We'll have to come up with a plan."

The waitress appeared with their dinners which interrupted their shop talk. Each ordered a second margarita and, while they dined, the conversation shifted to each other's personal history. Eliot talked about growing up on a Texas cattle ranch, being a bronco rider on the southwestern rodeo circuit for three years, and duty as a border patrolman in New Mexico and Arizona for five years, until he migrated north to Leadville and became a county deputy sheriff. He had never married and admitted that it was too easy just drifting along.

Sharon's life history was in clear contrast with his. A native of St. Louis, she grew up in the well-to-do suburb of Creve Coeur and went to junior college for two years. The law interested her so she trained to be a paralegal, followed by a position in a large downtown firm. However, after five years of a stifling office routine and a failed romantic relationship, she decided that a major life change was in order. She moved to Kansas City, MO, applied to the city's police academy, and was accepted.

Sharon loved police work and her career prospered in Kansas City for eight years. However, realizing that getting promoted to detective there would probably never happen, she began checking other places around the country that might offer better opportunities. She lucked out in Pueblo, hired on during a city campaign to get more women into the police department. Now, with twelve years in Pueblo, the last five as a detective, she felt comfortable in her role. Moreover, for the first time in her professional life, she didn't feel a restless urge to move elsewhere.

The waitress took away their plates and asked if they were interested in dessert. Sharon promptly spoke up, "None for me, thanks."

Eliot gave the waitress his credit card and she went away.

"I'm surprised you don't want a sweet," he said.

"Really? Why is that?"

"Do you recall us having lunch in Denver after we talked to Mrs. Moore? You had a monstrous chocolate sundae that day."

She laughed. "Sure, I remember. And at that very same lunch, I believe you mentioned something about dancing. Didn't you ask if there was a place in Pueblo where we could do some two-stepping?"

"Good memory, Sharon."

"Well, are you up for it?"

He stuck his right foot out and away from the table, wiggling a hand-tooled, red and white cowboy boot. "Check this out. I'm ready for some boot scootin'."

CHAPTER TWENTY-ONE

WHAT IS WRONG WITH THAT WOMAN?

On Friday afternoon, while Sheriff Waters was driving to Pueblo for dinner with Detective Hardcastle, Andrew received a telephone call from Emmaline Dolan.

"Good news, Andy. Mr. Sebastian accepted our offer on those three lots. Praise the Lord, I do believe this is the start of blessed things for you and Miriam." She consistently used her daughter's first name when Sarah wasn't within earshot.

"That's *great* news. Were the negotiations difficult?"

"Not at all. In fact, it gets even better. He wants an immediate closing, as fast as it can be arranged."

"He must need the money. How soon can you make it happen?"

"I'm working with the escrow people in Pueblo right now, trying to have it next week. How's your schedule looking?"

"Not a problem. We don't need Sarah for this, do we? She's working day shift at the hospital."

"Not at all," she said. "I'm having Roscoe do a limited power of attorney so you can sign on behalf of RBC."

"Sounds good."

"Oh, I forgot, there's something else. Mr. Sebastian is paying *all* the closing costs to make this happen."

Andrew paused. "You know, we might have got those properties for less money. That guy sounds like he was super-motivated to unload them."

"Now, Andrew, no buyer's remorse. I won't have it. We did good and you're going to put up some nice houses on those lots."

"You're right. Now the fun begins."

"Good attitude. I'll let you know the where and when real soon."

Over the weekend, Leslie focused on teaching Julie all the features of her Mercedes CL 550. Julie settled in quickly with the driving part, both in small towns and on the *autostrada.* The only tricky item was the navigation system, an LCD color screen on the dashboard that used GPS technology and maps for detailed driving directions. Leslie made Julie read the instruction manual first before letting her press a single button. After a few trial-and-error episodes, Julie felt confident enough to proclaim that no way would she be getting lost in Italy.

Leslie also exchanged several e-mails with Roger Halliday, bickering back and forth about who would arrive first in Colorado Springs. Roger pleaded unspecified business obligations that prevented him from immediate travel but offered instead to make reservations for her at the Broadmoor whenever her travel plans firmed up. He went so far as to suggest that, since the accommodations would be in his name, she should check in as

Mrs. Halliday, thus granting her a modicum of personal security. Leslie liked his idea for several reasons but stipulated that they should have a luxury suite and he should pay for it.

Leslie booked her flight from Rome with British Airways. She would leave at 7:50 AM on Wednesday, stop briefly in London, and arrive in Denver at 3:25 PM. She'd continue with United Airlines and get into Colorado Springs at 6:10 PM. She included this information in an e-mail to Halliday and hinted that he'd best not let her wait alone too long if he knew what was good for him. His reply mistakenly revealed that he took her threat as a joke.

Leslie took Julie into Siena on Monday morning and opened a joint account at the same bank that Leslie used. Julie also applied for a credit card and Euro checks on the same new account. After the necessary financial transactions were completed, mother and daughter spent the rest of the day shopping for groceries and last minute clothing items for Leslie.

Julie did the driving honors on Tuesday morning and took Leslie to the Hilton Hotel at the Rome airport where they had a long lunch. Leslie, trying hard not to sound like a nervous mother, had a difficult time keeping the conversation alive. Julie filled in the gaps with talk about Lucia and her French banker. Julie had learned that Lucia's romantic weekend with him was a resounding success. Nevertheless, Lucia missed Julie's company and hoped that she could return soon to Milan. When Julie mentioned to Leslie that she'd probably go back on the train next weekend, Leslie was pleased and noted that it was a good idea instead of driving such a distance. She also reminded Julie to let Maria Borelli know so she could keep an eye on the villa during her absence. After lunch, they retrieved Leslie's two suitcases from her car in the adjacent parking structure and wheeled them into the hotel's lobby. Leslie gave Julie a long goodbye hug.

"Have a good flight, Mom. Hope this trip works out for you."

"So do I. I'll call you, let you know how things are going."

"Hey, you didn't tell me where you'll be staying."

Leslie paused, recalling that she had conveniently dodged that issue. Julie was under the impression that her mother was flying only as far as Denver. "Oh, I'll be at the Brown Palace, but that's only temporary. I'll probably relocate to a more convenient place once I get the lay of the land."

"Call me when you know something."

They hugged again. As Julie headed for the hotel's front door, Leslie waved and called out, "Drive safely." Julie walked out and soon disappeared.

Once in her room, Leslie unpacked a few items from one of her suitcases. She took a moment to look out the single window at some kind of industrial hodgepodge of stacked lumber and machinery below. She'd chosen an ordinary room for her one night alone instead of picking a suite like the one she and Roger Halliday had reveled in a short time ago. *There's no way to find that same pleasure right now. I'll just have to wait until we're together again.*

Roger Halliday left Washington's Dulles Airport late Monday afternoon on a United Airlines nonstop to Denver. While airborne, he again read all of Clarke Layton's reports that Leslie had given him. Layton had accumulated a great deal of information on Andrew and Sarah. Although Leslie was unhappy with Layton, Roger knew that it was because of Andrew's actions, not the lack of good work by Layton.

One small detail had not been resolved: a photo showing Sarah wearing wedding rings. Roger knew that she'd divorced Tom Rickenbach and was sure that she had not remarried. *Why was she still wearing them?*

Thanks to Layton's work, Roger was able to check both Andrew's and Sarah's history of activity on their respective computers. Andrew still e-mailed but it was mostly work-related and not very illuminating. Sarah used Facebook occasionally but it was normal stuff.

The only interesting piece of information Roger found pertained to Sarah's bank account. He discovered that $2,105,278 had been deposited in her account by a Pueblo brokerage firm on February 9th. Four days later, an even two million was withdrawn. He figured that such a large sum must have come from the sale of Digger dot com stock. *What was the outgoing two million for? Probably too much to buy a house. Maybe some type of alternate investment? Like starting a new business?*

Roger landed just after 7:00 PM, picked up his rental car, and drove to a motel near the giant shopping mall complex at the confluence of Interstate 25 and the C-470 Beltway. Once in his room, he set up his laptop computer and checked his e-mail. There was one from Leslie, peevishly demanding to know when he'd arrive in Colorado Springs. He sent her a short reply, saying he was working on a sensitive issue and would be delayed for several more days. He didn't mention where he was at the moment but implied that he was still in Virginia.

The next morning, Roger dressed in an expensive gray suit, a white shirt and a maroon silk tie. He stood before a full length mirror and checked his appearance, taking a moment to carefully comb his silver hair and clean his glasses. Satisfied that he could pass as a successful businessman, he slipped on his dark blue overcoat, checked out of the motel, and drove to a nearby restaurant for breakfast.

About ten o'clock, he entered the Cherry Hills residential area and easily found Leslie's house, thanks to Layton's notes. He passed it before turning around and parking some fifty yards away. It had snowed briefly the night before but it was melting in the morning's bright sunshine.

Roger walked up to Leslie's house and found a uniformed policeman removing yellow plastic tapes that had been used to secure the premises. He was impressed by the imposing view, a house that spoke of an upper class life style, but the lack of visible damage to the exterior, aside from darkened windows, seemed curious. Even more startling was a thought that Andrew Krag had abandoned this mansion to live in a Leadville mountain cabin. *Quite a change for him.*

He walked up one arc of the circular driveway but stopped when a short man wearing a bright red down jacket came out the front door. He gave Roger an inquisitive look and said, "Can I help you?"

"I heard this property is for sale. I came by on the off chance I could see it."

The man stepped off the front portal and extended his hand. "You're in luck. I'm Alan Morris, the listing agent. There's some damage to the inside but I'm getting it taken care of. Should be shipshape in a few weeks."

"What happened?"

"Oh, nothing serious. Some homeless folks broke in, started a fire in the living room and it got out of hand. Lots of smoke and ash but no structural damage."

"Would you mind if I walked around?" said Roger.

"C'mon inside, I'll show you the place."

Morris gave him a complete tour of the house. Roger expressed keen interest, but more as a secret accomplice in Leslie's schemes than a wealthy man looking for an expensive home.

After the tour, they stood outside near the front door. "Thanks, Alan, for your time. It's a beautiful home in spite of the fire damage. I like it."

Morris gave him his business card. "Call me if you have any more questions. At my office or on my cell phone."

"I'm curious about something," said Roger, "the cause of the fire. Could it have been intentionally set?"

"You mean . . . like arson? Oh no, that was ruled out real quick after the fire department and police gave the place a close inspection."

"Well, all right then." Roger began walking away. "Thanks again," he called out. "I'll be in touch."

He got into his rental car and drove away. While heading east on Arapahoe to I-25, he chuckled. *Never had to give him that phony name I dreamed up.*

Roger pulled into Leadville in late afternoon. Heavy gray clouds hugged the mountains as daylight faded, portending the probability of heavy snow. He drove slowly through the city along Harrison Street, looking right and left, becoming familiar with the town's buildings and layout. At the southern edge of the city, he turned around and went back, exiting on the north side.

He found the site of Andrew's cabin, drove up the driveway and parked so he could get a complete view of the remains from inside the car. He took out a photo of the cabin, one that Clarke

Layton had taken before Leslie's arson had consumed it. Gazing at the remaining concrete foundation, the stone fireplace and chimney, he shook his head in disgust. *Leslie didn't need to do this. It was totally unnecessary. What is wrong with that woman?*

He got out of his car and walked completely around the lot, not sure what he was looking for, but trying to understand Andrew Krag a little better. No clues in that department either, except he figured that Krag liked the mountains, living a simple life, and being the master of his own fate.

He was about to get back into his car when another vehicle came up the driveway and stopped near him. When the driver emerged, Roger noticed the man's cowboy hat and dirty tan duster. As he came closer, Roger became nervous when he spotted a shiny lawman's badge pinned to the duster. "What brings you out this way?" the man said.

"I heard this property might be available and thought I'd take a look." Roger extended his hand. "I'm Jack Thompson."

"Sheriff Waters," he said, shaking Roger's hand. "You from around here?"

"No, I live in Denver. I'm thinking this would be a great place to come in the summer. Do some hiking and fishing. Get away from the rat race."

"What kind of work is that?"

"Export import, mostly food and beverage products. And way too much travel out of the country to keep things moving."

"I think you'd enjoy the area," said Waters. "Plenty of places to ski or snowshoe if you're into winter sports."

"I'll be looking into them, too," said Roger as he got in his car. "Think I'd better find a room before it starts snowing."

"Try the Silver King Inn on Poplar, a nice place to stay. And you'll get a fine meal at Quincy's on Harrison."

"Thanks for the tips, sheriff. I'll check 'em out."

Roger breathed easier as he drove down the driveway. However, if he'd taken a moment to look in his rear view mirror, he would have seen the sheriff writing something into a small notebook and would not have not felt all that secure.

CHAPTER TWENTY-TWO

DOES IT SNOW IN COLORADO?

Eliot Waters leaned back in his chair, boots propped up on his desk, while he stared out the window into a deepening darkness. He twisted the end of his mustache between his thumb and forefinger, an unconscious habit that took over when he was trying to understand a puzzling situation. There was nobody left at the station he felt comfortable talking to so he picked up the phone and dialed.

"Detective Hardcastle," she answered after two rings.

"Hello, Sharon. Hoping I could catch you before you left."

"Hi Eliot. I'll be here a while longer but you can always get me on my cell phone. Is this personal or business?"

He chuckled. "A bit of both, I suppose. How are you?"

"Fine, keeping busy. And you?"

A bit perplexed. Thought maybe you could help me out."

"All right, try me."

The way she said "try me" made him wish that he could reach out and hold her close, like the way they danced several nights ago. But he willed himself out of his daydream. "I drove up to Andrew Krag's cabin this afternoon, something I do every now and then. Checking up on it, make sure nothing is going on. There was a man up there looking the place over. Said he heard it was available and was shopping around for a vacation property."

"And this bothered you?"

"It didn't but it does now. First of all, the property is not actually up for sale. And if it was, Emmaline Dolan would have been right there alongside him. I didn't bother to ask but . . ."

"How did he look?"

"Wealthy, like he could afford it. About my age, a nice looking fellow all decked out in an expensive suit. Said his name was Jack Thompson from Denver, in the export import business."

"I don't see anything wrong with that."

"Yeah, but I ran his plate number and this is where his story starts to fall apart. The car's a rental from the Denver airport, signed out to Roger Halliday from Virginia. Now why do you suppose a gentleman like him would lie to the Lake County Sheriff about his ID?"

"Sounds suspicious, Eliot. Like the guy might be hiding something."

"Which brings me to the business part of my call. I'd sure like to know more about him and wonder if you have time to help."

"For you, certainly. Give me everything you have and I'll do some digging." He gave her Halliday's address in Vienna and his driver's license number. "Are we done now?" she said.

"Not quite. When will I see you again?"

"This weekend is good for me. How about Saturday?"

Saturday is good. I'll come down and we can have dinner again. Something other than Tex-Mex though."

"No, let me do the driving this time. I'll come up Saturday morning and you can show me that fish hatchery you've been bragging about."

He laughed. "That won't take long. How about skiing or snowshoeing? Work up a big appetite for the dinner I'll cook."

"You can cook?"

"You wait. My cuisine rivals the best Paris has to offer."

"OK, I'll wait *and* see. And I'll throw my ski gear in the car."

"There's also a place we can do some dancing if you've a mind."

"That's very nice," she said in a sultry voice, "but let's not waste all our energy on *outdoor* events."

Eliot's pulse quickened. "You're right, we'll have to pace ourselves."

Roger found a parking spot on Harrison Street near Quincy's. He picked up a copy of the Leadville *Herald Democrat* from a sidewalk box, entered the restaurant and was seated at a small table in the back. When the waitress appeared, he ordered a scotch on the rocks with a lemon twist and the only entree available during the week, filet mignon, medium rare, with a loaded baked potato.

While sipping his scotch, he flipped through the newspaper until an article caught his eye. Roscoe Bartlett, head of RBC, Inc., had announced the expansion of his company. Bartlett's niece, Miriam S. Dolan of Pueblo, also the daughter of local residents Sam and Emmaline Dolan, would be a partner in the new enterprise. The article concluded by noting that Geo-Tech Engineer

Andrew Krag would manage the Pueblo operations with home construction in the Pueblo West area.

Having only snacks while driving from Denver, Roger ate quickly when his meal arrived. There was room for dessert so he had a chocolate sundae and a cup of coffee. He thought again about the news article and figured that Sarah had used her two million dollars as an investment, not only in RBC but in her future with Andrew Krag. He laughed quietly to himself. This would be good news for everyone involved in the new venture. But he knew one woman in particular who would be outraged at Andrew and Sarah's prospects for a happy life together.

He paid the modest bill and drove to the Silver King Inn on Poplar that Sheriff Waters had recommended. While sitting in front of the hotel with the engine idling, Roger had second thoughts. *Might not be a good idea staying here in case the sheriff came looking. In fact, it would be smart to avoid this town altogether.*

He put the car in drive, turned around and headed south on U. S. 24. When he reached Buena Vista, he took a room at the Best Western Vista Inn. After taking a hot shower, he made himself comfortable in bed with his laptop and checked his e-mail. There was a long rant from Leslie which she'd sent from the Rome airport's Hilton Hotel near midnight. She was lonely, angry, and probably drunk.

He shut down the computer without answering her e-mail. He knew he had to do something, either *about* her or *for* her. But first, he'd do something physical *with* her. He hoped the 'about' and 'for' would logically follow.

Later that evening, Eliot Waters was at home watching Jay Leno when the telephone rang. "Hello, Sharon," he said, noting her name on the caller ID screen. "Hope you're not going to tell me you're not coming up on Saturday."

"No, no, nothing like that. I've got some information for you on Halliday."

He sat up straighter and muted the TV's sound. "Already? How in the heck did you manage that?"

"I have a bud in the FBI and she owed me a favor."

"Hold on, let me get something to write with."

"No, let me give you the highlights. I'll send an e-mail with all the details."

He relaxed again. "Go ahead."

"All right. Roger Lee Halliday, forty-nine, divorced, does live in Vienna, Virginia. His father was career Air Force but was shot down over North Viet Nam in 1968, died in prison there. He went to the Air Force Academy, served for ten years but resigned as a captain in 1995. He couldn't pass the flight physical so they sent him to the Technology Institute at Wright-Patterson where he earned a masters in computer and communications engineering. When he left the Air Force, he moved to Palo Alto and worked for a software company called Digger Dot Com for six years."

"So far, so good," he said. "Sounds like a solid citizen."

"It gets better. In 2001, he quits Digger and moves to Vienna, and becomes an agent with the CIA. Gets all kinds of special intelligence security clearances."

"Uh, oh. I'm almost afraid to ask what kind of *projects* he worked on."

"Not to worry, I couldn't tell you anyway. My friend doesn't have that kind of visibility into his activity there."

"Is he still on the payroll?"

"No, he left four years ago. And now we get to the mystery part. He has no employer but travels all over the world."

"He did mention being in the export import business."

"Yeah, but what are his products?" she said. "Food? Wine?"

"Could be. Or maybe weapons or drugs."

The line went silent for several seconds. "What do you think, Eliot?"

"He appears to be a law abiding citizen, but there's no good reason for him to be in this part of the country. Or one we know about."

"Any idea where he might be right now?"

"I recommended the Silver King Inn as a nice place to stay tonight." He glanced at his watch. "Think I'll mosey on over there and have a chat with Mr. Halliday."

"Be careful, Eliot. He could be dangerous."

"Talk to you soon."

Halliday's Wednesday started out well. A fresh two inches of snow had fallen during the night but, because of a bright sun and brisk wind, the roads were coated with a shallow film. He found a small cafe that had been converted from a railroad dining car and had a big breakfast of eggs, bacon and hash browns.

On the road again, he cruised south until he reached U. S. 50 and headed east. He turned off at the community of Pueblo West and toured various home neighborhoods. Moving on to Pueblo, he drove around the perimeter of Parkview Medical Center and then to Sarah's house next to Walking Stick Golf Course. There were no surprise encounters with people whom Leslie Krag loved to hate. If he was still a CIA employee, his morning activities would be part of a larger exercise, making a reconnaissance and getting a feel for the situation and the terrain.

His next destination was Colorado Springs. He decided to surprise Leslie at the airport when she arrived that evening but had several hours to kill. A visit with mother at the Shady Elms Retirement Home would be a good thing to do.

He arrived shortly after she'd had lunch in the central dining room. He helped her walk to a communal recreation room equipped with jigsaw puzzles, board games, books, and a TV tuned to a loud news channel.

The facility was pleasant enough, decorated in maroon carpeting and maple wainscoting along light green walls, but Roger hated it. The building had a faint odor that felt like a preliminary step in the embalming process.

His visit with Elise Halliday didn't last long. She peppered him with the same questions asked during dozens of previous visits: What have you been doing? Are you dating anyone? When are you going to settle down and get a wife? And how about a couple of grandchildren before I go to meet the man upstairs? He laughed at the last question; his mother forgot that he would be fifty in less than a year.

Roger was vague about his business activities but let slip that he'd met a lovely woman recently in Italy. This was a big mistake; it only generated more questions and ramped up her dismay that he couldn't find a nice mountain girl right here in Colorado. The unspoken hint was that he should live in Colorado Springs with a house big enough for himself, his loving mother, and a growing family. He gave her a hug and a kiss, promised he'd think about her suggestions, and left.

He drove downtown and stopped for a leisurely lunch at The Ritz Grill near the Antlers Hilton. Over a beer and a hamburger, he thought about the next several days with Leslie, in particular what would happen tomorrow. He believed that she was on a collision course with disaster in her deranged quest for justice and revenge against Andrew and Sarah. Somehow, he had to steer her in another direction and, if he couldn't do that, he'd have to end their relationship.

Roger checked in at The Broadmoor under his real name and dropped his suitcase in the suite that Leslie had *requested.* He slipped the bellman a twenty dollar bill with a request for a felt tip pen and a large piece of white cardboard, and was soon making a sign that read, WELCOME MRS. HALLIDAY.

At the airport he took up a position in the waiting area for greeters. Leslie's plane was on time. When she came through the revolving door, Roger thought she looked like she'd just gotten out of bed but needed to go back for more sleep.

He held the sign so it covered his mouth, the top edge touching his nose. When she spotted him and read the sign, her face cycled through several expressions ranging from confusion to disbelief and finally settling on tearful joy. She ran and crashed bodily into him, causing him to drop the sign. "Damn you, Halliday, I hate you." She hugged him hard and kissed him three times, tears flowing freely. "Why didn't you tell me you were coming? And where have you been?"

He returned the hug and gave her a hard kiss. "Just wanted a surprise. Are you glad to see me?"

She grabbed the back of his neck and pulled him into another kiss. "Does it snow in Colorado?"

Roger laughed and squeezed her waist. "I have a car and I've already checked us in. How was your flight?"

"Like it would never end."

"You must be exhausted."

She gave him a loopy look. "Strangely enough, I just got my second wind."

CHAPTER TWENTY-THREE

I CAN'T GET ENOUGH OF YOU

Sharon Hardcastle arrived at her office early on Thursday morning. She'd had a restless sleep the night before, mulling over and over the appearance of Roger Halliday at the Leadville cabin site. *What was he doing there and what's his connection to Andrew Krag?*

She had fourteen new e-mails when she logged in but she opened the one from Eliot Waters first.

Hi Sharon,

Thanks again for the details on Halliday. Makes for interesting reading. Turns out he didn't take my recommendation about the Silver King Inn. In fact, I called around and learned he didn't stay any place in Leadville. Not too surprising, right? I'll check in with Emmaline Dolan and see if she talked with Halliday. Any news from your neck of the woods?

I'm planning Saturday's dinner and thought I'd ask what you're partial to. Beef, chicken or fish? I'm handy in the kitchen with any of them.

Saw an interesting article in the local paper about Andrew Krag's company. RBC is expanding in Pueblo and Sarah Dolan's becoming a partner in the business. Looks like happy days ahead for the young lovers. I've pasted in a link to the article and you can read the whole thing if you're interested. http://www.leadvilleherald.com

Looking forward to Saturday,
Eliot

Sharon made a snorting laugh. "Young lovers," she said aloud. "Wonder what the prospects are for old coots?" She read the article and had to agree with Eliot's appraisal about the future for Andrew and Sarah. But she also wondered about the significance of Sarah becoming a partner in the new business entity. *Why did that have to happen? Did Roscoe do this out of the goodness of his heart? A way to leave a legacy to his niece since he doesn't have any children?*

She spent most of the morning out of the office, following up leads on the rental scams case. Back in her office around noon and having a sandwich at her desk, she again read the *Leadville Democrat* news article. *We need to get Andy involved in this.*

She dialed Sarah's home number but it rolled over to her voice mailbox. She next tried Andrew's cell phone and he picked up right away.

"Hello, Mr. Krag. This is Detective Hardcastle, Pueblo PD. We've never met but I've spoken to your friend, Sarah, a couple of times."

"Is something wrong? Is Sarah OK?"

"Nothing's wrong, Mr. Krag. I'd just like to have a talk with *you.* Are you free later today? I can meet you most anywhere in Pueblo."

"What's this about, detective?"

"It's not serious, I just need some information, talk to you in person rather than on the phone. When can we get together?"

He paused. "Aw hell, OK," he said. "Five o'clock at Sarah's place would work. You know where she lives?"

"Sure do. See you at five."

My God, that was fantastic," moaned Leslie. "I can't get enough of you."

She and Roger lay side by side and breathing hard. They'd just finished a prolonged lovemaking session, the second time within the last twelve hours.

He made a humming sound, lightly brushing his fingers across her breast.

After several minutes, Leslie flung a leg over his knees. "I'm hungry."

"You want to go out for breakfast?"

"What's the weather like out there?"

"Have no idea," he said, "let me check." He wiggled out of bed and pulled back the edge of a drape. "A little snow on the ground but the sun is out."

"Let's have room service. What would you like?"

"Surprise me," he said, turning into the bathroom.

Their elaborate breakfasts came a half hour later and both ate with little talk. They were having a second cup of coffee when Roger asked, "What would you like to do today?"

"Nothing specific, I wasn't sure when you'd be joining me. Maybe get used to each other, get over jet lag, make some plans for dealing with Krag and his whore." She speared a strawberry and popped it into her mouth. "You look all bright and bushy-tailed. When did you get here?" Her question was the first instance of concern about someone other than herself.

"Yesterday. Spent some time with Mom before meeting you."

"How is she?"

"Physically, fine for her age. But she's not too happy with her dutiful son. She keeps wanting me to settle down and give her some grandchildren."

"Well don't look at me."

Both laughed hard. "She forgets," said Roger, "about all the times I've told her that it wasn't going to happen. But I did tell her about you."

"Me? What did you say?"

"Only that I'd met a lovely woman in Italy."

"I suppose that's enough for now. Do you want me to meet her?"

"No, it's too soon for that. We need to talk about a few things first."

She placed her pyramid-shaped napkin on the table. "No time like the present."

"All right then. First, I told you about getting to Colorado Springs yesterday. That's true enough, but I didn't mention that I flew into Denver on Monday."

"Really? What have you been doing since then?"

"I went by your house the next morning."

"What the hell? I didn't ask you to do that."

"I know," he said, "but I wanted to have a look for myself. As your partner, so to speak."

"A partner who apparently doesn't trust me."

Roger let it slide. "I met your agent and he gave me a complete tour of the place. Like I was a prospective buyer."

"What did it look like?"

"Not as bad as I expected. A week or so and it should back on the market."

"Are you satisfied now?" she said.

"Almost. He said the police and fire department have ruled out arson. Completely. Finito. All done."

"That's bullshit," she yelled. "Nancy saw the place right after the fire, talked to the firemen. It was arson and Andrew Krag did it. End of story."

"You can go on believing that but it's not going to help the situation."

Leslie sat still for a moment, her arms folded across her chest as a brooding scowl covered her face. "What kind of trouble did you get into next?"

He made a crooked smile. "I drove to Leadville and looked at Andrew's cabin. Or what was left after you torched it."

"Are you crazy?"

"I ran into an old friend of yours as I was getting ready to leave. Does the name Eliot Waters ring a bell?"

"Yes, that damn cowboy sheriff." She started to get up. "This is not good."

"Not to worry. I gave him a phony name."

"He's not stupid, Roger. What if he connects you with me?"

"There's no way for him to do that. I pretended to be interested in buying it as a vacation getaway. Didn't stick around long and spent the night in Buena Vista."

"I still don't like it. There's no reason to take risks like that."

Roger began putting on a sweat suit. "I'm going out for a run. My conditioning program is all screwed up because of the traveling."

Leslie moved around the table to be closer. "What about *us,* Roger? Do you care *anything* about me?"

"Of course I do. You're the main reason I came to Colorado, to be with you and help you. But let me ask you a question. You remember that jade Buddha I gave you in Rome? And his message about revenge?"

"Yeah, yeah, I remember."

He opened the door and lightly kissed her. "Be back in an hour or so."

Leslie collected the breakfast dishes and set them outside the suite. She was about to take a shower when she noticed Roger's suitcase resting on a luggage rack. *Now would be a good time to do some searching.* She went through its interior, looking for a gun, but came up empty handed. Finding one would have suited her fine, allowing her to take the initiative in her vendetta against Andrew Krag.

She began tidying up, collecting newspapers spread about the room. She found the Leadville *Herald Democrat,* folded in such a way that she could see the article about RBC's expansion in Pueblo.

Leslie was engulfed by a wave of confused emotions. The idea of Andrew's success and partnership with Sarah infuriated her, causing her to ball up the paper and throw it across the room. But she had second thoughts: *Information is power.*

A plan began to materialize in her mind; an attack on a target so lucrative that its destruction would be a mortal blow. *Destroy*

*the RBC presence in Pueblo and forever ruin Andrew and
Sarah's chance for success and happiness.*

She placed the paper ball on the breakfast table and spread
out the crumpled pages, restoring them close to their original
condition. She moved on to the bathroom and, as she was climbing
into the shower, had another thought. *Roger didn't share that
news article with me. What reason would he have for
withholding it? Because he didn't want to hurt me anymore,
make me suffer?*

Leslie hummed a tune as she let the warm water run over her
body. *He does care for me and shows it by his actions instead
of mere words.*

Andrew answered the door promptly when Sharon arrived. She
held up her ID card to eye level and said, "Detective Hardcastle,
Mr. Krag. We've never met but I've talked with Sarah a couple
of times."

"C'mon inside, Detective. Care for something to drink?"

"No, thanks, I'm fine."

He hung her coat in the foyer closet and showed her to a
comfortable chair in the living room as he sat on the couch. "So,"
he said, "am I in some kind of trouble?"

She smiled. "Not at all. Just wanted to talk with you about a
few things."

"All right, shoot. No, wait. You don't say *shoot* to a police
officer, right?"

Sharon made a polite laugh. "First, congratulations on your
new business in Pueblo. I just read an article about your company's
expansion."

"You did?"

"Sure, the Leadville newspaper. It also mentioned that Sarah would be a partner. Quite promising for both of you."

"Sounds like Roscoe—he's my boss—hired a press agent. Well, I guess any kind of publicity helps."

"I was surprised about Sarah," she said. "She seems dedicated to nursing."

"That won't change. She's a silent partner, cashed in a lot of stock and bought a minority share in RBC."

"Ah, I get it." She paused and crossed her legs. "Do you know a man named Roger Halliday?"

The sudden change in subject surprised Andy. "No, the name doesn't ring a bell. Should I?"

"A man showed up at your cabin site on Tuesday afternoon. Sheriff Waters talked to him there for a couple of minutes but he gave his name as Jack Thompson. He also said that he'd heard the place was available and was interested in it as a vacation getaway."

"I'm losing you, Detective. The guy has two names? The property is not on the market, I don't know where he got that."

"OK, Sheriff Waters traced the guy's car back to a rental agency at the Denver airport. That's how he learned his real name is Halliday. The sheriff also called Emmaline Dolan and she confirmed that you're only rebuilding the cabin for now."

"Sounds weird," said Andrew.

"Yes, very mysterious. I ran a background check on Halliday. He's a former government employee, lives in Virginia, and doesn't have any verifiable source of income. So why would he be coming to look at your place in Leadville?"

He shrugged his shoulders. "Wish I could help but I'm totally in the dark."

Sharon uncrossed her legs, preparing to get up. "Are you absolutely sure that you've never heard of Roger Halliday?"

Sarah suddenly appeared in the doorway. "Hey, been a while since I've heard *that* name. What's up with Roger?"

Andrew looked puzzled. "You know him?"

"Sure, I know him." Sarah looked straight at Detective Hardcastle. "Has something happened to him? Is he in trouble?"

Andrew and Sharon were so dumbstruck that they could only stare at her.

"Whaaat?" said Sarah.

CHAPTER TWENTY-FOUR

YOU'RE TWENTY-SIX AND GOING ON EIGHTEEN

After Leslie had taken her shower and dressed, she stuck her head out the door of the suite. The weather was crisp, sunny, and dry, but her jogging lover was nowhere to be seen. Back inside, she checked the time. It was about eleven o'clock and, if she remembered correctly what Roger had told her, it would be near 7:00 P.M. at her Castellina villa. *This would be a good time to call Julie.*

"Hi, Mom," she answered. "You sound like you're right next door."

"Yes, it's a good connection. How are you making out?"

"Fine, cooking a little something when you called. How was your flight?"

"Long and boring," said Leslie, "just like every other flight across the Atlantic."

"Where are you staying?"

Leslie hesitated, wondering what to say, before deciding to tell the truth. "At the Broadmoor. Decent weather we're having, almost like Italy this time of year." Leslie hoped that Julie would assume the Broadmoor was in Denver, thereby relieving her of explaining why she was in Colorado Springs.

"Hey Mom, I found some funny looking pajamas. Cream colored with blue bamboo shoots all over. You actually wear them?"

The abrupt change of subject startled Leslie. "Where did you find *those*?"

"I did some laundry this morning and they were in the dryer. Cute duds."

"They keep me warm on cold nights." *That damn Halliday. Must be his idea of a practical joke.* "Just fold them up and stick them in my bedroom."

Julie giggled at her mother's white lie. "Sure thing, Mom."

"Have you heard anything from Lucia? Has Maria Borelli come by?"

"No to both questions. But I did have an interesting visitor this afternoon. A guy named Marco."

"What did *he* want?" Marco was another of Leslie's lovers, a much younger man whom she hadn't seen in months.

"He was looking for you, said he was a friend. You know him?"

Another hesitation, longer this time. "Yes, I do. What did you tell him?"

"That you were out of the country and would be gone for a couple of weeks. He was disappointed but got over it real quick."

"What do you mean by *that*?"

"He took me for a ride on his motorcycle, showed me some

beautiful places in the country. Really a nice guy."

"Um, Julie . . ."

"And he's taking me out for dinner tomorrow night."

"What?"

"Nothing fancy. Can't wear dressy clothes riding a bike in February."

"Need I remind you of a small detail that you seem to forget? You're a married woman, Julie, and should be working on your relationship with Harper."

"Mother, I'm an adult, almost thirty."

"Damn it, you're twenty-six and going on eighteen. I want you to stay away from Marco. He'll only cause trouble."

"What's he to you? You have something going with this guy?"

"That's none of your business. I'm calling Maria and . . ."

Julie laughed. "So she can be my jailer? No, no, no. I'm going to hang up now, Mom. Call me back when you calm down."

Leslie was about to give her cell phone a major league pitch when Roger came back. "Uh oh," he said, "looks like you got some bad news."

"Big mistake," cried Leslie, "leaving her in Italy by herself. Should've dragged her kicking and screaming all the way back to JFK."

"What did she do now?"

"And *you*, my loyal partner. Leaving those idiotic Asian pajamas at my place so she could find them. You think that's funny?"

Roger bristled with smoldering anger. "So she found them, big deal. It's not the end of the world, Leslie. I lost them and now I know where they are."

Leslie threw up her hands and muttered an expletive.

"I need a shower," said Roger. "Anything you'd like to do this afternoon?"

She picked up the Leadville newspaper and held it up so he could see the article. "Yes, I'd like to drive around Pueblo West and see what kind of pleasure domes asshole Krag is going to build."

Roger gave her a worried look. "First, I have to do something on my computer. Then we'll go out there."

Detective Hardcastle called Sheriff Waters after meeting with Andrew and Sarah. "Big news, Eliot. You are *not* going to believe this."

"I have something, too," he said, "but you go first."

"That article about RBC's expansion in Pueblo got me thinking. A strange man shows up at Andrew Krag's place in Leadville, lies to you about his name, and then sort of slides off the map. I'm thinking maybe Andrew knows something about this guy so I called him and set up a meeting. I just got back."

"Does Krag owe Halliday some money?"

"Not at all. Andrew never heard of him before today. But Sarah knows him. He worked at that software company in California with Sarah's ex-husband, Tom Rickenbach, the CEO of Digger.com. Sarah and Tom socialized with Halliday and his wife for several years in the late 1990s. That is, until Sarah divorced Rickenbach and moved to Pueblo. Halliday left the company about a year after that."

Sharon paused but heard nothing from the other end.

"Are you there?"

"That's one helluva coincidence, Sharon. Halliday checks out Andrew's cabin site, Sarah knows him from long ago, but Andrew doesn't. You think Halliday is trying to reconnect with Sarah? Like maybe they had an affair and he wants to take up where they left off?"

"Don't think so, Eliot. She talked about him like he was only a good friend, a big brother type."

"Did you mention Halliday working for the Feds?"

"Only that he moved to Northern Virginia for a job in Washington. I didn't think they needed to know about him and the CIA."

"Good move," he said. "How'd you leave it?"

"Open. Said I'd get back if I heard anything. You know, they're both a bit nervous after what Leslie did to Andrew's cabin."

"Can't blame them a bit."

"You said you have some news."

"I do. It occurred to me that if Mr. Halliday was interested in a burned up cabin in Leadville, he might also have been curious about a big house in Denver that recently caught fire."

"You mean?"

"I called the real estate agent handling Leslie's house and asked him if anyone contacted him recently about buying it. He was at the house Tuesday morning when a well dressed man came up and asked if it was still on the market. He gave the fellow a guided tour but failed to get his name. The description the agent gave me matched Roger Halliday when I saw him that afternoon, wearing the exact same clothes."

"Good work, Eliot. I think Halliday must be connected to Leslie."

"But how would she know this man? The geography doesn't make sense."

"With all her money, Halliday might be working as a hired

gun, former CIA agent and all that."

"We need to find Halliday," he said.

"What's he doing, Eliot? Coming all this way to look at burned up homes?"

"Gathering information, getting the lay of the land."

Sharon exhaled a whoosh. "Where do we start looking for him?"

"Not sure, but I reckon Andrew and Sarah ought to keep a sharp eye."

"I'll give Andrew a call," she said.

"He *could* be dangerous?" said Sarah. "She actually said that?"

"Could be, might be. Something along those lines." Andrew had just got off the phone with Detective Hardcastle.

Sarah sat on the other side of the dinner table, a facial storm warning broadcasted to her dining partner. "This whole business is crazy," she said, "and I'm not liking it. What the heck is Roger doing? Coming to your cabin and now we hear that he happened to stop by your old place in Denver? It doesn't make sense. Except for the fact that your nutty ex-wife is involved and still out there on the loose."

"The detective was just giving us a heads up. She and Sheriff Waters will be looking for him and have plenty of questions."

"What Roger's doing doesn't fit him at all."

"Can I ask you a personal question?" he said.

"If you must."

"What kind of relationship did you have with him?"

"It was *not* a relationship. Like I said before, we were friends. Good friends. I think he may have had a secret crush on me but I never encouraged him."

"He was married at the time, right?"

"Yes, and she was something else. Always had him under her thumb. I also got the idea that she was pretty stingy with the bedroom action."

"He told you that?"

"Not in so many words," she said, "but I'm a good listener. You told me that yourself, remember? On our first non-date, snowshoeing up to Turquoise Lake, and the next night at the Dew Drop Inn?"

Andrew laughed. "You're right and you have a good memory, too."

"Roger was under a lot of pressure in those days, just like Tom and all the other guys at Digger, putting in sixty to seventy hour weeks."

"Not good for a peaceful home life."

"I'm not surprised Roger went to D. C., getting a job with normal hours and work-free weekends. He was a patriotic guy, an Air Force vet who loved his country. He probably left with lots of Digger stock so he has plenty of money."

"Yeah, so he can snoop around Colorado like he owns it." Andrew got up and started collecting dinner dishes. "Hey, maybe he'd like to invest in RBC."

Sarah joined him at the kitchen sink. "Not funny, Mr. Krag."

"So what's Roger Halliday really like? From hearing you talk and what Detective Hardcastle said, he doesn't sound like much of a man."

"You are dead wrong, Andy. He's very quiet, unassuming, but Tom told me several stories about Roger. He used Roger as a negotiator in difficult contract discussions. He said that Roger became a different person: vicious, argumentative, dictatorial, anything to accomplish the mission. Tom also kidded Roger a lot about being an Air Force vet. Said that with his killer instincts, he should have been a dog face in special ops. Whatever that means."

"Wasn't Tom an Army officer?"

"Yes, and in Iraq the same time I was."

Andrew stopped loading the dishwasher, put his arms around Sarah and pulled her close. *No 'could be' or 'might be' about it, Halliday is dangerous.*

CHAPTER TWENTY-FIVE

I'D LIKE US TO HAVE A PLACE IN ITALY

Leslie and Roger drove south on I-25 and took U. S. 50 west when they reached the Pueblo exit. They entered the Pueblo West community near the Desert Hawk Golf Course and drove through several neighborhoods, looking at houses with different architectural styles. Rambling single-story adobes sat next to two-story McMansions.

Leslie kept silent for most of the tour, prompting Roger to ask if she had any opinions so far. "Just a random bunch of boxes," she said. "Nothing to compare with Cherry Creek."

Roger just grunted and kept driving. They eventually arrived at an area south of the state park where only a few homes dotted the landscape.

"What's out here?" she asked.

"Patience, we're almost there."

She looked around and made a tsk-tsk sound.

He pulled over and stopped the car. "*Regardez*," he said, pointing to two signs sticking out of the ground on a vacant lot.

"OK, this lot's sold. So what?"

"Look at the other sign."

She got out of the car and Roger followed. "Future site of an affordable and quality home by RBC," said Leslie, reading the sign's block letters.

Roger reached into a clear plastic container attached to the sign, pulled out two color brochures and handed one to Leslie. "Andrew Krag's new business venture."

She unfolded it. "Very professional. I'll give him that."

Roger spotted Sarah Dolan's name at the bottom, listed as chief designer, but thought it wise not to call Leslie's attention to it.

"How'd you know about this, Roger?"

"Just doing my computer thing. I saw that article in the Leadville paper about this new business and the lot sales are a matter of public record."

"You do good work, Roger. Both in and out of bed."

He laughed and put an arm around her shoulder. "Always happy to please."

Leslie returned the brochure to the box but Roger put his in his pocket.

"I'm getting cold," she said, "can we go back now?"

"Sure."

They pulled away but Roger hit the brakes after turning a corner. "Whoa, check that out."

"A trailer? My God, I hope they're not putting mobile homes out here. You'd have trailer trash moving in from everywhere, stinking up the place and dragging down property values."

"It's not the kind you live in." He pulled up closer to get a better view. "It's a temporary workplace to oversee the home building that's about to happen out here. Krag must be eager to start putting up those houses."

"How do you know it's him?"

Roger checked some handwritten notes scribbled on a Broadmoor pad from their suite. "This is another one of RBC's three lots." He glanced over at Leslie and was surprised to see her smiling, the first positive emotion shown during the drive. "You all right?"

"Yes," she said. "Why do you ask?"

"Just curious."

"Let's take a walk, Roger. I'd like to get a better look."

He shut off the engine and they got out. The ground was hard, free of mud and snow, allowing them to circle the trailer without getting much dirt on their shoes and jeans. Nobody was in the trailer so they were able to get up next to it, look in the windows and check the locked door. Roger was still surprised at Leslie's good humor and now her curiosity, like she was on a shopping trip at Nordstrom's and had a credit card at the ready.

When they got back inside the car Leslie said, "Thanks for showing me all this. Anything else to see of Mr. Krag's enterprise?"

"Nope, that's it for today."

"Let's stop at a drug store on the way back. I need a few things."

Andrew Krag went into Walgreens and searched for shaving cream and razor blades. He found what he needed and headed for the checkout counter near the store's entrance. But as he turned a corner and was about to step into the main aisle, he stopped when he saw a familiar figure looking intently at a small bottle in her hand. *My God, that woman looks just like Leslie. But it couldn't be her. Or could it?*

He backed up, turned the corner, and waited for several moments. *It could be her, traveling with this Halliday guy. And if it is her . . .* He peeked around the corner and studied the woman's appearance and movements. *It has to be her. Should I confront her? No, the woman's crazy and she could have a gun. But I have to do something. I have to call the police.*

He reached into his coat pocket, searching for his cell phone, but couldn't find it. It wasn't in his shirt or trouser pockets either. *Damn, I left it in my truck.*

He looked around the corner again, saw Leslie heading his way, and had a mild panic attack. Backing up and turning into the adjacent aisle, he dropped his shaving cream and razor blades on a shelf holding office supplies and marched swiftly out the front door. Once in his SUV, he found his cell phone and punched a number he read from a card pulled hastily from his wallet.

"Detective Hardcastle," she answered.

"It's Andy Krag, I just spotted my wife here at Walgreens. I mean my ex, right here in Pueblo. She's here." The words came out in a rushing stream.

"OK, Mr. Krag, take it easy. Where are you?"

"I'm in my truck, sitting in front. She's still inside, I think."

"Which Walgreens are you at?"

"The one on Bonforte Boulevard."

"And you saw Leslie inside the store? How did you know it was her? Did you talk with her?"

"No, I didn't talk to her and I'm pretty sure she didn't see me."

"And you're sure it was her."

"Absolutely."

"OK, I'll be right there. You just sit still and don't do anything crazy."

Minutes later, Hardcastle pulled into the parking lot. When Andrew saw her get out of her car, he ran over. "You're too late, detective. She got away."

"Are you kidding? I got here as fast as I could."

"She came out right after I called you. Got into a car and drove away. A man was driving but I didn't get a good look at him."

"Damn," she said. "I wanted to see the look on her face when I arrested her."

"I did get the license number." He handed her an old cash register receipt with the number scribbled on the back.

Hardcastle reached into her car, pulled out a notebook and flipped it open. "It tracks, she's with Halliday. Now we have to figure out where they're hiding."

Heavy snow began falling in late afternoon. Roger and Leslie decided to stick close to home that evening with dinner at the hotel's Penrose Room.

Both ordered vodka martinis, straight up with an olive, from their tuxedoed waiter and asked for more time to study the comprehensive menu. When their drinks came, Leslie raised her glass in a toast. "Thanks for taking me out to Puberty West today. Seeing what Mr. Krag's planning to do fits nicely with my own ideas."

"Really? How so?"

"We blow up that trailer office or set fire to it. Plant land mines in all his building lots." She made a cackling laugh. "And that's just for starters. A message to let him know we're coming and we're royally pissed."

Roger shook his head and put his martini glass on the table. "You keep forgetting what I've told you several times already. Nothing illegal. The inclusive 'we' you're using is totally off target."

"All right then, wise guy. You got any better ideas?"

"Yeah, drop the whole thing."

"You're no help. I thought you were on my side."

"I am, Leslie, believe me. But it's time to face facts. Andrew Krag did not set fire to your house. Period. This is reality. Do you understand?"

She scowled and raised her voice. "And you are wrong, wrong, wrong. I came halfway around the world for this, left my daughter in that mausoleum of a villa, and now you're turning traitor on me. Why?"

He reached out but she pulled back her hand and drank most of her martini. "I honestly care for you," he said, "and we could have a wonderful life together. In Italy, Virginia, or someplace else. Doesn't really matter one way or the other as long as you're with me. But you've got to give up this vendetta. It's consuming you and we'll never have any kind of relationship unless you get past it."

She pulled a tissue from her purse and dabbed her eyes. "Maybe after we're finished with those two. Yes, I'd like us to have a place in Italy. It has so much to offer and you wouldn't have to go hopping around the world."

"Not *after* we're finished. I want you to end it *now*."

"Let's sleep on it. Talk about it some more in the morning."

The waiter reappeared and was ready to take their order. They agreed to share a chateaubriand accompanied by a bottle of

Napa's finest Cabernet.

Conversation during dinner shifted to more pleasant topics, thanks to the delicious food and a second bottle of Cabernet. Roger suggested moving out of the Broadmoor to minimize the risk of being found by the police. Leslie agreed that it was a good idea and offered The Brown Palace in Denver or ski resorts in Aspen or Vail as suitable alternatives. However, no decision was reached.

They were winding up the meal with a rich chocolate cake and fresh raspberries, along with coffee and cognac. "An excellent dinner," he said. "The best I've had in quite a while."

She gave him a flirty smile. "And there's more to come."

"I couldn't eat another bite."

"I'm not talking about food," she said.

He grinned. "Tell me more."

"Remember that black nightgown I wore at the Rome Airport Hilton?"

"The one I missed because I fell asleep?"

"Yes, I'm giving you another chance."

"So that's it, huh? Sex is the answer?"

She made a throaty laugh. "That's correct. But it's like the *Jeopardy!* game. You have to ask the right question to win a prize."

Their lovemaking turned out to be a dull and passionless event, thanks to the copious food and alcohol consumed. Without indulging in a post mortem, they decided to call it a night and get some sleep.

Shortly before dawn, Leslie had a vivid dream. She was hiking along a high elevation trail in the Colorado Rockies with Andrew Krag. It was a bright summer day and he had gone ahead, out of sight around a rocky outcropping. Leslie stopped to take a drink of water from a plastic bottle when she saw Andrew running toward her, a frantic look on his face.

He yelled, "Run for your life, Leslie, it's a bear."

Andrew kept running and soon disappeared down the trail from where they'd come. Moments later a huge brown bear came galloping toward her, sending tremors of fear throughout her body. The bear stopped for a moment a few feet away and advanced slowly on all four paws until it reached her. The bear stood and hugged her in a firm but gentle way.

"No, no, I don't want this," she cried out, trying to break the bear's embrace.

"Relax and enjoy it," said the bear, as the surrounding mountain scene morphed into a darkened room and the bear's voice became ominously familiar.

Leslie was fully awake. "Roger," she cried out, "what are you doing?"

"I want you . . . trying to get inside."

She squirmed. "This is crazy, I was sound asleep."

He put his mouth on her left breast and raked his front teeth over the nipple. "Open your legs, dammit."

She could feel the repeated jabs of his hard penis and was powerless. He was much stronger and her attempts to push him away only made him more insistent.

She reluctantly parted her legs and he entered quickly, pumping and thrusting, both hands gripping her buttocks hard. It was over quickly. He rolled over onto his back and breathed heavily.

After several moments, she called out, "Are you satisfied now?"

"Yes," was the subdued reply, his passion spent.

"What the hell was that about? I can't believe you're horny after what we did a couple of hours ago."

Roger got out of bed and started for the bathroom. "It's a guy thing."

After he returned, Leslie went into the bathroom to clean herself up and check for injuries. When she crawled back into bed, Roger was asleep. That was a humiliating and degrading experience, she thought. We'll have to talk first thing in the morning and establish some new ground rules about sex.

CHAPTER TWENTY-SIX

A NASTY WOMAN, I'M NOT SORRY TO SEE HER GO

"You saw her?" said Sarah. "Where was this?"

"At the Walgreens on Bonforte," said Andrew.

"The woman's here in Pueblo? What did you say to her? I hope she's in jail where she belongs." Sarah had just come from the hospital and was standing next to Andrew as he washed leaves of Romaine lettuce at the kitchen sink.

"I didn't talk to her. I called Detective Hardcastle and she came right over. But Leslie was gone before she got there."

"And you let her get away? I don't believe this."

"It wasn't my idea. She could have been armed and I didn't want a shootout right there in the drug store."

Sarah scoffed. "Was she alone?"

"In the store, yes. But I saw her get in a car and drive away. I gave Hardcastle the license number and it was the same car Halliday rented at the airport."

Sarah paced back and forth, talking to herself, "Not good, not good."

Andrew placed a full salad bowl in the refrigerator. "Let's go into the living room and relax a bit before dinner."

They took their glasses of Merlot to a love seat and sat close to each other, warmed by flames in the gas log fireplace.

Sarah said, "So now we know that Roger and *that woman* are together. I'll never understand how that happened. What the heck does he see in her?"

"Ah, the mystery of romance."

"How old is Leslie?"

He rubbed his chin. "She'll be fifty-two next month. Does that matter?"

"Just thinking. I doubt her money could be the big attraction. I'm sure he has plenty of Digger stock so he can't be hurting financially." She took a sip of wine. "What are the police going to do now?"

"Hardcastle's putting out an APB, now that they know the two are together and the car they're driving. She's also going to call Sheriff Waters and check some leads on where they might be hiding."

"Maybe your pool-shooting buddy can track her down. Rhonda Awesome, was it?" Sarah was referring to Patrolwoman Rhonda Dawson, an acquaintance of Andrew's before he met Sarah, the same officer who'd responded to Leslie's auto wreck in early January. "Why don't you give her a call?"

"Maybe," said Andrew, not taking the bait.

"Dammit, I feel so helpless. Like the guillotine blade is about to fall."

He squeezed her hand. "I know, but we have to let the police do their job."

Sarah sighed. "OK, forget all that. How was your day, otherwise?"

"Pretty good. Got my office trailer delivered this morning and set up on our lot. I'll start moving some things into it tomorrow. Get ready for lot clearing and staking next week."

"It's kind of isolated out there, don't you think? Someone could do considerable damage to your office one night if she were so inclined."

"Point taken," he said. "I'll give Hardcastle a call and see if the Pueblo PD can keep an eye on that area for us."

Leslie awoke the next morning to see bright sunshine streaming through a vertical gap in the bedroom's heavy curtains. She rolled over in Roger's direction but his side of the bed was empty.

She went into the bathroom, thinking that he'd probably gone out for the papers or a quick jog before breakfast. But when she came out and looked around the suite, things didn't look right. An unsettled feeling came over her. None of his clothes were in the closet, no personal items lay on the dresser, and his suitcase was gone.

She began bustling about the suite, looking for clues that might explain his absence. Her worst fears were realized when she spotted a hotel envelope on the living room desk with her name printed on the front in block letters. *Oh God, no.*

With trembling fingers she ripped open the envelope and began reading the enclosed note. But after only a few moments, she ran out the door, clutching the note in her hand, the edges of her peach-colored bathrobe flapping in the winter wind. Leslie's goal was the general location of where he'd parked the car yesterday afternoon. *Please God, get me there before he leaves.*

She ran around the parking lot in growing desperation. *He's gone, he left me.* Out of breath and her tears flowing, she stood in the center of a vacant parking lot and began a rambling monologue of pleas, curse words, and utterances that made little or no sense. Once she exhausted her limited vocabulary and her supply of angry energy, the freezing temperature made its presence known with tiny needles stabbing her face, hands, and exposed legs.

She sprinted back to the suite, wanting to get back into its warmth, but faced a new problem when she discovered the door was locked. More angry curses followed as she pounded on the door with her fists. A woman pushing a maid's cart came up to her. "I have a key, one minute, please." The woman opened the door and said, "It happens all the time." Leslie barged into the suite and slammed the door without even a grateful word to the stupefied maid.

Leslie found a partially full bottle of vodka in her suitcase, one that she'd kept a secret from Roger, and took a big swig. She threw herself on the bed and wiped her eyes with the edge of Roger's pillow as the vodka burned her throat. After her tears finally dried, she sat up and pulled Roger's note from her bathrobe pocket and read it more slowly this time.

Dear Leslie,

I know this is not the best way to leave but you gave me no choice. I said everything I had to say last night so the rest is up to you. You know how to reach me.

Love, Roger

P. S. I haven't checked out with the front desk so you can

stay longer. But I think you should move out soon in case the
police come looking.

She crumpled up the note and screamed, "Fuck you, Halliday. Who needs you anyway?"

She lay on the bed as the minutes clicked by, thinking about her predicament and all the men she'd loved, the same ones who dumped her when things didn't go their way. Richard, Andrew, Clarke Layton, Paul Harrington, and now Roger. *Whatever happened to good old-fashioned love, respect and loyalty?*

Leslie got out of bed, took off her robe, and filled the bathtub with hot water. She eased herself into the wet warmth and began to think. *I need to get out of here, but where can I go? I can't expect any help from Nancy. She'd turn me down in a New York minute. I should get packed up and have breakfast somewhere, along with a Bloody Mary or two, and think about my next move. But I'm not going back to Italy without giving Krag and his slut the full measure of misery they deserve.*

Sharon Hardcastle was in the middle of a Cobb Salad when her cell phone rang. She recognized the caller's ID and said, "Eliot, how are you?"

"Fine, Sharon. Where are you?"

"In The Springs, having lunch."

"Kind of out of the way for you, isn't it?"

"It is, but I learned something this morning. Roger Halliday's mother lives here in a retirement home. I'm heading over there shortly." She expected Waters to say something but heard nothing. "Eliot?"

"Might be too little, too late."

"What do you mean?"

"Just talked to a young man at the airport rental car agency, the same fellow who gave me the info on Halliday a couple of days ago. Seems he turned his car in this morning, probably heading back home. I'm going to check with the airlines flying to D.C. and see if he was a passenger."

"Was Leslie Krag with him? Can you find out?"

"I asked but he didn't know about any woman."

Sharon paused. "Sounds like they're running scared, Eliot. Maybe they saw me at Walgreens yesterday."

"But you told me they left before you got there."

"Yeah, I know. Grasping at straws."

"I suppose we can rest easy for a spell. You still coming up tomorrow?"

"Sure am. What did you decide to cook?"

He chuckled. "That will have to remain confidential. But I will have a nice dessert for you."

"That's the ticket. The bigger the better."

"You're a wonder, keeping so fit and trim. What's your secret?"

"Chasing bad guys and having a high metabolism rate."

"I'll let you get back to your lunch. Say howdy to Mrs. Halliday for me."

She ended the call and laughed to herself. *Might as well have that meeting with Mrs. Halliday, as long as I'm here. After that, I can think about a carefree weekend with Eliot without worrying about Leslie Krag on the loose somewhere in Colorado.*

An hour later, Detective Hardcastle left The Shady Elms. After a rambling conversation with Elise Halliday, Sharon had learned only two relevant pieces of information: Roger was seeing an Italian woman and was now staying at The Broadmoor Hotel in Colorado Springs.

She sat in her car for several minutes, debating about returning to her office or going by The Broadmoor. *What the heck, I might as well check it out.*

Fifteen minutes later she was showing her badge to a uniformed woman behind the hotel's registration desk. "It's about one of your guests, a Roger Halliday. He checked out earlier this morning."

The woman tapped her keyboard several times while staring at her computer screen. "Yes, we have the Hallidays, but they're still with us."

"They?"

The woman gave Sharon her sincerest hospitality smile. "That's right, room 2304." She pointed to a laminated map on the counter. "They haven't checked out yet. Can I call them for you?"

"No, don't call," said Sharon. "Thanks much, you've been very helpful."

Sharon got into her car and felt the adrenaline kick in. *If Halliday went back to Virginia, why didn't he check out? Could Leslie still be here? And if she is, why did he leave without her?*

She drove to a parking slot near Halliday's room and walked slowly to the door, pulling her service pistol from its holster, and looking right and left in case Leslie Krag made a sudden appearance. A maid's cart was parked nearby.

Sharon gently pushed the door open with one hand while keeping her pistol low and snug against her leg. "Hello?" she called out.

The maid, who was stripping the bed, spotted Sharon. "Can I help you?"

"The woman who was here. Where is she?"

"She's gone," said the maid. "She packed up and left."

Sharon holstered her pistol and the maid's eyes opened wide when she saw the gun. "My name's Hardcastle, Pueblo police. "You have any idea where she went?"

"No, maybe she took a taxi. A nasty woman, I'm not sad to see her go."

"OK then." Sharon looked around the room, realizing the adrenaline rush was gone and her chase of Leslie was back to square one. "Please go about your work," she said to the maid. "I'll have a look around and get out of your way."

She went into the bathroom and noted toilet articles sitting in various places. Every item was for a woman. *She must have been in a big hurry.*

Back in the living room, Sharon bent over to retrieve a crumpled slip of paper from a wastebasket. She read the note and smiled. *So the mystery lovers are no longer a couple. How very sad. Roger Halliday is a lot smarter than I thought, dumping her before the proverbial shit hits the fan. And I think that Leslie Krag has just about run out of luck.*

CHAPTER TWENTY-SEVEN

YOU SURE KNOW HOW TO WELCOME A GIRL

Leslie partially unpacked her luggage, hung clothes in the closet, and placed the few remaining cosmetic items in the bathroom. In a special suitcase compartment, she found a large brown envelope and dumped its contents on the queen-size bed. She spread out several checkbooks, traveler's checks, credit cards, and driver's licenses made out to both Leslie Krag and Faye Aronson, the one for Faye acquired last year when her relationship with Clarke Layton went sour. She also had two envelopes containing dollars and Euros in various denominations. *Thank God I had the foresight to have things made up for both identities.*

Leslie had convinced the taxi driver who'd picked her up at the Broadmoor to drive north on I-25 to Denver and deposit her at the Courtyard Marriott near the Arapahoe exit. She gave him a $100 tip in addition to the hefty one-way fare.

She stuffed some dollars, her checkbook, and her Faye

Aronson driver's license into her purse and went into the office where she asked the registration clerk to call a taxi. She also inquired about the closest location of a reputable auto dealer where she might buy a good used car.

Leslie was in no mood to haggle with the young salesman who met her at the door when she arrived at Pinnacle Motors, two miles east of the hotel. She found a dark blue Buick sedan in excellent condition, about two years old, and agreed on the salesman's price to pay with cash and a personal check. The most important feature was its readiness to drive off the lot. She had a nervous moment as the paperwork was being completed because the name on her check was different than her driver's license. She explained it away easily, saying that she had recently remarried and hadn't bothered to get down to the DMV. Luckily for her, the Cherry Hills address was the same on both.

When she drove away from the lot, she felt a new sense of independence and power. She could now travel freely with little danger of apprehension because the police wouldn't have a good reason to suspect this woman in a dreary second-class sedan. She would later change her appearance, a further step in her plan to gain even more personal security.

She found a French restaurant and had an early dinner; a delightful salmon preceded by a vodka martini and accompanied by a full bottle of *Sancerre*. Her thoughts veered to Roger Halliday while sipping the martini. *What a coward, sneaking off in the middle of the night. He's a damn hit man for God's sake, but afraid to stand up to a woman.* After she'd finished about half the wine, her attitude became more dismissive. *Some friend he is. I'm probably better off without him. So why do I miss him so much?*

Back at her hotel, she called her real estate agent, Alan Morris.

"Leslie," he said, "good to hear from you. And what a good connection, like you're almost next door."

"Pretty close, I'm in Denver at the airport. Just got in from Rome after a long and tiring flight."

"I didn't think you'd be coming back, but this is a nice surprise."

"I hadn't planned to, but I have some things to take care of in person."

"I have good news on your house," he said. "The cleanup is going well and should be finished in several days."

"That's why I'm calling. Is there any chance I can stay in the house while I'm here? It would only be for a short time."

"I don't see why not, it's your home. The guest room on the east side had no damage and you wouldn't be interfering with the work crews. But you might have to time-share the kitchen around lunch time."

"Sounds wonderful, Alan," she said. "I'll come over tomorrow after breakfast. I'm too exhausted to go anywhere tonight."

"Give me a call and I'll meet you at the house. Anything else I can do?"

"You've been absolutely divine," she said. "Just one small favor. Please don't tell anyone I'm back. It would spoil the surprise."

"Got it. See you tomorrow, Leslie."

She laughed after hanging up. *My own home, the last place they'd look.*

Sharon Hardcastle pulled into Leadville on Saturday around noon. She found Eliot's office and parked in the lot adjacent to the building. When Eliot saw her walk through his office door, he almost jumped across his desk to join her. He gave her a bear hug and planted a kiss on her lips while her eyes opened in wide surprise. "Whoa," she said, "you sure know how to welcome a girl."

He relaxed his embrace and stepped back slightly while looking her over. "You look great, all set for some outdoor adventures."

"That I am." She pointed to her blue ski trousers and jacket, both made of a tightly woven smooth fabric. "I've got my layers here, assuming we'll be doing some cross country or snowshoeing."

He cocked one eye. "Sounds like you've done this before."

"Don't worry, Eliot. I won't embarrass either of us."

He chuckled. "Should we have some lunch before heading out?"

"Actually, I'm good to go. Had a late breakfast and put snacks in my day pack." She smiled. "Even brought some for you."

Out in the parking lot, they transferred Sharon's gear to Eliot's vehicle. They drove out of town, south on U. S. 24, and passed the Lake County Airport. Eliot glanced over and said, "Just a short ride to the famous fish farm."

"I can hardly wait," she said, her voice betraying a stifled laugh.

Five minutes later, they arrived at the Leadville National Fish Hatchery. A woman at the entry desk greeted Eliot as an old friend and he touched the brim of his Stetson as a salute. Eliot and Sharon walked around the information gallery and glass tanks that demonstrated the various processes for mating, hatching, and growing fish that were later transplanted to lakes, streams and rivers.

Without any words spoken, she took his hand as they strolled about the galleries, holding it for most of an hour. They eventually came back to the entrance and, before going outside, Eliot said, "We haven't talked about our favorite criminal. I'm thinking we ought to get that out of the way before going much further."

"Sure." She folded her arms. "After I called yesterday, I spoke to my TSA friend at the Colorado Springs Airport and gave him both names that she uses. He's asked the airlines to monitor outgoing passengers in case she tries to leave like she did two months ago. Don't want *that* to happen again."

"Guess you haven't heard anything."

"No, nothing. But I've checked with taxi companies, trying to find out if she got picked up at the Broadmoor and where she went. Do you have any idea how many taxi companies there are in The Springs?"

"More than you'd like, I'm sure."

"So I've got dispatchers checking with other dispatchers who were on duty yesterday morning. And talking to drivers who had pickups at the Broadmoor for any kind of woman matching her description."

"I'm guessing you'd have heard by now if she caught a flight out."

"Better than a guess," she said. She moved closer and linked her arm with his. "You know something? It's nice having a date with another police officer. You never run out of conversation topics."

"Sad to say, it's likely to be talk about our experience with bad guys."

"And bad girls, too."

Eliot chuckled and said, "You'll hear something about her soon.

First, I have some spectacular scenery to show you. Let's get your day pack and check out one of my favorite hiking trails."

On Saturday morning, as Leslie entered her home's circular driveway, Alan Morris stepped out of the door and onto the front steps. He met her at the car as she got out. "Hi Leslie, welcome back."

She took his outstretched hand and gave him a peck on the cheek. "Thanks for meeting me, Alan." She looked around and said, "Are the cleaners here today?"

"Not on the weekend, but they'll be here Monday morning. Couple more days ought to do it."

"Would you mind? I've got two heavy suitcases in the trunk."

He took one in each hand. "What happened to your Beemer?"

"Oh, I sold it when I moved to Italy. Bought a Mercedes, a more practical car for me over there."

He took her luggage to the foyer. "Let me show you what we've done to restore your house. I'll take your bags to the guest room later."

"Fine, lead the way."

He took her into the living room where she was pleasantly surprised at how good it looked. "There's still some touchup painting to be done. Then they'll clean the windows, wipe everything down and do a last vacuum."

They toured the dining room and kitchen where it was not readily apparent that there had ever been a fire. Leslie made a few sniffs, trying to catch some scent of the smoke, but didn't get enough to comment. Alan noted that waxing the dining room furniture and mopping the kitchen floor were on the agenda for next week. Leslie was irritated when she saw the empty space previously occupied by the table and four chairs that Andrew had taken to Leadville. Alan had compensated for this problem by moving some pieces from the living and dining rooms, a realtor's technique for insuring a better showing of the house.

After looking over the damaged rooms, Alan grabbed her suitcases. As they passed the master bedroom, Leslie had an anxious moment, recalling the passionate lovemaking with Andrew and the meaningless sex with her private detective, Clarke Layton. *I could never sleep comfortably in that room again.*

They arrived at the guest room that Leslie would occupy. "Anything else I can do for you today?" he said, signaling his intent to leave.

She came closer. "Thank you so much, Alan, for all you've done. It's been a stressful couple of months for me with the divorce and then the fire." When he started to edge away, she grabbed his sleeve. "I do have a question. Where can I buy a gun?"

"A gun? Why do you need a gun?"

"I'm living alone and don't feel safe. There's also been some trouble with my ex and the woman he's living with. I need protection. From her, not from him."

"I don't know, Leslie. Seems like a bad idea."

"You don't think I can handle one? For your information, I have a gun at my place in Italy. And I know how to use it."

"Well, there's hunting and outfitter stores around the city. Check out the yellow pages, I'm sure you'll find a place that'll be glad to sell you one."

"I'm not talking about that," she said, the angry impatience rising in her voice. "That would take too long. I need something now."

He stared at her for a moment. "Sorry, Leslie. Can't help you."

She turned and opened a suitcase. "Goodbye, Alan. Have a nice weekend."

Sharon and Eliot sat close to each other on his living room couch, sipping Merlot and keeping conversation to a minimum. A steady warmth came from the fireplace while Eliot massaged her feet, her legs resting on his knees.

After visiting the fish hatchery that afternoon, they had taken a short hike to the north where they could view a solidly frozen Turquoise Lake populated by several fishing shacks. A sweeping panorama of snow-covered fourteeners gave them a majestic view, the vast ring of peaks surrounding a winter paradise. Following this easy hike, they drove to the Tennessee Pass Nordic Center and skied cross-country for two hours. Eliot was a plodding, grind-it-out sort of a skier, but he kept pace with her. Sharon showed a natural athletic ability, plenty of stamina, and a polished technique with graceful kicks and glides.

She finished her wine and wiggled her toes. "Great dinner, Eliot. I never knew lamb chops could taste so good. And the salad was perfect. The bits of apple, cranberries, walnuts and feta cheese were ingenious."

"Hope you saved some room for dessert."

"Let's wait a few minutes, if you don't mind."

He rubbed his thumb along the instep of her foot. "Anything special you'd like to do tomorrow?"

"Please don't think I'm crazy, but I'd like to see Andy Krag's cabin. Or rather what's left of it."

"It's not crazy, but definitely an unusual request. Why the interest?"

"Oh, I don't know. Get a better feel for the people involved in

all this drama. What it's like to be a cabin dweller at 10,000 feet."
She grinned and added, "Maybe get some more clues about you."

Eliot slid his hand inside the leg of her warmup pants and
massaged her calf muscles. Sharon's cell phone, resting on a nearby
end table, suddenly awoke with a musical ring tone. "Don't stop,"
she told him, reaching out to pick up the phone. "Hardcastle," she
answered.

Eliot heard only her half of the conversation. When she cried
out "Denver?" he stopped massaging her leg and said, "What
happened?"

She held up her palm to his face and kept talking on the phone.
"OK, I got it. Thanks much for the help, I'll take it from here."

Sharon ended the call and turned to Eliot. "Leslie took a taxi
to Denver. The driver dropped her at a Marriott on the south
edge of town."

"Why would she go to Denver?"

"To catch a plane for Italy?"

"Doesn't fit," he said. "The taxi could have dropped her at
any airport hotel."

"She might still be at the Marriott. I'll give them a call." She
got back on her cell phone, heard the hotel number from directory
assistance, and called. After a few minutes, she hung up and said,
"Too late again, damn it. She checked out this morning with a
different clerk and left no forwarding address."

"That's too bad. We could have driven over and arrested
her."

She raised an eyebrow. "You'd do that tonight?"

He chuckled. "Are you impressed by my devotion to duty?"

"Ha. You're only saying that because she's not there."

"Ah, you broke the code."

"The only good thing is we don't have to go looking for her right this minute."

He raised his glass. "I'll drink to that."

"Say, what about this fabulous dessert you mentioned?"

"Coming right up." He went to the kitchen and brought back an oval-shaped dish containing multicolored scoops of ice cream, chocolate syrup on the vanilla, and chunks of fresh fruit.

"What have we got here?" she said.

"A super duper banana split, big enough for two."

He sat down again while she held the dish on a tray resting on her knees. "Fresh strawberries and pineapple," she said, "you outdid yourself." She took a bite of chocolate ice cream and moaned in pleasure.

They had taken several bites when he said, "What's Leslie up to?"

"I was going to ask you the same thing. About all I can figure is that she's on the run, no doubt thinking we're coming after her."

After they ate everything in the dish he said, "We have to outsmart her, anticipate her next step."

Sharon leaned toward him, draped an arm around his shoulder and kissed him. "Let's sleep on it. And hope for inspiration in the morning."

CHAPTER TWENTY-EIGHT

JUST NEED A LITTLE MORE PRACTICE

Leslie was hungry after unpacking and getting everything settled. She rummaged through the kitchen pantry and plugged in the empty refrigerator. *Of course there's nothing to eat or drink. Nobody lives here anymore.*

Her first stop was the P. F. Chang restaurant in the Park Meadows shopping center, only ten minutes away. Once she was seated and had ordered a vodka martini, she remembered it was not only the same place she'd met Clarke Layton several months ago, but it was also the same table where she'd hired him after a short conversation. *Should have done a more thorough investigation of him, the stupid loser. Wonder what rock he's hiding under?*

Her next destination was a thrift store in nearby Littleton. She found boots, male trousers, an overcoat, and a man's felt hat, the most unfashionable things she'd ever seen. *Perfect. When I wear these I'll look like a homeless old bag lady.* They seemed to be clean but had a faint beer and cigar odor. She resolved to air them out before ever putting them on. In another part of the store, she placed six different pairs of eye glasses into her shopping cart and rolled on to the checkout counter. The grand total at the register for her treasures was a whopping $37.50. She gave the elderly woman cashier a $50 bill and told her to keep the change as a donation.

As she headed for the exit, she laughed and sang opening parts of *Pennies from Heaven.* The cashier only shook her head in disgust.

Leslie drove to a liquor store on County Line Road and picked up a huge bottle of Grey Goose vodka and a half dozen assorted bottles of wine, including white vermouth for her martinis. Her last stop was a King Sooper supermarket to buy hair dye, snacks, eggs, bacon, muffins, cereal and milk.

Later that afternoon she set up her own makeshift beauty parlor. Knowing the hair dye's unpleasant odor and likely mess, she chose a bathroom a good distance away from her new bedroom. As she gazed in the mirror and tugged at her hair, she thought of cutting it first. She decided against it, fearing she'd butcher the job and it would make her stand out even more. *I can wait until I get back to Siena.*

After Leslie had finished the job and restored her now dark brown hair to its original shape, she tried on various pairs of glasses. One pair reminded her of the actress, Carol Channing, but she judged them too bizarre. People would remember her and she didn't want that. She chose a pair with round lenses and tortoise shell frames. They distorted her vision but she could live with it for several days.

The sun had set and snow was forecast for later that evening. She dithered about plans for dinner and finally decided to stay in. Maybe she'd have some bacon and eggs. While having a vodka martini and toasting her new look, which she thought made her look much younger and more attractive without the glasses, she thought about calling Julie and Maria Borelli. She tried to remember what Roger had told her about the time difference but couldn't figure it out. *They're probably asleep anyway. I'll call in the morning.*

Some time before dawn, Eliot rolled to the right and faced Sharon, outlined by a faint blue light coming from a small lamp on a corner dresser. As he slowly awoke and could focus, he realized she was smiling. "You're awake," he said.

"Brilliant deduction, Sherlock." She stroked his cheek with three fingers.

"Just wanted to make sure you didn't hightail it south."

"Um, no . . . we've got too much weekend ahead of us."

"Been awake long?" he said.

"Not long."

"You OK?"

"I feel wonderful," she said, "so relaxed. I was pretty nervous when we came to bed, wondering how it would be."

"And the verdict?"

She draped her arm across his neck and kissed him. "Guess."

"I was kind of edgy myself. It's been a while."

"You are a sweet, sweet man, Eliot. So kind, loving and patient. I appreciate that more than you know."

He kissed her. "I can always do better. Just need a little more practice."

She giggled. "Then we can have more *practice* together." She pushed her pelvis against him to emphasize the word.

He slowly caressed her back, moving his hand from the base of her neck, down to her waist, and on to her thighs and calves. "You're very well put together, you know. Beautiful legs which you manage to keep hidden. I sure like touching you, anywhere and everywhere."

"Well, Mr. Waters, I try to take good care of myself. I also have the benefit of not having to nurse old rodeo injuries."

"That's because you've led such a sheltered life. Might have to get you exposed to some cattle roping and Brahma bull bashing."

"I think not. But let me ask you something. I know you like music, the western and pop stuff. How about the classics?"

"You mean like Beethoven and Mozart?"

"Exactly. Would you go to a symphony with me some time?"

"Sure, I'll try most anything once."

"I'll check the Pueblo calendar but we may have to hear one in Denver."

"No problem," he said. "We can make it an overnighter."

She sighed. "Looks like we'll have to do some driving to see each other."

"I don't mind. Being with you is what counts."

Sharon rolled over to be on top of him. "You know, Andrew and Sarah had a similar situation but look how it turned out. He gets to kiss her goodnight and good morning, every night and every morning."

"True enough, but his home burned to the ground. Moving in with her was the right thing to do."

"Just saying." She kissed him and added, "Am I too heavy?"

"I might have to cut you back a bit on the banana splits."

She laughed, they rolled around tightly entwined in each other's body, had some more *practice*, and slept soundly until well after sunrise.

On Sunday morning, Leslie awoke with one of the worst hangovers of her life. Her dinner last night was a buffet of honey roasted cashews, cheese sticks, and peanut butter on crackers, all washed down with plenty of Grey Goose.

She'd had an erotic dream featuring herself with Roger Halliday, a brief inconclusive scenario where they were on the verge of a simultaneous orgasm but were interrupted for some vague reason. When she reached a state between the dream and wide awake reality, she masturbated to get some degree of satisfaction. But after she was finished, she felt more forlorn than ever. Not because of any moral concerns or psychological guilt, but because she was angry and disgusted with herself for not having a man in bed that would perform this essential service. What the hell is the world coming to? she wondered.

Leslie padded to the kitchen in her bathrobe and pulled out the bottle of Grey Goose and a container of orange juice. She dropped several ice cubes into a glass and poured the two liquids over the ice, more screw than driver. It tasted so good that she mixed herself another. *Time to call Julie and see what she's up to.*

No answer. After five rings, she heard her own voice—a strange sensation—saying that she was not available at the moment and to please leave a message. She hung up, thought for a moment, and called back. She left a message for Julie, asking her to call back soon.

Leslie tried Maria next and connected after two rings. "Hello,

Leslie, I have been thinking about you. Are you all right?"

"I've been better. What time is it there?"

"About seven o'clock in the evening. What about your house? Have they arrested your husband?"

The question caused Leslie to hesitate, trying to recall what she'd told Maria before leaving Italy. *Have to be careful, the lies are piling up.* "It's complicated, Maria. They've questioned him but haven't actually arrested him. I think they're trying to gather more evidence before making a formal charge. I'm trying to help them."

"Then I wish you luck and a quick return to Italy."

"I just tried to reach Julie," said Leslie, "but only got my answering machine. Have you talked to her lately?" The line went quiet. "Maria? Are you there?"

"Yes, I am listening."

"Well, have you seen her?"

"Please don't be angry with me, but I feel a delicate position."

"What does that mean?"

"I saw Julie this morning. I had baked some special bread and took it to your home but I did not stay long. It was awkward."

"Why? What happened?"

"Julie was still in sleeping clothes but she was not alone. A young man was there. He was rude and would not speak to me but rode away on his motorcycle."

"Marco," she yelled. "I told her not to have anything to do with that man. What am I going to do with her?"

After a pause Maria said, "I wish I could help."

"It's all my fault, I shouldn't have left her alone. I made it too easy for her."

"You must not blame yourself, Leslie. Would you like me to

go back tonight?"

"Thanks, but no." Leslie felt calmer. "Maybe she'll call me."

"Do not be harsh with her. You would not know about this if I had not taken the bread to her."

"Yeah, you're right. Not a lot I can do about it being so far away."

They talked for several more minutes. Afterwards, Leslie thought hard about this latest situation. She'd given Julie a great deal of financial help, permitting almost unlimited freedom, and now it was coming back to haunt her.

Leslie placed another call, this one to Julie's cell phone. She left a message when it rolled over to voice mail.

"Hello, my *darling daughter.* Now that I know I can't trust you after all, here's the deal. You get yourself a one-way plane ticket back to JFK right now and get yourself back to your husband where you belong. You've got twenty-four hours before you turn into a pumpkin with no money. I'm calling the bank in Siena tomorrow morning and canceling that account I set up for you. Leave my car at the villa and catch a ride with Maria to the airport. Or maybe you could bum one with your buddy Marco and freeze your ass off speeding down the *autostrada* on his motorcycle. Don't call me. I have nothing more to say to you."

After calling her villa and leaving essentially the same message, Leslie took a shower and dressed to go out. She felt her spirits lifted, having dispatched the problem with her daughter and getting her away from the Italian predator who had enjoyed the bodies of both mother and daughter, probably in the same bed. *If I ever see that man again, I'll castrate him.*

She drove to a nearby restaurant that was so crowded she had to take a stool at the bar. The bartender, a lean man about sixty named Mike whom she recognized from previous visits, gave her a warm welcome. She had a breakfast of scrambled eggs, wheat toast, fresh fruit and a screwdriver.

After Mike had presented the bill, Leslie motioned him to come closer. "Mike," she said, "I need a favor."

"Sure, what can I do for you?"

"I need a gun, right now. Where can I buy one?"

The smile disappeared as he shifted backward. She slid a hundred dollar bill across the bar. "I need protection, Mike. My husband left me and his bitchy girlfriend is stalking me. Can you help me?" She slid another hundred toward him.

He palmed the bills and said, "Hold on a minute, I'll be right back." He went off to a back room and came back with a slip of paper. "Call this number and ask for Ray. Tell him you got it from me. He'll probably have you meet him somewhere to pick it up. You have any idea what you're looking for?"

"Yeah, a Glock. I had one before but I lost it in a car wreck."

"You can trust him. You'll get a piece with no numbers on it."

She gave him another hundred. "Thanks, Mike, you're a prince."

"Thanks, but you never got that number from me."

"Got it," she said. Leslie felt her cell phone vibrating and looked at the screen. It was Julie. She finished her screwdriver and left the bar without answering the call.

CHAPTER TWENTY-NINE
YOU TWO HAVE A GEOGRAPHY PROBLEM

Sheriff Waters stepped out of his office about noon. Last night's four inches of snow was turning to slush. He spotted a familiar figure heading his way, a man holding tightly to a dog's leash.

"Hey there," he called out, "your dog taking you for a walk?"

Andrew Krag pulled up next to Waters. "Yeah, he's a real handful. God only knows what he'll be like when he grows up."

The sheriff bent over and gave the dog a couple of head pats. The animal was mostly black with a white vertical blaze down his face that continued on and through his chest. "He's beautiful, Andy. What breed is he?"

"A Bernese Mountain Dog. Saw an ad in the paper by a breeder over in Pueblo West." The dog's frolicking in the snow and straining the leash interrupted Andrew. "He's just a puppy now but thc guy who sold him to us said his weight will probably double by the time he's an adult."

Waters laughed. "A good pooch for fourteener country. And you'll need to make lots of trips to the supermarket to keep him happy. What's his name?"

"Haven't decided yet. Maybe Barney, like Barney Bernese, but Sarah's thinking Monty or Moses suits him better. She's counting on him for protection whenever I'm away on business."

"Classic names, I like 'em all." He turned slightly. "I'm heading for the Cloud City Cafe for lunch. Care to join me?"

"I would, but I'm not sure about *Barney*," said Andrew.

"Bring him along. I'll get him a burger and fries. That'll keep him happy."

Once at the cafe, Sheriff Waters used his influence to get a corner table in a back room where the threesome could be accommodated. The dog seemed comfortable sitting under the table, wagging his considerable tail and sipping water from a pan brought by their puppy-loving waitress.

Over lunch, Waters asked, "What brings you up to Leadville?"

"Had a meeting with Roscoe, gave him a progress report on the Pueblo branch. We bought three building lots and I've got a trailer on one of them for a field office. I'll be working out of it when we start building spec homes."

"I'm happy for you and Sarah, things turning out well in spite of the fire."

"I was by my cabin site after the meeting. Not much going on there right now because of the weather."

"I dropped by yesterday," said Waters. "Sharon wanted to see it."

"Sharon?"

"Uh . . . Detective Hardcastle, that is."

"She came to Leadville on a Sunday to see my cabin?"

Waters was on the verge of blushing. "Actually, she came up on Saturday. We did some cross country and I cooked her one of my famous chuck wagon dinners."

Andrew was silent for a moment until a wide grin spread across his face. "Well, I'll be. You and the pretty blonde detective. That's terrific."

"Kind of crazy, huh? But she's a fine woman and we have a lot in common. Loving the outdoors, dancing, good food and conversation, plus a great respect for the law and a burning desire for justice to be served."

"That's wonderful," said Andrew. "Sarah will be so happy when I tell her." He paused and rubbed his chin. "But you two have a geography problem, just like Sarah and I had before the fire."

"We've talked about that. But no hurry to do anything about it. For now, we'll take turns visiting each other on the weekends."

"I wish you two the best of luck."

After they'd finished lunch and were waiting for the check, the conversation drifted to the ongoing hunt for Leslie Krag. Waters said, "Detective Hardcastle learned that she and Roger Halliday had been staying at the Broadmoor in The Springs. But when Sharon got there, Leslie'd hightailed it to Denver in a taxi. Halliday had already flown the coop and gone back to Virginia."

"They split up?"

"Yep, seems they had some kind of a lovers' quarrel. The taxi dropped her at a hotel on the city's south side but she stayed only one night. After that, the trail got cold and we're not sure where she is right now."

"I don't get it," said Andy. "With him leaving her like that, why didn't she grab a flight out of The Springs like she did before?"

"We're thinking she has some unfinished business in Colorado."

"Like me and Sarah."

"Sad to say, but I think you're right."

"Maybe she'll take a flight out of DIA and go direct to Italy."

"Sharon and I think the taxi from the Broadmoor would have taken her to a hotel next to the Denver airport. If she's all that fired up to leave the country."

"Makes sense."

"You know her better than we do, Andy. Any ideas on where she might be?"

Andrew pondered for a moment. "How about Nancy Moore? Or maybe that idiot private detective she hired?"

"Layton moved away from Denver," said Waters. "And Mrs. Moore isn't having anything to do with her. At least that's what she tells us."

"Do you know how bad the fire was at her house?"

"Not all that bad. I talked to Alan Morris, her real estate agent, and he's hired a cleaning crew to get it back in shape."

"Maybe she's hiding out there. After all, it's still her home."

"Why do you suppose she'd do that?"

"Isn't it the last thing you'd expect? Leslie is a pretty sneaky woman and has done some weird things in her life."

"Gimme a for instance," said Waters.

"I'll give you two. Leslie's first husband worked on Wall Street and had an affair with a much younger woman in his office who's now his wife. About the time she divorced him, Leslie collected a bunch of those pullout cards you see in magazines and signed up the new wife for subscriptions. She told me this story one night when she was loaded. Leslie's ex-husband suspected that she was behind it and had the NYPD pay her a visit but they never could prove anything."

"That adds up to lots of aggravation but isn't too serious."

"There's more. Leslie always had a fractious relationship with her daughter, Julie. At our wedding, both of them were drunk and got into a physical knockdown at the reception. So she vowed revenge for that little fracas and got even when Julie got married two years later. Leslie hired some actor buddy to show up at the church. You know that part in the ceremony when the minister asks if anyone knows why these two shouldn't be joined in holy matrimony? Speak now or forever hold your peace? Well, this actor guy marched down the aisle and pretended to be Julie's jilted lover and, from all accounts, put on quite a show."

"Now that's downright mean, but I can believe it happened."

"And burning down my cabin fits the pattern."

The table was silent except for Andrew's dog flapping his tail on the floor. "I'll give Morris a call when I get back to the office," said Waters.

Leslie set her clock to wake up early on Monday. She wanted to call the Siena bank before it closed and also talk with Maria Borelli. She made a small pot of coffee, and turned on her cell phone. She had two messages in her voice mailbox.

The first message was from Julie, short and to the point. "Bitch," she yelled.

"Takes one to know one," said Leslie, immediately deleting it.

The second message was from a man with a low voice that sounded like a snow shovel scraping a sidewalk. "This is Ray. I have the item you need with everything that goes with it. Six hundred bucks, cash. Small bills, nothing over a twenty. If you're still interested, meet me at Chubby's Mexican place tonight at eight o'clock. It's on 38th Avenue across from Longo's Tavern. I'll be parked in the back. Light blue Volvo wagon with a big dent in the rear fender. Don't be late or the deal's off."

"Judas priest," she said aloud. "I'll have to get a city map."

She collected her financial papers and made the call to her bank in Siena. After identifying herself and being passed to several officers in serial fashion, she was finally ready to conduct her financial transaction.

"I want to close the account," she told the man. "You can mail a check for the balance to my home in Castellina."

"It will not be necessary," he said. "The other owner, Miss Julia Grantham, has already done that earlier today. She withdrew all the remaining funds."

That little shit. "All right, there's a credit card and Euro checks associated with this account and I want them canceled immediately."

During a small delay, she heard the man tapping a keyboard. "There are a number of outstanding charges on this account. Almost three thousand Euros. How do you wish to settle them?"

"Take it out of my personal account and pay the damn things off." *She's my daughter all right, trying to resuscitate the Italian economy single-handed.*

"I shall take care of these matters personally, Mrs. Krag. We value your business greatly. Will there be anything else I can help you with?"

"No, that's enough for one day."

She fixed herself breakfast, took a shower and dressed in casual clothes. The cleaning crew showed up, two dark skinned women named Dora and Josephine who spoke mostly in Spanish or with halting English. Leslie stayed out of their way, hanging out in her bedroom watching TV.

She made her call to Maria and asked, after the usual exchange of greetings, "Have you heard anything from my daughter? I thought she might be contacting you about a ride to the airport."

"No, Leslie, she has not called. And I have not returned to your villa. I don't wish to see that man again."

"I don't think there's a danger of that. Julie has surely moved on. I'd like you to go over there, check on my car, and make sure everything's OK. Will you do that for me?"

After a pause, Maria said, "All right, Leslie. This time I will do as you ask. But please call me back in three hours. It is so expensive for me to call you. I should have more information for you then."

"Thanks, Maria, I'll call you later. You are a sweet person and a dear friend."

Alan Morris was not in his office when Sheriff Waters made the call but was able to reach him on his cell phone.

"Hello, Sheriff. Are you calling about that guy who looked at the house last week? He hasn't been back."

"No, a different reason this time. It's about the owner, Leslie Krag."

"What about her?"

"Have you been in touch with her recently?"

There was no answer.

"Mr. Morris?"

"Yes, I've talked with her. Is something wrong?"

"When did you talk with her last?"

"Uh . . . yesterday."

"And where was she when you talked to her?"

More silence. "Is she in trouble, sheriff?"

"I need to find her, talk to her. Now if you know of her whereabouts, I think you should fess up right now and tell me."

"This is not good, sheriff. You're putting me in a terrible spot. She told me it would spoil the surprise if I told anybody."

"I'm waiting," said Waters.

"OK, she's staying at the house, in a guest bedroom. She promised to stay out of the way so the cleaning crew could finish up their work."

"Now that wasn't so hard, was it?" Waters continued, "Now you are not to tell Mrs. Krag that we've had this little talk. I'll be coming to see her pretty soon and I want to be sure that she'll be there. And if she's packed up again and moved . . . well, that would not be in your best interests."

"I understand, sheriff. Please don't tell her I told you. I need that commission."

CHAPTER THIRTY

SHE'S GOING TO BE ONE SORRY LITTLE GIRL

An anxious Leslie called Maria again two hours later but only received her answering machine. She tried again and again, still getting the same recording, sweetly inviting the caller to leave a message. Finally, about five hours after Leslie's initial call, Maria answered the phone.

"Did you get over to my place?" said Leslie. "Is it still standing?"

"Yes, it's there. It looks fine from the outside."

"What do you mean by that?"

"I'm afraid the inside was not very nice. Julie left a large mess so I've been cleaning things up."

"You didn't need to do that, but thanks anyway. I would have reimbursed you to have a professional cleaning outfit come in."

"I understand that," said Maria, "but there were things that shouldn't be seen by anyone. As I've told you, this is a small village. People will talk."

"Then you'd better tell me what you found."

"Your daughter and *that man* must have had a big party for themselves. Many parties. Empty bottles of wine and whiskey, male and female underwear scattered everywhere and condoms hung like Christmas tree ornaments. I don't understand why they didn't throw it all into the trash. It was disgusting."

"Julie was sending me a message. I'm so sorry you had to see all that."

"No matter, it's finished. I removed linens from all the beds, washed them and cleaned up the rooms best I could."

"All the beds? They used more than one?"

Maria changed the subject. "There is good news, Leslie. Your car is perfectly fine, in the garage with keys on the floor."

"Thank you, my friend. I truly appreciate all you've done."

"There is another thing," said Maria. "Julie left a note but it's for Lucia. The envelope was not sealed so I read it. Would you like to know what she wrote?"

Leslie sighed. "Of course."

"She says, 'Hey Lucia, I'm on the road again, this time with a really hot guy named Marco. Thought it would be a good idea to get out of here before you-know-who comes back or the caribeaners show up with rubber hoses.' Maria paused to add, "I think she meant to say *carabiniere*. 'I may be out of touch for a while but I'll call you. I want to follow up on the job with your bank. Hugs, Julie.'"

"Just toss that garbage in the wastebasket."

"I have already read it to Lucia and I told her about the mess Julie left. She needs to know those things."

"You're right, Julie is living in a fantasy world. She needs to go back to her husband and get her life straightened out. When this little fling with Marco comes crashing down to earth, and it will, she's going to be one sorry little girl."

There was another pause before Maria spoke again. "When are *you* coming back to Italy, Leslie?"

"I need a couple of more days to wrap things up. Are you getting tired of solving all my problems there?"

"There's another reason, a personal one."

"Which is?"

"Marcello has asked me to go on holiday with him. I would like to say yes but I would feel bad about leaving while you are in America."

"For God's sake, Maria, do it and have a wonderful time."

"Thank you, Leslie, it could be a very important time for us. I think that Marcello would like to ask me a big question."

"Then I'm happy for you. Go for it."

After the call, Leslie thought about Julie's latest escapade. *Wonder if I can pack the Glock in my suitcase when I fly back to Rome?*

Leslie had her usual vodka martinis before and during a makeshift dinner while watching the six o'clock news. She was also pondering what she would wear tonight for her meeting with Ray at Chummy's. *Should it be normal clothing or my disguise?* A call from Alan Morris interrupted her deliberations.

"What do you want, Alan?"

Her brusque manner caused him to hesitate. "Uh . . . how are you getting along over there, Leslie?"

"All right, why do you ask?"

"Something's come up. A bureaucrat from the health department called. Your house has to be fumigated and inspected before I can offer it for sale again."

"Never heard of that before, but OK."

"I've scheduled it for tomorrow. It will take a couple of days and then the fire department will have to look the place over and sign off on the clearance."

"What are you trying to tell me?"

"You'll have to move out while this is going on. Wouldn't be good for your health, breathing in those noxious fumes."

"Can't you do this after I leave? It should only be a couple of more days and I'll be going back to Italy."

"Sorry, Leslie, but I've got everything set up. Too late to cancel now. They'll be there bright and early in the morning."

"You know something? You are a giant pain in the ass sometimes. All right, I'll move to a hotel later tonight."

She hung up and checked the time. She could still get dressed and find Chummy's before eight o'clock. After picking up the pistol, she'd come back to the house, pack up, and get a hotel room along I-25 on the south side of Denver.

Sheriff Waters called Detective Hardcastle right after his telephone conversation with Alan Morris. His adrenaline was rising for two reasons: the increased likelihood of apprehending Leslie Krag and seeing Sharon again soon.

"Hey, Eliot, nice to hear your voice. Having separation anxiety already?"

"That and more, Sharon. I have some news about Leslie Krag."

"What's she done now?"

"Where's the last place you think she'd be?"

"Don't play games, Eliot."

"All right. Had lunch today with Andrew Krag and I gave him

the big picture. Told him about your visit to the Broadmoor and how you tracked her to the Marriott in Denver. He thought her next stop would be Cherry Hills."

"Her home? Why would she do that?"

"Probably thinking it was the last place we'd look. So I called that Morris fellow again. He was pretty cagey but, after a little pressure, he admitted she's there. Sleeping in a guest room while they clean up all the fire debris."

"Won't he tell her about your call?"

"Don't think so. Managed to convince him it would be a bad move."

"She sounds pretty mobile," said Sharon, "like she's making it a point not to be in one spot too long." She paused. "What are you thinking, Eliot?"

"I think we should pay Ms. Krag a visit tonight."

"We?"

"Can't do this alone, Sharon. Too risky."

"Guess I could come up tonight. But I wouldn't do this for any old lawman, you know. Are you bringing Denver PD in on this?"

"Rather not," he said. "Just want to take her into custody and book her into the Lake County jail. Show her all the comforts of home."

"We're on a slippery slope here," she said, "neither one of us being on home turf. Where should I meet you?"

"You remember Benedict's, the place we had lunch about two months ago? It's west off the I-25 Arapahoe exit, then a couple hundred yards on the right."

"Got it. I can probably get there about seven-thirty."

"Sounds good," he said, "and don't forget to bring your

weapon."

"You really think I'll need it?"

"The woman's unpredictable. Remember the pistol they found in her car?"

"Yeah, I remember. She put some rounds into Andy's bed before she burned up his cabin."

"See you at seven-thirty. We'll make a plan and I'll buy you dessert."

"You'd better, Eliot. Can't be 100% without dessert."

Leslie decided to wear her thrift shop outfit when meeting Ray. She thought he might pressure her for more money if she wore expensive clothes.

Leslie drove along 38th Avenue, saw Longo's Tavern, and turned right into Chummy's parking lot where she found a place in the rear. None of the cars in the dimly lit parking area looked like the light blue Volvo wagon that Ray was supposed to be driving. She checked the time; ten minutes before eight o'clock. She'd have to wait for him to show.

Leslie sat in her darkened car as the temperature got colder. It had started to snow an hour ago, lightly at first but now much harder. Twenty minutes after her arrival, her teeth chattering and her feet freezing, she saw the Volvo pull into the lot and park against the rear wall of the restaurant and next to a dumpster. She got out, sprinted to the Volvo and rapped on the driver's side window. The driver, wearing a Greek sailor's hat, sporting a scruffy gray beard and smoking a cigarette, opened the window about two inches. He flicked the cigarette through the gap and barely missed her left ear. "Get in the car," he rasped.

"Are you Ray?"

"No, I'm the goddamn sheik of Arabia. Get in the fucking car."

Leslie walked around to the passenger side and got in. The sudden warmth was nice but the residue of cigarette smoke almost gagged her.

"You got the money?" he said.

She pulled a wad of bills from her overcoat's pocket and handed it to him. He riffled through them and stuffed them into a pocket.

"Aren't you going to count it?" she asked.

"I already did." He reached behind his seat and grabbed a dirty rolled-up towel off the floor. He unfurled it until a black pistol and a small cardboard box of bullets were visible. "Here's your weapon," he said as he handed it to her. "The mag's in the grip but no rounds loaded. Ammo's in the box."

She gripped the Glock and smiled. "Feels good, just like the one I had before."

"I'm happy for you, lady. Now get the hell out of my car."

She got out, the pistol and ammunition tucked into her pockets, and walked quickly back to her own car. "That was a pleasant experience," she muttered as she got inside.

Leslie removed her fake glasses and drove carefully on her way back to Cherry Hills. She knew it would be a disaster if she was stopped by a police officer for the slightest infraction. Overall, she was pleased with herself, managing to acquire a weapon and now prepared for the final step in her quest. However, as she got closer to her house, she had a nagging feeling. *Was it really necessary to move out of the house during this sudden fumigation? How come I never heard of such a thing before? And why didn't Alan Morris have this done earlier if it was really necessary?*

She slowed the car as she entered her neighborhood, something inside telling her to be careful. Her fears were realized as she got closer to her house. Two vehicles were parked in her circular driveway, a black SUV and a light-colored sedan, nose-to-nose as if they were kissing.

Leslie drove past her house, turned around and parked about fifty yards from the driveway, headlights off but the engine still running. *Alan wanted me out of the house. He was trying to warn me.* She turned on the dome light and began feeding bullets into the Glock's magazine. *Whoever my visitors are, I'm ready for them.*

Once the pistol was loaded, she placed it on the passenger seat and continued her vigil, hoping for something to happen. *Where are these people? If they broke into my house, I could have them arrested. Or if they're police, they broke the law if they don't have a search warrant.*

A short time later, she spotted two figures coming from the side of the house and approaching the SUV. One person was a man wearing a long duster coat and a western hat. "It's that goddam Leadville sheriff," she said.

The two got into the SUV but nothing more happened. Are they going to sit there all night? she wondered.

After ten minutes, the SUV's lights went on and white smoke started coming out the tail pipe but the vehicle didn't move. *Dammit, they're going to sit there and wait me out. Well, screw them. Let's see who can wait the longest.*

Ten more minutes passed and Leslie was losing patience. A glance at the dashboard panel revealed that her gas tank was almost empty. She'd have to leave but she didn't want these two following her. Ever again. She'd give them a message, a full bundle of 9 mm messages.

She chambered a round in the pistol, opened her window all the way and inched the car forward, still with the headlights off. She stopped when the car was even with the two vehicles and placed both hands on the window ledge with the Glock in her right hand. She steadied her arms, took a deep breath and emptied the Glock's magazine with quick shots aimed at the tires of both vehicles.

Leslie zoomed the car ahead and got all the way to University Boulevard before raising the window and turning on the headlights. "The poor stupid bastards," she said aloud, "they don't know who they're dealing with."

CHAPTER THIRTY-ONE

THE WOMAN'S CAR INSURANCE MUST COST A FORTUNE

Eliot and Sharon sat in the front seat of his SUV, talking quietly about their progress, or more appropriately the lack of same, in the search for Leslie Krag. At one point, Sharon glanced left to look at Eliot and noticed something beyond, a dark automobile on the opposite side of the street, no headlights on, and moving slowly in their direction. She was about to say something when the car stopped and she saw flashes from the driver's window, followed instantly by the *pop-pop-pop* of a gun being fired. A split second later, when the SUV's rear window was shattered, she reacted with a frantic yell, "Someone's shooting at us."

At the same moment, because of similar experience with Border Patrol incidents, he lunged over and covered her with his upper body, pushing her towards the floorboard at the same time. They heard more bullets being fired, not thinking to count them, but praying the assailant would soon run out of ammunition.

After what seemed an eternity, the shooting stopped and Eliot sat up. "You OK?" he said while she struggled to uncoil herself.

"I'm fine, what about you?"

"I'm all right." He looked backward at a million tiny pieces of glass scattered across the rear seat. "Gonna get pretty cold in here real soon."

Sharon got out and made a quick inspection of her car while Eliot did the same for his SUV. When they met up again, she said, "I'm not going anywhere in that thing tonight. Got a flat in front and a busted window on the passenger side. Anything serious on your vehicle?"

"Tires are OK, only the back window is out. Let's get rolling."

They got back inside and Eliot started the engine. "No problems under the hood. So far, anyway."

He backed out of the driveway, turned around and headed toward University Boulevard. "Where are we going?" she said.

"After her."

"You think it was Leslie."

"No doubt in my mind. I told you the woman's unpredictable."

"Eliot, she was shooting at us."

"Now aren't you glad you brought your weapon?"

Leslie pulled into a gas station on University near County Line Road. Her credit card was rejected at the pump with a brief message: SEE CLERK INSIDE.

She let fly several curses, went inside, and found a young black woman at the cash register. "The damn thing wouldn't take my card," she yelled.

The clerk, her short hair an experiment in blond and pink, gave Leslie an irritated look for being bothered with such a trivial matter.

"I'm in a hurry," said Leslie. "How do I get some gas?"

"Gimme some cash, lady, and I'll turn it on from here."

Leslie tossed two $20 bills at her and stormed back outside. While her tank was filling up, she went back inside to use the bathroom.

The pump had shut off when she returned. She started up the engine and pulled over to the far side of the lot where there was less light. With the engine still running, she released the Glock's magazine and loaded it with fifteen more bullets.

She returned the magazine, pulled back the slide and chambered a round. *Now I'm ready, but where do I go next?*

Leslie glanced at the dashboard clock. 9:08 P.M. It would take about an hour to the airport, park the car and get to the ticket counters. *I've got money and my passport so I can catch a flight to Europe.*

As Eliot made a left turn at University, Sharon said, "That car was a dark color. I think it was a four door."

He grabbed his cell phone from the center tray. "Steady the wheel for me." Sharon placed her left hand on the steering wheel while his call went through. "Alan, Sheriff Waters. Does Leslie Krag have a car?" Pause. "Got it, thanks."

Eliot put the phone back and placed both hands on the wheel. "Good eye, Sharon. It's a dark blue Buick, four door sedan. He thinks it has Colorado plates."

"That narrows things down a bit."

They pulled up to County Line Road and stopped at the intersection for red traffic lights. "Eliot," she said, "over in that gas station. Might be her."

He craned his neck to get a look. "Let's check it out," he said, making a sharp U-turn to the left in front of two oncoming cars just getting the green light.

But once they'd made the turn, the dark blue sedan sped away from the station and zipped through the intersection as the lights were turning from green to amber.

"She's spotted us," said Eliot. "Hold on tight."

Sharon reached inside her coat and found her cell phone. "I'm calling the State Patrol, giving them a heads up." She made a report and placed her phone next to Eliot's in the console tray. She pulled her weapon from a shoulder holster, checked to see that it was loaded, and held it as they tried to close the gap.

Leslie jammed her foot on the accelerator when she saw the black SUV making its U-turn. "Dammit," she said, "I missed his tires."

She passed under C-470, swerved around two cars waiting to turn left and accelerated up the onramp. Once on the three-lane highway heading east, she drove even faster at close to 80 mph. The wind was blowing falling snow directly at her windshield and creating a disorienting effect. "What's wrong with these damn wipers?" she yelled, "they're not going fast enough."

She glanced at the rear view mirror and could see the black SUV coming up fast behind her. Suddenly, she started to skid and lose control. On the verge of panic, she took her foot off the accelerator for a moment, regained control and continued moving forward.

Her loss of speed allowed the black SUV to come along side. "Oh no you don't," she yelled, lowering the driver's side window. She grabbed the pistol, stuck the barrel out the open window and fired shots downward at the SUV's tires. The SUV slowed momentarily, making her think she hit one of the tires, but it only took a position behind her.

Leslie could barely make out the huge I-25 intersection looming ahead. This is the big moment, she thought. I have to find the right lane off this highway if I'm going to make it to the airport.

As Eliot's SUV came abreast of the blue Buick, Sharon glanced to her right. "She's shooting at us, back off."

He slowed and swung to the right and in back of Leslie's car. "I'll just keep up, try to figure where she's headed. She has to make a decision pretty soon."

As they approached the I-25 intersection, Eliot let the distance between them increase so he'd have enough reaction time. They watched carefully as Leslie approached the interchange, still at high speed, with no clues about which way she'd turn. As she headed up a long left-curving arc of cement and steel, she got too close to a guard rail on the right, causing sparks to fly.

Leslie's car kept moving but swerved to the left and bounced off another guard rail, sending her sharply to the right, entering multiple lanes of I-25 heading north. She corrected but lost control when trying to avoid several vehicles merging into the northbound lanes from other ramps. An oncoming car slammed into her rear fender, rolling her car several times, and landing it upside down in the center lane.

When Eliot saw what was happening, he took his foot off the accelerator, fearing a disastrous skid if he applied the brakes. Other cars approaching the wreck were not as savvy; a monumental traffic jam was soon in progress. Sharon got on her cell phone again and called the State Patrol, this time giving their location and the urgent need for an ambulance. Eliot turned on the

SUV's hazard lights as they pulled up close to the multiple car pileup.

Eliot and Sharon stared through the falling snow. Over a dozen tail lights blinked their warnings, headlights pointed at bizarre angles, and white smoke rose out of Leslie's engine compartment.

After a long moment he said, "What are you thinking?"

"The woman's car insurance must cost a fortune."

Eliot grunted. "I'm getting out, see if we can help with this mess."

"Right behind you, partner."

They made their way to Leslie's overturned car as others emerged from their vehicles. Sharon held out her badge, telling everyone to stay back, and that help was coming. Eliot got on his knees to look inside. "She's in the back. God only knows how she got there."

"Can we get her out?"asked Sharon.

"Don't think so. Better wait for the ambulance."

An hour later, Eliot and Sharon arrived at the Sky Ridge Medical Center, several miles south of the accident site next to I-25. They identified themselves to the Emergency Room receptionist and asked about a woman who had been brought in from an auto accident. The receptionist made a telephone call and said that someone would be out right away.

'Right away' in hospital terminology became twenty minutes in real time. A tall woman with a brown ponytail and a stethoscope around her neck, dressed in light green hospital scrubs, came out to meet them. "I'm Dr. Lanier," she said, extending her hand to Sharon.

"Detective Hardcastle, Pueblo P. D. Sheriff Waters here is

from Leadville."

Eliot touched the brim of his hat. "We've wanted to talk with Leslie Krag for some time about arson and conspiracy to commit murder. Tonight she fired a couple dozen bullets at us so that adds a few more items to the list. We believe someone will have to keep a close eye on her."

"She's in bad shape, sheriff. No danger to anyone except herself."

"Can she be interviewed?" asked Sharon.

"Not now. She's unconscious and has some pretty serious injuries. My two areas of concern being her head and spine."

"When will you know something definite?" said Eliot.

"Check with us tomorrow. We'll be doing lots of tests. EKG, MRI, CAT scan."

Sharon and Eliot looked at each other. "Let's find a motel," she said. "I'm running out of gas."

"Thank you, doctor," he said. "Tomorrow it is."

Eliot awoke at eight o'clock the next morning with Sharon cuddled up next to him. He felt good, in spite of all they'd been through the night before.

She soon stirred and opened one eye. "Looks like a new day has arrived."

"Another opportunity for greatness," he said, planting a kiss on her cheek.

"Had a crazy dream last night. Leslie was chasing me around a department store waving a big butcher knife. Had to throw suitcases at her in self-defense."

He chuckled. "Was I in your dream?"

"I kept looking but you weren't in the picture." She draped

her arm across his chest. "What's the plan, Eliot? Do we have one?"

"Let's have breakfast at the next door IHOP, go back to the hospital and see what the doctors found out."

"Sounds good," she said. "I'd like to take a quick shower, then call my supervisor. Don't see how I'll be able to get back to my office today."

"And while you're getting cleaned up, I'll check my truck to make sure the cardboard window panel is still in place."

They returned to Sky Ridge Medical Center about ten o'clock. Leslie had been moved to Intensive Care but was still unconscious.

A male doctor about sixty with white bushy hair met them. "I'm Dr. Kehoe and I'll be her primary care physician while she's here." He pointed to a consultation alcove where they could sit and be comfortable.

Eliot said, "What can you tell us about her condition?"

Dr. Kehoe removed his glasses. "I think she'll live but the injuries to her spine are severe. She'll have a long period of recuperation and therapy in our spine and joint center, one of the best in the country."

"The woman's a criminal," said Sharon, "an arsonist who tried to kill both of us last night. She escaped from the Pueblo hospital and we don't want that again."

"You could certainly station a guard next to her room but I don't see the point. She's not going anywhere for a long time."

"That bad, huh?" said Eliot.

"She may never walk again and could spend the rest of her life in a wheelchair. Nursing care around the clock. Maybe not the kind of justice you folks want but she'll be in a different kind of prison. One of her own making, you might say."

Eliot and Sharon exchanged disappointed looks. Eliot gave Dr. Kehoe one of his cards which prompted Sharon to do the same. "I'd like you to contact either one of us," said Eliot, "if something dramatic happens. I'll be checking with you myself from time to time."

Dr. Kehoe pocketed their cards. "Would you know if she has a family?"

Eliot said, "Her ex-husband lives down in Pueblo and she has a good friend here in Denver. We'll tell them."

Dr. Kehoe said goodbye but Eliot and Sharon remained seated. Sharon took a moment to lean forward and place her head in her hands. "So that's the way it ends? After all the hell we've been through with that woman? People need to know about her and what she's done."

Eliot took both of her hands. "Afraid so, but look on the bright side. She won't be hurting anybody else now. Aside from the damage to our vehicles, we're in pretty good shape. Could've been worse, you know, all those bullets flying around us like bees."

"I like your style, Eliot. Always able to put a positive spin on things."

"Happy to oblige," he said, leaning over and giving her a kiss. "Think I'll give Mrs. Moore a call, let her know what happened. Why don't you call Andy Krag? He'd probably like to know that he and Sarah don't have to worry about Leslie anymore."

"I'll go out to the lobby," she said, "and find a quiet corner."

Eliot called Nancy Moore on his cell phone. After identifying himself she said, "I don't have any information on Leslie, sheriff."

"Well I do, Mrs. Moore. She's in pretty serious condition over here at Sky Ridge Medical Center. Thought you'd like to know."

"What? Are you serious, Leslie's in the hospital? What happened?"

"Kind of a long story. We tried to meet with her last night but she had other ideas. Wrecked her car on the interstate and they brought her to Sky Ridge. That's where I am right now."

"Have you talked to her?"

"She's still unconscious but I did speak with her doctor. What I'd like from you is information about her family. If she has any, that is."

"Oh God, I don't know. Let me think." Several moments later she continued, "She has a daughter, her name is Julie. She's married and lives in New Jersey somewhere. Don't know what her last name might be. Oh, and a close friend in Italy. I can call her."

"That's a good start."

"What about Andrew? Have you called him?"

"Detective Hardcastle is making that call."

"Guess I should come over there, see how she's doing. I'm probably the only friend she has left."

"Better call first," he said, "and make sure she can have visitors."

"Thanks for letting me know, sheriff."

Waters went off to the lobby and met Sharon as she was ending her call. "Had an interesting conversation with Mr. Krag. Kind of a mixed emotions thing with him. He felt bad about Leslie's accident but relieved that she won't be bothering him anymore. Although he wasn't totally comfortable with the possibility of her eventual recovery when she could do more mischief."

Eliot briefed her on his conversation with Nancy Moore. He ended by saying, "Looks like our work here is over. Let's go back and see about your car."

She pressed her body up against his. "Put your arms around me, Eliot." He gladly obliged and she continued, "After we get the tire fixed, I want to follow you back to Leadville. I don't want to be alone tonight."

"I like that. I'll fix us another dinner, with dessert. How does that sound?"

"Can't think of anything better."

EPILOGUE

During an emotional transatlantic telephone call, Nancy Moore breaks the news to Maria Borelli of Leslie's latest automobile accident. Maria promises to get her daughter, Lucia, to help search for Julie.

Two months later, Julie phones Lucia, asking if she can come to Milan and spend several days with her. Julie is almost broke, needs a job, and Marco has tired of her; he wants her out of his apartment. Lucia tells Julie of her mother's accident and convinces her to return immediately to the Castellina villa and stay there until she can get enough money and fly back to New Jersey.

Julie returns to Harper, her husband, and they negotiate a shaky reunion. As a necessary condition to living with him again, Julie takes a low-paying intern position at a local bank so she can contribute to the family's expenses. She also agrees to couples counseling for patching up the cracks in their marriage.

Two days after the accident, Leslie regains consciousness. The day after that, she is visited by Nancy Moore. Leslie is bedridden and heavily medicated to relieve the pain in her neck and back. Dr. Kehoe privately tells Nancy that Leslie will live but will likely be confined to a wheelchair for the rest of her life.

Nancy visits Leslie often, bringing reading material and flowers. When Nancy tells Leslie about finding Julie and her return to Harper, Leslie is pleased but not interested in reconnecting with her daughter. "Julie can call me and apologize first," she tells Nancy.

Leslie insists that Nancy and her husband, Joe, take the promised trip to Italy and stay at her villa. Nancy reluctantly agrees and asks what she would like them to bring back from Castellina. The only item she wants from the villa is the jade Buddha carving that Roger Halliday gave her.

In May, Roger Halliday travels to Hanoi and receives his father's remains, thanks to some covert activities by the CIA and State Department in cooperation with the Vietnamese government. He takes the remains to Colorado Springs for presentation to his mother. Roger subsequently sells his home in Virginia, moves to a small town in Northern California, and begins writing a memoir.

Roger never learns of Leslie's misfortune and she makes no effort to contact him. She fears another rejection for the stupid actions which caused her disability and doesn't want his pity.

Andrew Krag and Sarah Dolan have a June wedding in a scenic mountain setting just outside Leadville's city limits. Roscoe Bartlett is Andrew's best man while Tanice Bartlett is Sarah's matron of honor. Sarah's brother, Bart, brings his family from San Diego for the celebration. Andrew's numerous climbing buddies form an archway with their ice axes for the happy couple's exit.

Andrew takes Sarah on a honeymoon to Europe. They spend

a week walking about Paris followed by a ten day cruise through the Greek islands. When they return to Pueblo, Sarah gives him a delayed wedding gift: private flying lessons so he can soar over his beloved Colorado fourteeners.

In August, Emmaline Dolan closes escrow on the sale of the first spec home built by RBC in Pueblo West. Andrew is already shopping around for lots on which to build more homes. His Leadville cabin is completely rebuilt in September but he and Sarah decide not to sell or rent it out. They will keep it as a weekend getaway when they come to Leadville with Barney, their beloved dog, for family visits.

Sarah often checks herself for breast lumps but she remains clean, playfully rejecting Andrew's offer to help her look.

Despite pressure by Sheriff Waters, Andrew decides not to press charges against Leslie for destruction of his cabin. Andrew believes that Leslie has suffered enough and, because of her accident, will not pose a threat to anyone in the future.

Waters and Detective Hardcastle investigate the possible prosecution of Leslie for various offenses associated with the catastrophic car chase and resulting accident. However, when confronted by the Arapahoe Country District Attorney about their failure to cooperate with local authorities, they reluctantly drop the whole thing.

Eliot and Sharon continue improving their personal relationship, working their respective jobs during the week and getting lots of *practice* on the weekends in either Pueblo or Leadville.

After nearly three months of rehabilitation at Sky View Medical Center's Spine Center, Leslie moves back into her Cherry Creek home. She's taken it off the market and has hired a contractor to make the house wheelchair-friendly.

She has several drinks every evening and enjoys looking at the jade Buddha carving. She often wonders what her future might have been if she'd agreed to quit thinking about revenge and try for a life with Roger in Italy or Virginia. She also hosts the occasional bridge party in her home for her women friends from the country club.

Besides the obvious damage done to her physical self, Leslie's only regret is that she didn't have a better plan for getting revenge against Andrew and Sarah.

AUTHOR BIOGRAPHY

Dick Reynolds has been a career Marine, a university teacher and a system engineer for a large defense electronics company.

Shortly after his retirement from the business world, he began a fourth career—fiction writing. His forty-plus short stories have appeared in such publications as *Literary House Review, Skyline Magazine, Barbaric Yawp* and *Imitation Fruit Literary Journal.* Two of his stories have been nominated for a Pushcart Prize. He has also published four novels, all romantic thrillers: *Averil, My Anchor, Mayhem in Mazatlan, Nightmare in Norway* and *Filling in the Triangles.*

Dick and his wife, Bernadette, live in Santa Fe, NM.

ACKNOWLEDGMENTS

I'm grateful to Nancy Moore Reynolds, Jane Schneider, Cindy Reynolds Pfeiffer, Don Whisnant, Dick Goodlake, Gerry Fabricius, and Dr. Thomas Kehoe M.D., who graciously allowed me to use their names for characters in the book.

Thanks also to my stepdaughter, Vicki Swab, for providing useful information about the greater Denver area.

Special thanks to my wife, Bernadette, who reviewed the entire manuscript several times and offered valuable critiques.